Who Are You, Calvin Bledsoe?

ALSO BY BROCK CLARKE

The Price of the Haircut

The Happiest People in the World

Exley

An Arsonist's Guide to Writers' Homes in New England

Carrying the Torch

What We Won't Do

The Ordinary White Boy

Who Are You, Calvin Bledsoe?

a novel by

BROCK CLARKE

ALGONQUIN BOOKS OF CHAPEL HILL 2019

Published by
ALGONQUIN BOOKS OF CHAPEL HILL
Post Office Box 2225
Chapel Hill, North Carolina 27515-2225

a division of
WORKMAN PUBLISHING
225 Varick Street
New York, New York 10014

This is a work of fiction. While, as in all fiction, the literary perceptions and insights are based on experience, all names, characters, places, and incidents either are products of the author's imagination or are used fictitiously.

Library of Congress Cataloging-in-Publication Data

Names: Clarke, Brock, author.
Title: Who are you, Calvin Bledsoe? : a novel / Brock Clarke.
Description: First Edition. | Chapel Hill, North Carolina :
Algonquin Books of Chapel Hill, 2019.
Identifiers: LCCN 2019005910 | ISBN 9781616208219 (hardcover : alk. paper)
Classification: LCC PS3603.L37 W48 2019 | DDC 813/.6—dc23
LC record available at https://lccn.loc.gov/2019005910

10 9 8 7 6 5 4 3 2 1
First Edition

For Ambrose and Quinn, my Maine Men

Let, therefore, pious readers learn to hate and detest those profane sophists, who thus deliberately corrupt and adulterate the Scriptures, in order that they may give some color to their delusions.

—John Calvin, *Calvin's Commentaries*

Perhaps, being lost, one should get loster.

—Saul Bellow, *Humboldt's Gift*

Who Are You, Calvin Bledsoe?

"Are we still on schedule?"

One

- - - - -

1.

My mother, Nola Bledsoe, was a minister, and she named me Calvin after her favorite theologian, John Calvin. She was very serious about John Calvin, had written a famous book about him—his enduring relevance, his misunderstood legacy. My mother was highly thought of by a lot of people who thought a lot about John Calvin.

2.

My father, on the other hand, was a high school coach—football in the fall, basketball in the winter, baseball in the spring. In the summer he ran clinics for athletes who would be playing their respective sports during the regular school year. His name was

Roger Bledsoe. My father has left this life, and he is also about to leave this story, so before he does, let me tell you a few things about him. He was seventy-seven years old when he died. He was bald on top and was always neatly dressed: pressed chinos, tucked-in oxford shirts—even his boat shoes were polished. His eyebrows were the only unkempt things about him: they curled and hung over his eyes like awnings.

So I remember what he looked like. I also remember his sayings. "You bet your sweet bippie," he liked to say, and also, when he needed to go to the bathroom, "I'm going out for a short beer." But mostly he liked to say, "This isn't my first rodeo, you know." Most of his pregame pep talks included that phrase. Most of his conversations did also. Several months before he died, I told my father that my wife and I were separating. This was after one of my father's baseball games. I was forty-seven years old, and I still went to all my father's games, went to all my mother's services, too. I have no memory of whether his team had won or lost that particular game, but I do remember that the wind was up, that my father's eyebrows were waving at me like cilia. "So, you're getting a divorce," he said.

I insisted that wasn't necessarily so. "Lots of people who get separated don't end up getting divorced," I said, and he squinted at me skeptically and said, "This isn't my first rodeo, you know."

3.

And then he died of a heart attack. Three days later my mother and I were in the cemetery, standing over his grave, next to the pile of dirt. The rest of the mourners had left. The hole was still open. The cemetery workers were waiting there with their shovels, their backhoe idling and rattling loudly behind them. This was in Maine. It was November. The air was filled with snow and with the feeling of last things. I wondered if the workers sensed this, too. This was probably the last hole they would be able to dig before the ground froze.

"That was a beautiful eulogy," I told my mother. In truth, the eulogy had surprised me. I'd expected it to be more, I don't know, *personal*. I'd heard her give nearly identical ones at the funerals of friends, members of her church, even relative strangers. Those eulogies, like my father's, had been filled with inspiring lessons about this life and the next as taught to us by the theologian . . . well, you know which one. It was strange: my mother and her book and her sermons always insisted that while Calvinists were reputed to be severe and full of judgment, John Calvin himself had been forgiving and full of love. But she always wrote and said this in a way that seemed severe and full of judgment.

"You must have always wondered why your father and I stayed together for as long as we did," my mother said—to me, I guessed, although she was looking at the hole. This surprised me even more than the eulogy. In fact, I had not wondered this at all. I had not ever even considered my parents' not staying together a possibility. I had not ever even considered my wife and me not staying together a possibility either until it actually happened. But I didn't say this to my mother. I wanted there to be peace between the living and the dead and also between the living and the living. "Why does anyone stay together for as long as they do?" I asked—rhetorically, I thought, although my mother answered anyway.

"God," she said, "family, fear, loyalty, sex, security, compassion, companionship, complacency, children, guilt, money, real estate, health insurance, not wanting to eat alone, not wanting to go on vacation alone, not wanting to watch television alone, not wanting to drink alone, not wanting to go on cruises alone, not wanting to go on cruises at all, not wanting to leave one person and find another person who then wants to go on cruises, not wanting to leave a person and not find another person at all, not wanting to find another person, not knowing what you want, not knowing what your problem is, love."

I had never heard my mother say anything remotely like this—it definitely didn't seem like a lesson she could have learned from John Calvin—but before I could say that, or anything else, my mother nodded in the direction of the cemetery workers, and they advanced on my father's grave with their shovels and their backhoe, and a few minutes later he was truly buried, and only then did it feel like he was truly gone.

4.

If you live, as I did then, in a small town in central Maine, there is no more visible a job than that of a high school coach or a minister. Is it any surprise that I chose a somewhat less visible job? I became a blogger for the pellet stove industry. You may not know that there is a pellet stove industry, or that it is has a blogger, but there is, and in fact it has two. I am the blogger who extols the virtues of the pellet stove: its cost and energy efficiency; the way it's good for the environment and the economy; the way it sits on the crest of the wave of the home-heating future. The other blogger is named Dawn, and Dawn's job is to spew vitriol at the makers and the sellers of the "conventional woodstove." This is what she calls it in her blog, always in scare quotes: the "conventional woodstove." All Dawn's Monday blog posts begin with a story of someone she's met at a "weekend party" who has asked her what's so wrong with the "conventional woodstove." If you're ever at a "weekend party" with Dawn, please don't ask her what's so wrong with the "conventional woodstove." Because she will say, "Oh, don't get me started." And if Dawn says that, it means she's already gotten started.

5.

Anyway, not six months later, my mother died, too, at the age of seventy-nine. Her car had apparently gotten stuck, or stalled, on the railroad tracks just outside of town and was hit by a north-bound train carrying propane tanks destined for Quebec. The train struck the car directly in its gas tank. Which exploded. As did the propane tanks. The propane-and-gasoline-fueled fire was so intense that even my mother's bones, even her teeth, had been burned into nothing. There was nothing left of her at all. The volunteer firemen said they'd never seen anything like it.

6.

There was nothing of my mother left to bury. But nevertheless, I buried her next to my father. It was May. The ground was once again unfrozen. My father's funeral had been attended by his athletes and his fellow coaches; my mother's, by her church-goers and also by the many fans of her work on John Calvin, including some of her fellow ministers who were also writers. This group was particularly gloomy: they frowned at me from behind their horn-rimmed glasses; they were like thistles among the just-blooming forsythia. They made me nervous, under-standably. I was expected to give the eulogy, and I knew it was expected that the eulogy would contain some words of wisdom and comfort from John Calvin. But what if I chose the wrong quote? For instance: "I consider looseness with words no less of a defect than looseness of the bowels." This was one of my moth-er's very favorite quotes from John Calvin. She often applied it to me when as a child, and even as an adult, I was taking too long reaching my point or if she suspected I didn't have one. But I didn't think it was exactly right for a eulogy, and I wondered how severely my mother's fellow writers and Calvinists would judge me if I used the word "bowels" to celebrate, or mourn, her passage from this life to the next. God, they were a cold bunch. I bet not one of them had ever felt the warmth of a pellet stove.

I don't know how long I stood there waiting for the right words to come to me, but just when I began to suspect that they never would, a voice called out, "You must submit to supreme suffering in order to discover the completion of joy!" I could not see who in the crowd had spoken, but I didn't recognize the voice: it was bright and warbly, a sweet voice that sounded like it came out of big body. Anyway, the crowd murmured approvingly—the quote was, of course, from John Calvin, and apparently the concept of supreme suffering was just the thing to bring them joy—and so all I said was, "Yes, exactly," and then, probably gratuitously, I added, "I love you, Mom." No one murmured approvingly at this. In fact, I had the definite feeling that later on I would be getting written critiques from my mother's fellow Calvinists, disapproving of the sentimentality and obviousness of my eulogy. But for now, they scattered. I nodded to the cemetery workers, and they moved forward and began to fill in the hole.

As they did, I noticed a woman walking toward me. She was tall and rangy, like one of my father's basketball players, and was wearing the kind of wraparound sunglasses that old people wear even when there's no sun (there was no sun), but her hair was a young woman's hair: it looked coarse and shiny, like horses' hair, and swept dramatically across her forehead, and was black—jet black, I'd say, although I've never actually seen a jet that color. Her face was dark brown and deeply weathered by the sun. She wore bright red pants that stopped just above her ankles, which were bare, and a green-and-red argyle sweater with a green turtleneck underneath, and old-fashioned bright white canvas tennis sneakers. Over the sweater hung a necklace, a silver clipper ship on a silver chain. The necklace was chipped and tarnished and faded as though the ship really had survived some sort of storm. The woman definitely did not look like she was dressed for a funeral. I judged her to be about my mother's age, and in fact she walked like my mother—like a stateswoman, like someone used to approaching and departing a podium—but in other ways she didn't look like my mother at all. Like most ministers, my mother had looked as if she were made in the winter, for the winter. Her clothes—heavy sweaters, loose skirts and dresses—were always gray, and even if they weren't, even if they were other colors, the colors were muted, as though the gray had somehow overpowered them. Perhaps the color came from inside her, because my mother's face had been gray, too. Of course, so had her hair, which she'd refused to dye, and when my father once had made the mistake of wondering why, my mother had glared at him and quoted fiercely, "There is no color in this world that is not intended to make us rejoice."

"Okay. Jeez, *sorry*," my father had said. He'd seemed surprised at my mother's fierceness, and I remember thinking, *Really?*, and I remember also thinking that, you know, maybe this really was my father's first rodeo, no matter what his favorite saying said.

You might be wondering why I'm comparing this stranger to my mother. I wasn't at the time; I am now, in memory, because of what the stranger said to me next.

"Pulverized by a train!" the woman said, and I recognized the bright voice that earlier had called out about suffering and joy. "A wonderful way to die. Although poor Nola probably didn't think so." She paused as though she expected me to respond. But what was I supposed to tell her? The truth, I suppose, which would have been "Probably not." "Tell me," the woman continued, "was she as cold a mother as she was a sister?"

I didn't say anything to that, not right away. I could see myself in her glasses. There was one of me in each lens. Both of me looked confused. "Sister?" I said. Because as far as I knew, my mother didn't have one.

"But what's wrong with that?" my aunt continued. "After all, the cold can teach us many things."

By the way, I soon learned that this was how my aunt spoke: she would say something, and then you would respond directly to what she had said, and then she would not respond directly to your direct response but instead would continue on with her original thought. Only when you consented to follow her thought would she then return to yours.

"What *can* the cold teach us?" I asked, and she smiled. When she smiled her upper lip peeled back and you could see plenty of gum, and I also noticed that she was missing a tooth. It was her left canine. But the missing tooth didn't seem to make her self-conscious. She smiled, happily showing gum and her missing tooth and her remaining teeth, which were as white as her sneakers.

"Twin," my aunt said, letting me know the kind of sister she was.

7.

My aunt's name was Beatrice Stark. Stark had, in fact, been my mother's maiden name. It had suited her so well. I never quite understood why she'd allowed marriage to change it.

"I've been reading your stories," my aunt said, and I noticed that she spoke like an elementary school teacher or an adult character in a TV show for children: her voice tended to go up at the end of her sentences no matter what the sentence was saying.

"My stories?"

"'My mother always said that her house never really felt like a home until she got a US Defender with a built-in blower and ash drawer,'" my aunt said, and I recognized the sentence from my blog. My aunt recited this sweetly and as far as I could tell not mockingly at all. But still, I was grateful for her sunglasses because as she must have guessed, the sentence from my blog was pure fiction: my mother had in fact always refused to get a pellet stove. She found the term "pellet stove" offensive and the word "blog" even more so. "It's a made-up word," she'd once said, and then I'd made the mistake of saying, "All words are made-up words, aren't they?" and then my mother had on the spot sermonized at length on the subject, and the gist of the sermon was no, they are not.

Anyway, my aunt had read my blog, and so she must have seen my post about the US Defender, which was also a post about my mother's death, which was how she knew to come to the funeral. I didn't ask from where she'd traveled. I didn't ask if she'd liked my blog. I didn't even want to say the word "blog"; I was afraid that my aunt would claim that it was a made-up word, too. The professional blogger basically has two fears: that no one reads his posts and that someone reads his posts and can't wait to tell him how much she doesn't like them. The noise of the backhoe and the cemetery workers grew more distant, and I realized, without paying attention, that my mother—or at least the idea of my mother, since there was no body to actually put in the casket; the train had made sure of that—was now fully underground, and as with my father, I'd once again missed the chance to say goodbye.

My aunt turned and began to walk away from my parents' graves. I did the same. We walked next to each other, and I wonder if she felt, as I did, like she wasn't sure what to do with her hands, her arms. I kept wondering if she was going to hook one of hers in one of mine. Well, she didn't. We soon reached my car and, parked in front of mine, her pickup truck: Indiana plates, beat up, rusty, more weathered looking even than my aunt's face. The fender appeared to be held to the rest of the truck by duct tape. It didn't seem like the kind of thing a woman my aunt's age would drive and was the first sign that she was not entirely what she appeared to be. Aunt Beatrice got in the truck. The door made an arthritic sound as it open and closed.

"How do you feel?" my aunt said through the open driver's-side window.

Alone, I wanted to say. But you don't say this kind of thing to an aunt you didn't know existed until a few minutes earlier, or to anyone else for that matter. "I feel all right," I said. She didn't respond to this. She was still wearing the sunglasses, and I noticed that there was another pair on the dashboard. I wanted to see her eyes, but I had the strange feeling that if I asked Aunt Beatrice to take off her glasses and she did, she'd be wearing another pair underneath. My aunt started the truck. It sounded surprisingly healthy—quiet to the point of being subdued. But the engine noise was at least loud enough to wake up a dog in the truck bed, because from the bed came a sudden violent barking. I took a step back, then another when I saw a large husky-looking thing stand up in the bed. It saw me and barked even more maniacally. When it barked, the dog's upper gum peeled back the way my aunt's did when she smiled. The dog, I noticed, had both its canines and all its other teeth, too.

"To recognize warmth," my aunt said, and only after she'd driven off did I realize that she'd finally told me what the cold can teach us.

Two

8.

To Recognize Warmth

Thank you, dear readers, for all your many consoling and comforting words about my mother's passing. I appreciate them. My mother would have appreciated them, too. My mother was a minister, after all, and she believed that God put us on this earth to console and comfort each other.

The pellet stove industry, of course, also believes in consolation and comfort! There are more and more of you satisfied pellet stove owners who know this to be true, and with help of new government green initiatives (like the two-thousand-dollar rebates on all the new Jutsol and Ironhorse superconductive models!), the pellet stove is more affordable than ever! In fact, my long-lost aunt Beatrice, who came to my mother's—her sister's—funeral and has decided to stay me for a while is so enjoying the US Defender that she just asked how much it costs. The question was idle, I think, but once she heard how low the purchasing price and how high the energy savings, well, it won't surprise any members of my virtual pellet stove posse to hear that I think she's strongly considering buying one of her own!

9.

Religion is rules, of course, and so is sports, and so is blogging for the pellet stove industry. Those rules dictate that I title my blogs and that I use exclamation points when writing about the pellet stove industry, or pellet stove models, or any happy feeling one might derive from a pellet stove. The rules dictate that I am allowed to use anecdotes about my family life as long as they are somehow related to the pleasures of the pellet stove. The rules also dictate that I never, ever, admit or indicate that I am merely writing into the void, but on the contrary act as though I have a large audience of readers, and that I begin my posts by referring to my readers formally as "dear readers," but then by the end of the post refer to them more familiarly as "my posse," and that I also refer to their kind correspondences even though I have never received one of these correspondences—kind or otherwise. Readers would know this, of course, because there is a comments section at the end of each post, and not once has anyone left a comment. But of course you'd have to read the post first to know that no one has left a comment.

So no one had ever left a comment. But at least I knew now that I had one reader: my aunt. She'd told me that she'd read my blog! And then she'd left without telling me where was she staying, when I would see her again, if I would see her again. That's why I wrote the post, in my car, on my phone, right there in the cemetery. At the time I chose not to wonder why I was writing these things, these lies. After all, I lied in my blog all the time. That was another rule: to think of lies as enhancements and not lies. But I know now why I lied. So that Aunt Beatrice would realize that she'd left without telling me where she was staying. So that she would know that I was wondering when I would see her again.

10.

It was eight o'clock as I made my way home through Congress. Let me tell you about the town, then, as I drive through it in memory now. The cemetery was behind the Congregational church. That was my mother's church. It was modestly steepled, white, clapboard. A church that would have been unassuming had it not been high on a hill, perfectly positioned to look down at the rest of the town. I took a left out of the cemetery, down the hill, and went past the ancient stone public library with its limited hours; past my father's school and its playing fields; past the charcoal plant; past the lumberyard; past the boat launch to

Lake Congress; into the center of town itself, which consisted of a town green, in the center of which was a gazebo and also a monument to our Soldiers and Sailors, and on the periphery of which were ten houses, all also white clapboard, and on the periphery of those houses were maybe a two dozen more houses, houses that used to be white clapboard but now were white and off-white vinyl siding.

There. I've told you about the town. Everything else in the town was actually outside the town, and everything outside the town was more or less the same as the things that are outside every town that more or less resembles the town of Congress.

11.

My parents' house was right on the green. I say "my parents' house," but except for my four years of college and then my two years of marriage, I'd lived there, too, and now that my mother was dead, I lived there by myself. I got out of my car and stood there on the porch, looking out on the green and listening to the town's nighttime chirpings and the faint motorboat noises coming off the lake. In her famous book my mother suggested that people in small towns were closer to God than people who lived in cities or in the country because at exactly this time of night, before they went to bed, they could sit out on their porches and sense the fine fellow feelings of their neighbors while at the same time appreciate the goodness and immensity of the natural world. I supposed that might be true, but it was also true that our neighbors seemed most prone to conduct their loud domestic arguments at dusk, and in fact once from this very porch I watched in the firefly-flicked gloaming a man chase his elderly father across the green and onto the gazebo steps, which is where the man caught and tackled his father and then beat him unconscious with a full plastic bottle of laundry detergent.

12.

Charles Otis. That was the name of the son. The father's name was Leland Otis. After Charles was done beating his father, he walked back across the green, past my house. As I said, I was standing on the porch. Charles saw me. But he didn't acknowledge me and kept walking. Several minutes later his father walked past my house, too. He was staggering, bleeding from the top of his bald head and also carrying the bottle of detergent, which, like his head, was dented. He also saw me and also, like his son, didn't acknowledge me. And why would they? And for that matter, why would I acknowledge them, what they had done, what I had seen? What was there to acknowledge? Because I already knew everything about them: they were Charles Otis and Leland Otis. And they already knew everything about me: I was Calvin Bledsoe.

13.

Anyway, I was thinking of this incident with the Otises, and of my mother, and of my father, and of my aunt, and of the empty green in front of me, and of the empty house behind me, when my cell phone rang.

14.

Earlier I mentioned Dawn, the other blogger for the pellet stove industry. It is time to admit that Dawn was the wife from whom I was separated. As my father had predicted, we'd gotten divorced, and then she'd moved away to Charlotte, North Carolina. But she still called me, pretty much every night. All that I had not mentioned. Because you cannot *mention* everything at once. This is yet another rule of blogging for the pellet stove industry.

"How was it?" Dawn asked. She was referring to my mother's funeral and burial. But her voice was pinched in a way that let me know that she already knew how it was. Dawn and my mother had not been friends. My mother tended to refer to her as "your scowling wife" and then, later, "your scowling ex-wife." For her part, Dawn hated my mother's sermons, and her book, which she thought was condescending in the extreme. According to Dawn, my mother's attitude toward grace suggested that we all want to be good people, or at least the best of us do.

"It was all right," I said, and I could picture Dawn scowling. "All right" was, according to Dawn, my favorite expression, and it was no coincidence that it was Dawn's least favorite expression. "My aunt Beatrice was there."

"Since when do you have an aunt?"

"She was my mother's twin."

"Since when did your mother have a twin?"

Since birth, I wanted to say. But I knew from long experience that it was useless to argue with Dawn. Not because I couldn't win, although I couldn't, but because Dawn didn't necessarily want to win either; she just didn't want the argument to end. She wanted it to go on forever. You'd think that divorce would have put an end the argument, but no.

I'm afraid I'm making Dawn seem awful. In fact, she mostly was. But still, since she'd moved to Charlotte, she sometimes appeared to me, the way God is supposed to. She didn't appear to me whole, but in parts. Her hair, for instance. Dawn had great hair. Spectacular locks. Many reddish coils springing from her head like ideas. Or her boots. Dawn liked to wear knee-high leather boots, riding boots, although she didn't ride.

15.

I say that we divorced. But in fact, it's Dawn who divorced me, because I wouldn't move with her to Charlotte in first place. This infuriated her. Dawn thought, what was the point in having a job that you could do from wherever you wanted if you all you wanted was to do it from where you were? In her kinder moments Dawn thought I didn't want to move to Charlotte with her because I didn't want to leave my parents and then, after my father died, my mother, in Congress. In her less kind moments she thought I didn't want to leave my parents and Congress and move with her to Charlotte because I was, in her words, "a big pussy." Now that my parents had died, she thought I would no longer be a big pussy and would finally leave Congress and join her in Charlotte.

"I'm wearing shorts," Dawn said. Like a lot of people who have moved from cold to warm places, Dawn liked to talk on the phone about how little she was wearing. This wasn't seduction. It was incredulity: Dawn couldn't understand why I wasn't living in a warm place from where I could then call people in a cold place and tell them that I was wearing shorts, too.

"I'm wearing shorts, too," I said.

"To your mother's funeral," Dawn said. I could hear typing noises, and I wondered if she was working on her blog. I could picture her curls fighting against the oppression of her headset.

"I changed." I hadn't; I was still wearing my gray funeral suit. I had left the porch and was now walking through the house. There, in the mudroom, were framed pictures of my father and his players in their official team photos. There, in the dining room, over the fireplace, was a painting of John Calvin, a portrait done by one of his contemporaries, which had been a gift from one of my mother's acolytes and which was worth more than the whole house. There, in my mother's study, on the north wall, were framed jackets from all the domestic and international editions of her famous book; on the south wall, her framed divinity degree. There, in the living room, on top of the piano, was a photo of the three of us taken right after my baptism. That was the only picture of the three of us on display in the house. Who knows why? Maybe more would have been considered idolatrous. But I knew that my mother kept a photo album in the piano seat. I opened it, and yes, there it still was. I flipped through until I found a picture of my teenaged mother in tennis shoes, and her parents (whom I'd never met—they'd died before I was born), and a teenaged girl also in tennis shoes. It was clearly Aunt Beatrice—even then her face was sun crisped, her black hair swept dramatically over her forehead. But my mother, when I'd asked her once who the girl was, had told me it was a distant cousin and to put the photo album back in piano bench, hurry up, we have to go to the field, or the court, maybe it was to the church, I can't remember which, and I can't remember if my mother had told me her cousin's name or, if she had, if she'd said it was Beatrice or made up a different name. In any case, it was definitely my aunt Beatrice. She wasn't wearing sunglasses either: her eyes were blue, I could tell that even with her squinting into the sun. And she was smiling. It was the same smile but less wolfish, more wholesome. Back then, she still had her tooth.

"When are you coming to Charlotte?" Dawn wanted to know, and I told her what I'd been telling her in the days since my mother died: that I needed to clean up the house, fix what needed to be fixed, put it on the market. I would come to Charlotte just as soon as I sold the house.

But the truth was that I wasn't going to do any of that. The truth was that I was never going to move to Charlotte. I was going to stay in my house in Congress. Alone. Forever. Earlier I'd wanted to say to my aunt that I felt alone. But that was all right with me. I wasn't afraid of feeling alone. I'd always felt alone. I'd felt alone when my parents were still alive, and I'd felt alone when I was married to Dawn, and I would feel alone if I moved to Charlotte to be with Dawn. The difference was, when you are alone with other people you have to pretend that you don't feel alone, the way a blogger for the pellet stove industry has to pretend he isn't writing into the void. I had to pretend to be a blogger. Other than that, I didn't want to pretend anymore.

16.

After I said good night to Dawn, I turned off the lights and went to bed. Several hours later I found myself awake and standing at the window, and I didn't know what I was doing there, but I was scared.

"I'm scared," I said to no one. Just then I heard several popping noises, and I realized that was what had gotten me out of bed and brought me to the window: I'd heard popping noises. The popping noises got louder and closer, and then I saw a skunk waddling down the middle of the street, and behind it were my neighbors, Charles and Leland Otis. They were holding BB guns and they were firing the guns at the skunk. Charles, the son, was wearing an oversized hooded sweatshirt, as usual, and Leland, the father, a flannel shirt, also as usual. Leland was very thin, and Charles was very fat—so very fat that I sometimes wondered if Charles was that fat on purpose; I sometimes wondered if his obesity was an intentional rebellion against his very thin father. I didn't wonder why they were shooting at the skunk: I'm sure the skunk had offended them in some way, because the Otises were always quick to be offended. I did wonder why the skunk didn't spray them. Maybe it already had. Maybe it was all sprayed out. The skunk went under my car, which was parked on the street, and the Otises kept firing and I heard the *ping ping* of the BBs hitting the car, and then the skunk emerged from the car and the Otises were pretty much on top of it by now and I could see the skunk lurch to the left and stumble and almost fall, but then it didn't fall; it managed to disappear down a storm drain, and then the Otises fired a few more rounds into the storm drain and then they strolled back across the green, past the gazebo, laughing and twirling their Daisys around their index fingers like gun-slingers. As they walked past my house I could have sworn both Otises looked at my house, looked up toward my bedroom, saw me standing there, stared at me staring at them. Then they kept walking. There was a thick fog rolling in from the lake, and the Otises disappeared into it. A second later I heard another gun-shot, and then I heard one of the Otises howl and then the other one laugh, and then the phone rang. I knew it was Dawn—she sometimes liked to call me in the middle of the night, when I was most likely to be confused and vulnerable—and in my con-fused, vulnerable state I thought there was a connection between the phone call and Otises; I thought that Dawn had hired the Otises to scare me. To scare me away from Congress and toward Charlotte. And it had worked. They had scared me so much that I was ready to say right then to Dawn on the telephone, *I will move to be with you in Charlotte. It is the wrong thing to do, but I will do it because I'm scared.*

"I'm scared," I said into the phone, and for several seconds I heard nothing, not even breathing, and I took the phone away from my ear and looked at the screen and saw the words UNKNOWN CALLER, and when I put the phone back to my ear, an automated man's voice said, "Clear sailing," and then he hung up.

Three

17.

As I said, in my middle-of-the-night muddledness, it seemed as though there was a connection between the Otises shooting at the skunk and the phone call. And in fact there was a connection. But I had no way of knowing what it was at the time.

18.

I woke up at nine in the morning, five hours after the phone call, feeling as though I were responsible for murder—my own or someone else's, I couldn't tell which. I sat up, sweating. My head was full of weapons: BB guns, of course, but also lasers, machetes, bazookas, coiled phone cords long enough to strangle someone. I don't only mean that my head was full of the thoughts of these things; I also mean that it felt as though these weapons were in my head, and they and their wielders were trying to get out. As though the Otises had turned their guns around and were with the gun butts trying to pound their way out of my forehead. Pounding, that's all I could feel and hear, pounding and more pounding, and then I realized it wasn't only coming from my head: someone was pounding on the front door.

I scrambled downstairs, opened the door, and there was my aunt standing there on the porch. She was wearing her sunglasses and the same very white sneakers. The rest of her clothes were only somewhat different from the ones she'd worn to my mother's funeral: her pants were green, her sweater blue, her turtle-neck a lighter shade of blue. I had the distinct impression that my aunt had a closet full of clothes that were different from one another only in their primary colors. Behind her I could see the truck and, in the bed, her dog, standing, pointed in my direction, alert.

The sun was dazzling and made my head feel even worse. I envied my aunt her sunglasses. She seemed, from behind those glasses, to be sizing me up. I realized that before I'd gone to bed I'd taken off my suit jacket and tie and shoes but had managed to fall asleep in my suit pants and my dress shirt. I must have looked like a dissipated businessman. Hotel rooms. Minibars. Rumpled sheets. I fought off the urge to tell my aunt that I rarely drank alcohol and that I never, except for today, woke up later than six thirty in the morning.

"I didn't sleep well last night," I explained to my aunt, then told her the story of being woken up in the middle of the night—first by the Otises shooting at the skunk and then the phone call from the automated man's voice saying "Clear sailing." My aunt seemed interested in the story. She adjusted her glasses and adjusted them again, and for a moment I thought she was going to take them off, but she didn't. Instead, she asked me to tell the story again. I did and added in this retelling that I'd told whoever was on the phone that I was scared, and I also mentioned Dawn, mentioned that I'd been on the phone with her before everything else had happened. I didn't tell my aunt that Dawn was my ex-wife, or that she was also a blogger for the pellet stove industry, or that she lived in Charlotte, or that she wanted me to live in Charlotte, too. I figured I'd save those details, and if my aunt asked me to tell her the story again, I'd add those details later. This is something else I'd learned blogging for the pellet stove industry: if you have to say something three times a week (I blogged three times a week), then you need to save some of what you have to say for the days when you have nothing to say.

But my aunt didn't ask me to tell the story again. She asked, "What were you so scared of?"

"I'd just buried my mother!" I said, and my aunt adjusted her glasses again, and I wondered if she knew that that wasn't the truth, or the whole truth. "He was an unknown caller," I said, talking about the man on the phone.

"Oh, there are no unknown callers," my aunt said in her usual cheerful way, and if I were more awake, I might have wondered how it was she thought she knew that.

"You're surprisingly bald, Calvin," my aunt added. Again, she said this brightly. My aunt had a knack for saying insulting things in a way that made them sound like they were happy points of fact, not insults at all.

"I shaved my head," I told her, and explained that a year or so earlier I had become highly conscious of the fact that I was losing my hair and that the hair I still had was gray and that this made me look older than I was or than I wanted to be. So as a corrective I shaved my head completely and grew a beard, which, I was now admitting for the first time, even to myself, was grayer and grizzlier and patchier than the head hair had been.

When I was through talking, my aunt said pleasantly, "I have never understood men." I waited for her to say more, but no, that was apparently all she had to say on that subject, and she was ready to move on to the next one.

"I thought you and I might take a little trip," my aunt said.

"I'd like that," I said. Maybe I even meant it. I had never been much of a traveler, not as an adult, and certainly not as a child. During the week my mother prepared for her sermons; on the weekend she delivered them. During the week my father prepared for his teams' games; on the weekend he coached them. The life of the cloth and the life of the whistle aren't so different. "Where?" I asked. I was thinking of somewhere close by, something that wouldn't be too tiring for an old lady: a day trip to a lake or a mountain; lunch at a historic inn in a nearby small town that compared to Congress was a somewhat bigger small town.

"Stockholm, Sweden," my aunt said.

"*Where?*" I said. My aunt adjusted her sunglasses and cocked her head in a way that I guessed was meant to say that she'd just told me where. "Why?"

Aunt Beatrice ignored this question. Maybe her sister's death had given her the right not to answer questions she didn't feel like answering. Did surviving give you rights? Only later did I begin to wonder what mine were.

"I've already bought the tickets," my aunt said. She reached into her back pocket and produced a ticket, which she handed to me. It was a real ticket, too—a stiff piece of off-white paper the size and shape of small envelope—not just a piece of paper you print from your computer. I looked at it. There was my name. The ticket said I was flying from Boston to Stockholm tonight.

"I can't," I said. My aunt didn't say anything. No doubt she was waiting to hear my reasons. I decided to try, at first, the most practical one. "I don't have a passport."

My aunt smiled as she reached inside her other back pocket and handed me my passport, too. "Tuck your ticket inside it," my aunt said. I did that, and she drew a deep, satisfied breath. "I do like to see an airplane ticket sticking out of a passport," she said.

19.

Later, it would seem ridiculous that I'd actually believed that someone who had gone ahead and gotten my passport without my Social Security number or signature or presence or permission had then so easily taken no for an answer.

"I'm sorry, I just can't," I said to my aunt. My aunt pursed her lips and nodded, as though I'd given her the expected answer. For a second it made me want to give her an unexpected answer. But only for a second. "I have so much to do."

"I understand."

"There's my job."

"Of course."

"And I have to get the house ready. I'm going to put it on the market once I get it ready."

"I understand," my aunt said again. I felt strangely accomplished. I'd given this excuse to Dawn many times, and not once had she said she'd understood.

"Well, you'll at least drive me to the airport," my aunt said, and then she held out her hand until I realized what she wanted—my passport and the ticket inside it—and I handed them back to her. Why she wanted the passport, I didn't know: she couldn't use it. But I know why I gave it back to her: because she had asked for it, and because if I didn't have a passport, then I would have another excuse not to go somewhere I did not want to go.

20.

I wonder how different my life would have been if I'd said no to my aunt's request. Very, probably.

But it's not easy to say no to an elderly relative's request that you drive her to the airport, especially if you've already denied her much bigger request. I didn't even attempt it. I said, "All right," and asked my aunt if she wanted to wait inside her old house while I got dressed. But she just shook her head and said in her disarmingly upbeat way, "The house of horrors."

It took me several seconds to realize that she was talking about my parents' house, which is to say, now, my house. When you are woken up in the middle of the night, you eventually make the trip from confusion through fear to annoyance. It had taken me five hours, but finally I'd completed the journey and was annoyed. I'd lived my entire life in this house. It was a perfectly all-right house. Nothing great had happened to me there. But nothing horrible had ever happened to me there either. "I saw a picture of you," I said to her accusingly, although I had no idea what the accusation was supposed to be. Aunt Beatrice didn't say anything to that. This annoyed me even more. Here she had appeared out of nowhere after being absent *my entire life* and then insulted my house, without even seeming to be curious about what it was like now or what picture of her I'd seen. "You had all your teeth then," I said to her, annoyed.

It was, up to that moment, the meanest thing I'd ever said. And do you know what it caused to happen? My aunt laughed, a laugh that sounded like a noise her dog would make. One sudden, sharp, hoarse *ruff*. It felt good being able to produce such immediate happiness. My blog certainly had never produced anything like that. I took silent note of what meanness could do. As John Calvin himself once said, "We must remember that Satan has his miracles, too."

21.

I was just about to walk into the house to get changed when my aunt called from behind me, "And who is Dawn?"

"Dawn is the other blogger for the pellet stove industry," I told her, perhaps too quickly, and without turning to face her. Aunt Beatrice said nothing to this. The silence was like a command to turn around. I did that. My aunt was leaning against her truck, arms crossed over her chest. "If you're ever at a weekend party with Dawn," I told my aunt, "don't ask her what's so wrong with the conventional woodstove." And then I told my aunt why not to ask Dawn this, and my aunt said in her happy way, "She sounds wonderful!" and then I turned and went back into the house, feeling like I'd gotten away with something.

22.

I came out of the house five minutes later, still stuck on what my aunt had said about it being a house of horrors. "She wasn't a bad mother, you know," I said to my aunt, who was still leaning against her truck. I was thinking of the time, right after I began blogging for the pellet stove industry, when I overheard my mother talking with one of her fellow writers and ministers. He wasn't from Maine. These people would come from all over the country, so eager were they to talk with my mother about how beautifully she wrote about how beautifully John Calvin wrote. Anyway, he and she were in the church, sitting side by side in a pew. I was in the balcony above. It was quiet in the balcony. I often liked to sit up there and think about pellet stoves and then with my thumbs type my blog on my cell phone. My mother and the minister had no idea I was sitting right above them. This is a good thing to remember in this life: no one ever looks up.

The other minister was asking about me. He had a slender, bent neck. Sloped shoulders. Terrible posture. I don't think I'd ever seen such a question mark of a man. "How's your boy?" he said. His accent was flat, and I assumed he was from somewhere flat, too.

"He's just started writing for the pellet stove industry," my mother said. I did notice that she said "writing" and not "blogging." But I also noticed some color in her voice, as though she were pleased enough to be reporting this news.

"He has," this man said in his flat, flat voice.

My mother gave me, as a child, an illustrated Old Testament, and in that book there is an illustration of the Garden of Eden, and in that illustration the serpent is looking menacingly at Adam and Eve with its neck flared out. Well, my mother's neck flared like the serpent's as she spat this quote from John Calvin at the flat-voiced minister: "There is no work, however vile or sordid, that does not glisten before God."

23.

"And your father?" my aunt said.

"My father was a good guy," I said. I believed this to be true. Also, this was what most people said about him. For instance, his former athletes and fellow coaches at his funeral: Roger Bledsoe was a good coach, they said, but more than that, he was a *good guy*.

"Have you ever noticed," my aunt said, "that whenever someone says someone else is a good guy, then no one ever wants to know anything more about it? But when someone gets called a bad guy, then that's not enough. We want to know exactly how and why."

I had not ever noticed this. It was probably worth noticing. But I was wondering about something else. "How well did you know my father?"

"Well enough," my aunt said.

"Did you know his sayings?"

Aunt Beatrice smiled and said, "This isn't my first rodeo, you know." Her expression was fond, and far away, very much like those people at my father's funeral, and I expected her to say that my father was a good guy, but she didn't.

"When was the last time you were . . ." And here I paused, because I'd been about to use the word "home," but I had the strong feeling that "home" wasn't the right word to describe the place I was about to ask her about. "In Congress?" I said instead.

"Around the time when you were born," my aunt said.

"Why didn't my mother ever tell me about you?" I asked my aunt.

"Because I was a bad guy," my aunt said, looking directly at me. Her expression wasn't at all far away anymore. Her mouth was closed, but I could picture her missing tooth.

My aunt was right: now that she'd said she was a bad guy, I wanted to know more. I wanted to know exactly how and why. "All right," I said instead, and we changed the subject.

24.

When did I begin to suspect that my aunt was really my mother and that the woman I'd thought was my mother was really my aunt? I don't know if it was right then, when my aunt said she was a bad guy. But I must have felt some sort of disturbance, because after this conversation I did something out of character. As I walked around the back of my aunt's truck I felt a strong desire to pet the dog. He growled when I stuck out my hand for him to sniff, but then he did sniff it, and then he did let me pet him.

Four

25.

We took my aunt's truck to the airport. I'd assumed, since she wanted me to come with her to the airport, that she'd want me to actually drive whichever vehicle we were taking. Old people are famously afraid of highway driving, and in fact my mother hadn't driven over forty-five miles per hour for the twenty years before she died. High speed was one of her few fears.

But no, my aunt wanted to drive. The dog stayed behind. I mean that before my aunt drove off, she lowered the gate on the back of the truck and the dog jumped out, ran up my front steps, and sat on my front porch in front of the door, as though the house were his to guard. I supposed when I came back from the airport, he would be my dog until my aunt returned. What would I do with him? I was planning on installing a pellet stove, and I could picture the dog sitting next to it. But then, I'd already pictured me sitting next to it. I wasn't sure if there was room enough in the picture for both of us.

26.

There, on the truck's bench seat, between my aunt and me, was my mother's famous book: *When I Was a Child, I Read John Calvin.* It was the paperback edition. On the back cover, I knew, was a photo of my mother shaking hands with the president of the United States of America. It was the president who'd said, upon first meeting my mother minutes before the photo had been taken, "So you're the little lady who wrote the great book that got us all talking about John Calvin again."

27.

I asked my aunt, "Did you read John Calvin as a child?" According to my mother's famous book, my grandfather—who was also a minister in Congress, as was his father—had had my mother read John Calvin as a child, and John Calvin had taught her everything: how to love, how to talk, how to think, how to write, how to live. But of course my mother had not mentioned my aunt in her famous book. Or anywhere else, for that matter. "Did you read John Calvin as a child, too?" I asked her.

My aunt answered by quoting John Calvin: "The effect of our knowledge . . . ought to be, first, to teach us reverence and fear." Which I understood to mean "Yes."

Because I, too, had been made to read John Calvin when I was a child, and I, too, would have used that quote to answer that question.

28.

Just as we were about to pull away from the curb, the Otises walked by. I mentioned before how different they were from each other. But they had one thing in common: they were always chewing on something. This morning, black coffee stirrers, which were bobbing out of the corners of their mouths. Other than that, and as usual, they didn't look like they could be related to each other. The morning light made Leland look drawn, weathered, and ancient, even more so than usual. I wondered if he was sick; he looked so thin in his tucked-in flannel; his shaved cheeks looked like they were being vacuumed from the inside. Charles, on the other hand, was full faced and unshaven and looked overstuffed in his enormous sweatshirt. His oversized sweatshirts always had outsized political messages on them. Today he wore a black sweatshirt. Its message, in large white block letters, read I'M 1776% SURE I'M KEEPING ALL MY GUNS'. There was usually something wrong on these sweatshirts, some typo or mispunctuation (in this case, the apostrophe at the end of "guns"), and these mistakes helped me hope that Charles meant the messages to be ironic. My mother, in her famous book, had made the famous argument that we should reject irony because irony is the death of hope. But one of the things my aunt taught me is that irony is essentially hopeful, especially if you need to believe that the things that other people think or say or wear are meant ironically.

"Bea," Leland said to my aunt around his coffee stirrer and through her open window. She didn't say anything back. Just looked at him from behind the barrier of her very large sunglasses. "Sorry about your sister," he added flatly, and still she didn't respond. Maybe because he didn't sound especially sorry. And in any case, my mother had never seemed especially fond of the Otises—they attended her church but always sat in the last pew, arms crossed, a picture not of devotion but defiance—and I wondered if my aunt disliked them, too.

"Nothing left of her at all," Charles said. He was on my side of the truck but seemed to be speaking not to me but to my aunt through my open window. I could smell a strong funk coming off him and I wondered if the skunk had gotten to the Otises after all, before the Otises had gotten to the skunk.

"Never seen anything like it," Leland agreed. They were talking about the manner of my mother's death. Because they were two of Congress's volunteer firemen who had gone to the scene of the accident and had discovered that there was nothing left of my mother to discover.

My aunt didn't say anything still. She fiddled with her glasses, and fiddled with them, but otherwise didn't seem inclined to respond. The air was full of the tension between people who haven't seen each other in forever but who nonetheless have known each other for too long and too well.

Meanwhile, Charles's skunk smell was starting to overwhelm

me. I considered telling him to take a step back, but we'd known each other all our lives—we'd even graduated in the same high school class together—and not once had I told him to do something, and I didn't think I could start now. So instead I asked in a whisper, "Did you know I had an aunt?"

Charles grinned around his coffee stirrer, which I took to mean yes, he did know.

"Why didn't you tell me?" I asked.

Charles stopped grinning and shot me a hostile, confused look, the kind of look you might direct at a stranger, and all of a sudden the truck was full of the tension between people who see each other all the time and who nonetheless don't know each other at all. "Why the *fuck* would I tell *you* that *you* had an aunt?" Charles said. He took a step back from truck as though I were the one who smelled.

"Well, Bea, I don't suppose we'll be seeing you again," Leland said from the driver's side, and my aunt then put the truck into gear as if to say, *I suppose not.* And then Leland Otis took a step back from the truck, too, and my aunt drove off.

29.

Two hours later we were on the highway, already near the New Hampshire border, making very good time. My aunt, unlike my mother, was not afraid of high speeds. Although I couldn't say exactly how fast she was going. The truck's speedometer seemed to be broken. The needle hadn't moved from zero. The gas gauge seemed to be broken also. Its needle hadn't moved from empty.

"Do you know what your mother was afraid of?" my aunt asked me.

You, I guessed in my head. *John Calvin*, I guessed in the same place. "High speeds," I said with my mouth instead.

"No," she said, "it was you."

This was a ridiculous thing to say—no one had ever been scared of me, least of all my mother—and couldn't be true. But I very much wanted it to be true, and it embarrassed me how much I wanted it to be true, how much I wanted my poor dead mother to have been scared of me. I wanted that so much that I was worried it would be obvious to my aunt, that the want would appear plainly on my face, like a pimple or a tic, and so to distract us both from it, I blurted out the first thing that came to my mind, which was, "Well, she should have been afraid of trains."

It was something my aunt might have said; I'd even said it in my aunt's bright tone of voice. My aunt smiled, in approval, I thought. And looking back, I realize what was going on: John Calvin had taught my mother how to love, how to talk, how to think, how to write, how to live, and now, my aunt was trying to teach me how to do those things, too.

30.

My lessons began immediately. One of the things my aunt taught me during the drive to the airport was to make sudden, sweeping generalizations, generalizations that would be hard to defend, which was why it was important that you made no attempt to defend them. For instance, just over the New Hampshire border, my aunt pointed out my window. There, in the middle lane, was a green sedan, and on the driver's-side door of that sedan were numbered buttons. You unlocked the door using a combination instead of a key or a remote control clicker. My aunt asked if I'd seen one of those combination locks before, and I said yes. My aunt asked if I'd ever owned a car with that kind of lock on the door, and I said no.

"Good," Aunt Beatrice said. "I find that people who have those on their cars are racists."

31.

As we crossed into Massachusetts Aunt Beatrice said, "You know, I liked that you wrote about me." She was, I realized, talking about my blog. I felt my head, my chest, filling up with warm liquid. No one had ever said they'd liked what I'd written. Not my parents. Not Dawn. Even my employers in the pellet stove industry were neutral on the subject. The sentence *Please don't go to Stockholm* popped into my head, and it might have then popped out of my mouth if my aunt hadn't added, "Of course, it was all lies."

"I'm sorry."

"Don't be," my aunt said. "That's what I liked about it."

32.

Some miles later I asked, "Aunt Beatrice, where have you been . . ." I was going to finish the question with "all my life," but that sounded like a thing you'd say not to an aunt but to a wife, or a future wife, although, as Dawn would be the first person to tell you, I'd never said it to her. Although in fairness, to myself, she'd never said it to me either. And in fairness to both of us, this was not the kind of thing you would ever say if you were a blogger for the pellet stove industry because the person would know where you'd been: you'd have been on your phone or your computer, blogging for the pellet stove industry. If you were that kind of person, then no matter where you were, that's where you'd been and that's what you'd been doing.

"All over the world," my aunt said. She brushed her hair away from her forehead, but then it fell back again immediately as though it could not be denied.

"Did you live in Stockholm?"

My aunt nodded. "I wanted to show you some of my old haunts," my aunt said, then added in voice much more pitiable than the one she'd been using, "before I die."

I didn't respond to that, perhaps because I began to suspect my aunt was manipulating me. But then we were getting closer to Boston, and like many people from small remote places, cities made me paranoid. Whenever I approached a city—and before I met my aunt I almost never approached a city—it was as though I were entering a question, a question directed at me, and inside the question was the answer to the question, plain for me to know, and yet somehow I knew that I would never know the answer. The trees thinned, the roads grew wider, the number of lanes multiplied, the traffic thickened and slowed, the billboards

proliferated. On one of the billboards was this message: YOU
CALL HIM "THE MAN UPSTAIRS." BUT HE HAS A *NAME*.

33.

Which is to say that earlier I was thinking of how I didn't want
my aunt to go to Stockholm, but now I was thinking about
getting her to the airport as quickly as possible and then getting
back to Congress, to my house, where I could write my blog for
the pellet stove industry and be alone.

But at each moment, when I should have been getting closer
to achieving that goal, something got in the way. For instance,
I'd supposed that my aunt would just pull up to the departures
curb, that she'd get out, and I'd say goodbye, then get into the
driver's seat and drive home. But instead my aunt ignored the
signs for departures and followed the ones toward parking.
When I asked her about it, my aunt said in that same pitiable
voice, "An old lady does like to be escorted into the airport."
Once again I felt manipulated—Aunt Beatrice's appeal to her
old age wasn't exactly convincing—but nonetheless, I didn't
argue as my aunt drove to the parking lot, which was full. So she
drove to the next lot, which was also full. Finally, she found a
spot in the economy lot. But then we had to take the shuttle bus
to the terminal. My aunt's terminal was the last on the shuttle's
route. And then, right before our stop, there were an extraor-
dinary number of cars, all of them dropping off people at the
departures curb (which was exactly what I'd planned on us doing
in the first place), including several cars that were parked where

the shuttle bus was supposed to stop. And the driver wouldn't let us off anywhere but the official stop. My aunt was very calm this entire time. But at each delay, my need to return to Congress felt more urgent but also more impossible. I'd had a kidney stone once that made me feel the same way. Very painful.

Finally, though, we got off the bus and stepped inside the terminal. I would have said goodbye to my aunt and driven back to Congress in the truck if two things hadn't happened.

"Does that man look familiar, Calvin?" my aunt said, and that was the first thing. She'd nodded her head in the direction of one of the large neon boards announcing departures and arrivals. There, standing in front of it, was a man reading the board. He was dressed in a suit, funeral gray, and was holding a hat in his hands, brimmed, old-fashioned, dented at the crown, also gray. His hair was likewise gray, not as thin as mine would have been had I allowed it to grow but still thin enough, combed to the side. His face was thin, too. The man looked hungry. He was looking at the board in the way of a turtle. By this I mean, his head was tipped back to look up at the board, but his shoulders and neck seemed to hook downward, like a shell, making looking up difficult.

And that's how I recognized him, from his terrible posture: it was the flat-voiced minister who'd been talking to my mother in her church while I spied on them from above in the balcony. I explained this to my aunt. I didn't find his presence in the airport unusual. I hadn't noticed him at the funeral, but then there were lots of gray-faced and -clothed ministers in the crowd.

Surely he'd been among them. Surely he'd flown into Boston, driven up to Congress for the funeral, and then driven back and was now waiting for the plane to take him back from where he'd come. I explained this to my aunt, too, and she nodded and said, "He followed us all the way from Congress to the airport in a 2012 Dodge Lumina, yellow, procured from the Hertz rental car agency. He parked the car in a spot eleven spots to the east of where I parked the truck." My aunt said this in her usual voice, but I noticed her fingers were lightly dancing on the strap of her purse as though it were an instrument.

I looked at my aunt, who was looking at the flat-voiced man, and so I looked at him. He was still looking at the board. Aunt Beatrice's accusation seemed unlikely. But it was also true that the man had been looking at the board for a long time now. And it was also true that his eyes seemed to dart in our direction, just for a second, before returning to the board.

"Huh," I said, and might have said more if the second thing hadn't happened.

34.

The phone rang. It was Dawn.

"I do love you, Calvin Bledsoe," she said. If she hadn't called me by name, I might have wondered if she'd meant to be saying this to someone else: Dawn had said those words—"I love you"—to me before, but until now she'd never sounded especially happy saying them.

"All right," I said. I mentioned earlier that Dawn hated that expression. To me, it meant that I was being agreeable. To Dawn, it meant that I didn't care. But what was I supposed to say? *I love you, too*—I suppose I could have said that. And I supposed Dawn would be the one to point that out to me. But no, she laughed. She laughed and said, "Under contract!" and I had to suppress the urge to say "all right" again. "Under contract!" she shouted. "Under contract!" Dawn sounded so happy, and I thought of my mother, who always distrusted loud public expressions of happiness. "Those who loudly insist on their happiness are rarely happy." Those were my mother's words. But Dawn's chanting of "Under contract!" made me also think of these words by John Calvin: "What shall we then say of chanting, which fills the ears with nothing but an empty sound?"

Meanwhile, Aunt Beatrice had turned away from the flat-voiced minister and was now looking at me. I wondered if she could hear Dawn's chanting. I shrugged in apology, mouthed the name "Dawn," then turned away from my aunt and back in the direction of the board, and I noticed that the flat-voiced minister was no longer there. And then Dawn said, "You did it!"

"I did?"

"Under contract!" Dawn said again. Those words were like the words on the billboard: I knew they contained a message meant for me, one that I should easily understand, but its meaning seemed very far away. In between it and me was Dawn's voice in my ear, chanting the message. I held the phone away from my ear and said to my aunt, "Under contract?"

My aunt thought about it a moment. Then she reached into her purse and brought out her own cell phone. It was the newest in the most sophisticated line: as long and wide as a folded map, as thin as a cracker. The phone was so expensive, so cutting edge, that even for a professional blogger it would seem like an indulgence. It was rumored to be the phone of choice for the intelligence and security communities. I wouldn't have been more surprised if my aunt had reached into her purse and brought out the newest, most expensive pellet stove, the Huntelaar from Germany, which cost upward of fifty thousand dollars and was able provide heat, for long stretches, without pellets.

My aunt spoke the words "under contract" into her phone, and seconds later a female British robot's voice said, "A term common to the real estate profession." The voice continued to talk, but I wasn't listening, because the coin for me had already dropped. I returned to my own phone. On it, I was supposed to be able to talk to someone and get on the internet simultaneously, but Dawn's voice coming out of it seemed to short-circuit its features and my fingers. Once again, I turned to my aunt and she handed her phone to me without me asking for it, and I handed her my phone without her asking for it either. Only after I'd handed my aunt the phone did I remember that I'd lied, or not told her the whole truth, about who Dawn was to me. But by then it was too late. Aunt Beatrice put my phone to her ear and immediately broke into a wide smile as though hearing the voice of an old friend. Her missing tooth made her look like a lunatic, and if I were a stranger walking by, I would have thought that she needed mental help even more desperately than dental.

Into my aunt's phone I typed "under contract" and then

my address, 41 Maine Street, Congress, Maine, and then hit the Search button, and I found what you might have already expected I would find: the website of a real estate company, Admiralty Realty, which reported that my house was not only for sale but was also already under contract.

35.

My namesake once wrote that "God tolerates even our stammering." It would be nice if that were so, because when my aunt handed me back my phone, I stammered into it. I knew what words I meant to say—they were "how" and "why" and "who"—but I suspect those weren't the words Dawn heard, because her word in response was "what." "*What?* I can't *hear* you, Calvin." And then, before I could try to make my questions clearer, she said, "Never mind. I'll be on first flight from Charlotte to Boston tomorrow."

"Why?" I said, and *that* she heard.

"*Why?*" she said with the incredulity she normally reserved for someone dense enough to wonder what was so wrong with the "conventional woodstove." "To celebrate!" she said. "And to help you pack up the house."

36.

After my mother met the president of the United States, she led a nondenominational service at the National Cathedral. The title of that sermon—"A Pilot Steers the Ship"—was also the title of one of the chapters in her famous book and was taken from these words by John Calvin: "Seeing that a Pilot steers the ship in which we sail, who will never allow us to perish even in the midst of shipwrecks." And I thought of those words right after Dawn said that she was flying up to help me pack my house. I remembered these words and thought yes, I am in the midst of a shipwreck, and yes, I need a pilot to steer me away from it. I closed my eyes and asked for a pilot. Whom did I ask? Whomever was listening: God, my mother, my father, John Calvin himself. I didn't expect anyone to listen, because as far as I could tell, no one ever had. But this time, someone did: a moment later, I heard a loudspeaker announce immediate boarding for a flight that would take its fortunate ticket-holding passengers to some distant place. And then I opened my eyes and there she was: dark spectacled, black haired, weathered face, gap toothed, my aunt, my mysterious long-lost aunt, both pilot and ship, waiting for me. She reached into her purse and withdrew my passport, with the ticket sticking out of it, and handed them to me.

"I was just going to call and tell you," I said to Dawn on the phone. "My aunt Beatrice and I are about to go on a trip!"

37.

One hour later I was still on the phone with Dawn. Yes, I told her, I really was going to Sweden with my aunt. Yes, I know it seemed sudden. No, I wasn't lying to her. Yes, I was coming back. Yes, I really was selling my house. No, I didn't like it when she called me a big pussy.

"It's time," Aunt Beatrice whispered into the ear that wasn't up against the phone. I assumed my aunt was telling me that it was time to board our flight, and so I told Dawn that I had to go, that my flight was boarding, that I'd text her when I got to Stockholm. Then I hung up, looked at the time, and saw that we had at least an hour before boarding. I looked to my aunt for clarification.

"It's time to grow up," she said.

"I'm nearly fifty years old," I told her, which was my way of saying *I already have*. But of course Aunt Beatrice heard it otherwise.

"It's never too late to grow up, Calvin," she said.

38.

Do you know that that was my first time on an airplane? When I was a child, my parents in word and deed and occupation suggested that we did not need to go anywhere; later, as an adult, my blogging for the pellet stove industry suggested the very same thing. But now, at nearly fifty years old, I was finally going somewhere in an airplane. The miracle of it! Not the miracle of flight, but the miracle of finally doing what so many people had already done.

39.

And do you know that it wasn't until we were already on the flight, already in the air, that I remembered my aunt's dog, which was waiting for us, or at least me, back in Congress?

"Aunt Beatrice," I said. "Your dog!"

My aunt seemed to consider these words, crunching the ice from her otherwise empty cup. Before she'd downed it, the cup had been full of scotch, as had the cup before, as had the cup before that. If I'd had that much liquor and that little water, I would have feared dehydration and the return of my kidney stones.

"Oh, he came with the truck," Aunt Beatrice finally said.

I said earlier that entering a city was like entering a question that contained an answer that you suspected was obvious to everyone else but was obscure to you. Entering a conversation with my aunt could be like that also.

"Where did the truck come from?"

"I stole it," my aunt said.

There was a man standing in the aisle. He had taken his suitcase out of the overhead compartment and then taken something out of his suitcase, and now he was shoving his suitcase back into the compartment. But when my aunt said, "I stole it," he seemed to pause in his labors, just for a second, before closing the compartment and retaking his seat. I was suddenly highly conscious of people listening to us. And now that I'd noticed the man and his suitcase, I finally became aware that my aunt was flying to Europe and yet she had no luggage, only a purse, which she'd slung over her head and left shoulder. The strap cut diagonally across her chest like a bandolier.

"Stole it," I said, and I was whispering now, "from whom?"

My aunt was flipping through the in-flight magazine. She

suddenly started to recite the name of each of America's Greatest
Steakhouses. She asked me, "Would you rather go to the original
in Chicago or the newest branch in Scottsdale?" and I knew I
wouldn't get an answer to my question until I answered hers.

"Chicago," I said, and my aunt nodded as though that were
the correct answer.

"I stole the truck from its owner, Calvin," my aunt said in
her normal voice, not whispering. When she said that—"I stole
it from its owner, Calvin"—it seemed to cost her nothing but
the breath she'd spent on saying the words. But I very much
wished she hadn't said the word "owner," because I immediately
pictured a woman (Why did I picture the truck's owner as a
woman? I don't know: maybe because a woman had stolen the
truck), a woman who had come out of a store or her house and
found not just her truck missing but her dog, too.

"You stole someone's *dog*," I said to my aunt.

"Well, as I said, he came with the truck," my aunt said to me.

Some people put on dark glasses when admitting their guilt,
or admitting to something that should cause them to feel guilt.
But no, that's when my aunt took off her dark glasses.

She took off her dark glasses. Her eyes were blue, like my
mother's, like mine, but the blue was somewhat muted, like the
sky seen through a tissue. Against her weathered, cracked face,
her eyes looked like two milky-blue marbles set in the sockets of
a dark clay mask.

"You shouldn't judge me, Calvin," my aunt said. I waited to
hear why not, but Aunt Beatrice had already put her sunglasses

back on and was clearly not going to tell me any more about how I should feel about the truck or the dog or her than she already had.

40.

I forgot to say: I suspected, even before she'd confessed to stealing the truck and the dog, that my aunt had something to do with my house being under contract, just as she'd somehow gotten my passport. But I wasn't going to accuse her of that. Not because I didn't care or because I wanted to be agreeable. But because I wanted to find out—not just how she'd done them, but why—and I knew if I asked, my aunt wouldn't tell me. Besides, you do not honor life's great mysteries by asking the mysteries to explain themselves to you. Those might sound like John Calvin's words. Or my mother's. But no, they're mine.

Five

- - - - -

41.

I woke with the airplane's bump and controlled skid of a landing.
In my shirt pocket was the form on which I was to declare that
I had nothing to declare. I blinked once, twice, then held my
eyes wide until they woke up, too. My aunt was already standing
in the aisle. Her right hand was on the seat in front of me, her
fingers drumming. The other hand was holding our passports,
fanned out like a pair of aces. The airplane had the faint stink
of people who have taken their shoes off and who have brushed
their teeth with their fingers. And everyone looked terrible, like
their faces had been dusted with chalk or cheese. In front of us a
man in a blue pinstriped suit was making circles on his chin and
cheeks and throat with a battery-powered electric razor. I looked

outside. It resembled the outside of the airport in Boston and presumably most other airports. But someone was talking to us over the airplane's PA system in Swedish, and then the man in front of us turned off his razor and started talking to his seatmate in that language. That was my first impression of Swedish: the language where something sophisticated sounds like it's always getting half caught in your throat.

42.

"It's time to grow up." My aunt's words were still bouncing around in my head. If Aunt Beatrice was right and I had yet to grow up, and it wasn't too late for me to do so, I thought I'd better start right away, with something small, and then I'd build up to bigger things. I stuck out my hand. "I should probably hold my own passport," I said. My aunt nodded, nodded gravely, as though this were a ceremony of some importance. "Probably," she said, and then gave me my passport.

We then exited the plane behind a boy and his family. He'd been crying since the plane had landed, and now he was trying hard not to and still somewhat failing. The mother was carrying the boy. "He's so tired," she said to the boy's father. Meanwhile, the boy was looking at us over his mother's shoulder. He was sniffling; his eyes were red, his face tearstained. My aunt unzipped her purse, reached in, and then extended her hand toward the boy. In her hand was a coin, a small brown coin with a hole in the middle. The boy rubbed his face against his mother's shoulder and then reached over the shoulder with his left hand and accepted the coin. And then the family turned left at the end of the ramp, and we turned right.

"That was very sweet of you," I said.

"I bought his happiness," my aunt said. And then what she'd done seemed less sweet. I searched my head for some relevant quote from John Calvin, or my mother, about not being able to buy one's way into heaven. Surely there was one. Surely there were many. But I couldn't locate one. Perhaps it was the jet lag, but John Calvin was already seeming far away. And besides, the boy did seem happier after he'd been paid off. I remembered my first impression of my aunt's voice, how she spoke like a character in a children's television show, or a teacher, and this encounter with the boy made it seem like my aunt did in fact have some experience with children.

"Were you ever a teacher, Aunt Beatrice?" I asked her.

"No," my aunt said, "but I was just thinking of the time when one of my clients requested that I pop his whore of an ex-wife right in her fucking gob."

We'd passed through passport control and were now walking through the terminal. I was trying to pay attention to everything: the signs, the restaurants, the people, what they were wearing, what they were saying. I didn't know much, but I wanted to know what the differences were between what there was to know in Stockholm and what I'd known in Congress. I didn't want to miss any of it. But when my aunt said . . . well, I'm not going to repeat it. You heard what she said. In any case, I stopped paying attention to anything else and paid attention only to her. I said earlier that my mother and my aunt walked in similar ways. But this is another way they were similar: they made me pay strict attention to what they were saying. Although of course they tended to say very different things.

"I'm merely quoting the client, Calvin," my aunt said. "And after all, this was what I got paid to do, and so this is what I did: I drove to her house, which before the divorce had been my client's as well. It is an estate of considerable size and little taste. Beige vinyl siding. No shutters. No chimney. Obscenely large garage. Many gazebos. Much statuary. A patio, brick. A grill, gas, with, on either side of the grill itself, two exposed propane tanks. It probably doesn't need pointing out that the tanks looked like testicles. The couple had had no children, so there was no athletic equipment, no sign of sport or play. Circular drive. Large sloping lawn with nonnative grass, unnaturally green, chemically treated. Flower beds with not enough flowers and too much mulch. A house with overmulched flower beds is an unhappy house, Calvin. It's true that this is a generalization. It is also true that most of the women I slapped lived on properties with overmulched flower beds."

"Aunt Beatrice, what are you talking about?" I finally asked, but of course she didn't answer me.

"I parked my car," she said, "on the downward slope of the driveway, facing forward. Remember this, Calvin: always make sure your car is facing forward. You never know when you might later need to flee. I walked to the door, rang the doorbell. I remember its lonely echo. The sound suggested a too-large house, underfurnished rooms." My aunt paused, perhaps still hearing that echo. I was hearing it, too. In one place or another (and there hadn't been many places), I'd always been hearing it. "I waited for a moment," my aunt continued, "then rang again. A man's voice boomed from the garage, which was attached to the house by way of a breezeway, so called (it had no windows, could admit no breeze), demanding that my client's ex-wife 'answer the door already.' This man was a real estate agent, who sold my client the house and then later stole my client's wife. My client wished me to strike the agent, too, but I'd informed him, firmly, no, I did not strike men; that is not what I did. That was one of my rules. If that was something the client wished done, then he would have to do it himself, or he would have to pay a man to do it. There may have been women who made their living slapping men on the behest of other men, but I had not heard of them, and I had not met them, although I would have liked to have heard of them, I would have liked to have met them: one should always welcome the wisdom, the experience, of a fellow professional."

My aunt paused again, perhaps to give me the chance to ask another question, which she would then not answer. When I didn't, she decided to finally answer my earlier one.

"I thought I'd made it plain," she said to me. "I was a woman who men paid to slap other women."

"When?" I said. "Where?" But of course my aunt ignored this and continued with her story.

"A few moments later, I heard footsteps from inside the

house. I took a step back, so that if my client's ex-wife were to look at me through the peephole, then this is what she would see: a lady of a certain age, short gray hair . . ."

"Gray hair!" I said triumphantly. I can tell you what I thought my triumph was: my aunt had earlier pointed out that I was very bald, and now I was pointing out that she dyed her hair. I didn't say it was much of a triumph. My aunt made that plain, too.

"There *are* wigs, Calvin," my aunt said, but I couldn't tell whether that meant she was wearing one now or then. "Short gray hair," she said again, "tan windbreaker, very white sneakers, large sunglasses, common among the cataracted." Aunt Beatrice adjusted her glasses to let me know that she was still wearing them. "Sometimes when I anticipated suspicion, hostility, I would wear a fanny pack. People find it impossible to suspect violence from someone wearing a fanny pack. But I was not wearing a fanny pack on this particular day. I was assured I would meet no resistance from my client's ex-wife. I understood from him that she is guileless. That was not the word he used. The words my client used to describe his ex-wife were 'the stupidest cow that I ever met in my whole entire life.'"

Aunt Beatrice didn't need to tell me that those were her clients' words, not her own. When she'd said them, her voice changed. It became lower—not like a man's voice but as though her voice were coming from somewhere deep inside her. It was as though one of my aunt's organs were speaking.

"The door opened inward," she said in her own voice, "and

when it did, I took a step forward. The ex-wife was standing there, right hand on the door, left on her hip. She was wearing a faded pink sweat suit."

I noticed that my aunt said the words "sweat suit" in that same subterranean voice, and so I interrupted and asked if those were her client's words, too.

"Those were not my client's words, Calvin," my aunt said. But she didn't then explain whose they were. It's possible she said them in that voice because she didn't wish the words "sweat suit" to be hers either.

"As I was saying," Aunt Beatrice said, and then she paused, dramatically, as though waiting for me to me interrupt her again, and for a second I felt as chastised as I'd been during all the many moments throughout all my life when my mother had used John Calvin to chastise me. But then my aunt laughed, and I saw the space where her tooth should have been, and the feeling evaporated. "I said the woman's name. Just to make sure that she was the right woman. The wrong women were slapped all too often in our business. It was a stain. The woman said, 'Yes?' and when she did I noticed a certain slackness around the mouth, a slackness that is proof, I think, not of age but disappointment. A mouth is very good at telling, especially when it doesn't talk. In any case, I slapped it, Calvin, with my right hand. Some of my colleagues, my competitors, wore gloves, but I did not. I preferred a bare hand, not for the feel but for the sound. A loud slap to the face is time interrupting. After I slapped a woman, the expression on her face tended to want to know not who are you, not what just happened, but where am I and what time is it.

"'It is nine forty-eight ante meridiem,' I said to the woman. I never told the women my name. I never told them the name of my clients. I never told them my purpose. I only told them the time so that they might have something by which to remember the experience, so that, even if they weren't sure what had happened or why, they at least knew when. And then I turned and left. I was rarely called after, never pursued. On the way to my automobile, I passed by the garage. In it, I heard the real estate agent on his phone, loudly deploying his argot. Something, he was saying, was a 'diamond in the rough,' and it also required an 'imaginative buyer,' and, in any case, it was 'definitely not a drive-by.' As I said, my rules forbade me from slapping men, but they did not forbid me from sometimes regretting my rules."

43.

I've already said much about how my aunt spoke. But in truth she spoke in many different ways. And here was another one: my aunt sometimes spoke in stories, which appeared out of nowhere and all at once. It's tempting to say that they were like sermons. But they were not like sermons. Sermons—at least my mother's sermons—were composed in advance and were meant to teach you a lesson. They were meant to teach you how John Calvin wanted you to live. My aunt's stories, on the other hand, were mostly there to tell you that she already had.

44.

Anyway, by the time my aunt finished her story, we'd reached our hotel. We'd exited the airport, gotten in a cab, were driven into Stockholm, and I'd missed all of it.

And since we never did make the return trip to the Stockholm airport, I couldn't have told you what that particular journey looks like. I assume it is watery. Stockholm is water. There might be parts of Stockholm that do not involve water, but I never saw them. For instance, there was our hotel and, in front of that, a broad stone-and-brick promenade and then water—rippling, sun-dappled water. I couldn't tell whether it was a river or a lake or the ocean. Ferries were everywhere, so many that I couldn't believe they weren't crashing into one another. I said Stockholm is water, but Stockholm is also islands. I could see a few of them even from where I was standing. I guessed the smaller ferries went to those nearby islands. But there were bigger ferries, too. I assumed they went to more distant places, and I was right.

45.

The man at the hotel's front desk greeted us in Swedish. "Hi hi" is what he said.

"Ohio," my aunt said back, startling both the man and myself. It took me a few moments to realize that Aunt Beatrice wasn't talking to him. No, she was finally responding to my earlier question, asking where and when she had slapped that woman. "I slapped that particular woman during the first

Clinton administration," my aunt said to me, although the man at the desk was listening, too. "A very frustrating time for the men of Ohio."

46.

And in this way, I began to piece together where my aunt had been all my life. This was in 2016. I was born in 1968. My aunt had been in Ohio sometime between 1993 and 1997. Earlier than that, at some point, for some amount of time, she'd lived in Stockholm. At that time that was what I knew.

47.

After saying "Ohio" in English (although I suppose it would have sounded the same in Swedish), my aunt spoke Swedish to the man at the front desk. I stood there with my head down, like a child. And then I understood the boy my aunt had earlier bought off. I mean, I understood why he was crying. Not because he was tired. But because he didn't understand the language. As I learned over the next few weeks, there's nothing like hearing people talking in the language of the country you've just arrived in to emphasize how incredibly little you know about where you are.

48.

The hotel room was actually two adjoining rooms, and in each room was a king-size bed, and in each room the beds were one of the few things that were not made of marble. And by the quality of the hotel rooms, I understood that my aunt was rich. And then I remembered the truck my aunt had stolen, and I wondered if my aunt was rich or if she'd just stolen from rich people, or if there was a difference. My aunt, I suspected, would say that there was no difference. As for John Calvin, he once said that "the torture of a bad conscience is the hell of a living soul." But I don't know, my aunt's conscience must have not have tortured her much if at all: she was already in her bed, white sneakers slipped off, sunglasses still on, fast asleep.

49.

To Grow Up

Dear readers, my aunt Beatrice and I are taking a trip. No small undertaking, for someone like me: as you know, there's nothing I like better than to stay at home and warm my toes by my trusty Traplodge AA and, oh, I don't know, maybe read a book or, more likely, tell my pellet stove posse about all the happy news (click on these links for rebates! service plans! model upgrades!) coming from the pellet stove industry.

But as you know, my mother has died, and when a parent dies, the world shrinks a little and becomes indistinct: Before your parent dies, you are their child, but after they die, then what are you? What are you supposed to be? What are you supposed to do? Luckily, I have my wise aunt on hand to tell me what I'm supposed to do: she tells me I'm supposed to grow up. She also tells me how I'm supposed to grow up: by going out and meeting the world. And it turns out that the part of the world I've gone to meet happens to be Sweden: the home of the mighty Lingonnaire, the original pellet stove, the pellet stove of all pellet stoves! You won't be surprised to hear that they're as common in Sweden as the pancakes and the meatballs. Even our hotel rooms have come equipped with them. My aunt is asleep in her room next to her stove, and I am writing to you in my room next to mine. And as my posse knows well enough, there is nothing like the even, radiant heat of a pellet stove to make wherever you are feel like home.

Expect more from me soon! In the meantime, keep your correspondences coming!

50.

After I wrote and posted, I crawled into my own bed. My aunt's conscience might not have tortured her, but mine tortured me: when I closed my eyes I saw her sitting in the driver's seat of her stolen truck. Her hair was gray, short. She was wearing her sunglasses. The truck's driver's-side window was open. Suddenly, as though someone had called her name, Aunt Beatrice turned toward the open window, and through the open window came a fist, a gloved fist, and it smashed into my aunt Beatrice's face. I opened my eyes and I was in my hotel room. The curtains were open. It was the middle of the day and the sun blasted in. I got up, closed the curtains, stared at the ceiling. There was a chandelier above my bed, and at the base of the chandelier was a circle of raised yellow-and-white molding that reminded me of a wedding cake. I closed my eyes again, and again there was my aunt, and she was once again facing forward in her forward-facing truck, and then once again she turned toward the open window, as though someone had called her name, but this time she said, "You shouldn't judge me, Calvin." When she opened her mouth I could see her missing tooth, and then I said quickly, "I won't!" and then willed myself to sleep before the gloved fist once again came through the open window and found its mark.

Six

51.

My dream (if you can call the vision before you fall asleep a dream) seemed to suggest that there was a connection between my aunt's missing tooth and her business in Ohio. But in fact there was not a connection, and in fact that was not how she lost her tooth. But I didn't find that out until later.

52.

I realize that I keep saying that I did not find this out and that out until later. But eventually I did, and eventually, I promise, I will tell you all about it. As John Calvin himself says, "Whenever the Lord holds us in suspense and delays his aid, he is not therefore asleep, but, on the contrary, regulates all His works in such a manner that he does nothing but at the proper time."

53.

Anyway, I woke up what seemed like many hours later, feeling as though I'd been struck on the head with the world's most enormous hammer. Where am I? I wondered, and then I did what most of us—professional bloggers or not—would do: I consulted my phone to orient myself.

54.

I had two texts waiting for me.

One was from Dawn: *You haven't texted me from Stockholm. I'm really pissed off, Calvin.*

And one was from the pellet stove industry. I could tell never tell who exactly from the industry was texting me. I'd worked for the industry for more than ten years and had gotten thousands of texts from the industry, and not once had the industry texter mentioned his or her name. The industry had hired me to blog because the industry thought the industry needed to be a little more personal, and the industry was probably right about that. The text said: *Dead ma = traffic!!!*

Well, I knew what "dead ma" meant. It took me a few seconds to understand how it, or she, equaled traffic. Traffic meant that someone had commented on my blog post. Maybe that's why I didn't register the term "traffic" at first: because I'd never had any.

55.

The traffic was in the form of the people at Lingonnaire, the Swedish pellet stove company, the first among firsts. "So wonderful that you and your relative are in our wonderful country," the comment on my blog said. I noticed the lack of exclamation points. A very rare thing, in our country, to see, in a blog, a claim of happiness not followed by enthusiastic punctuation. But I thought that maybe this was an example of the famous Scandinavian reserve. "And that you're enjoying our stoves," the comment went on to say. "In what hotel are you staying?"

I ended up learning so many things from my aunt. And one of those things was to always wait three seconds before responding to anything that might be important. This was why she so often adjusted her glasses. To buy her those three seconds. So that she'd make sure to take the time to decide whether the first thing she'd wanted to say was the right thing.

"Hello! We're staying at the Admiral Sonnenberg," I immediately wrote, and that famous Scandinavian reserve must have already rubbed off on me—you'll notice I only used one exclamation point before I hit Send—but make no mistake: I was excited. Not just that someone had responded to my post but also that it was someone from the pellet stove industry. As my aunt had said—and she was right—one should always welcome the wisdom, the experience, of a fellow professional.

56.

My aunt called my name from her room a moment or two after I'd hit Send. Although at first I thought it was not my aunt's voice: it was sharp, a cry more than a call. When I walked through the connecting door she was standing at the window, leaning forward, her hands on the sill, which was waist high. My aunt's posture reminded me of someone who'd just been punched in the stomach. The morning light was rushing through the windows: the light was harsh, and not for the first or last time I wished I had my aunt's glasses.

"Are you all right?" I asked my aunt. She didn't say anything at first. She took one hand off the sill and with it adjusted her glasses, and then adjusted them again. The sun was so powerful that it made her look as though she were lit from within.

57.

I do not like to remember this moment, my aunt bent over as though in pain. You could say it's foreshadowing, but if you read John Calvin as a child, then you know that it's *all* foreshadowing. Except the end isn't coming, it's already here.

58.

My aunt didn't answer. She pushed herself back from the sill and, with obvious effort, straightened up. For the first time since I'd met her, she seemed her age. Physically, but also mentally. Clearly, the trip had taken something out of her. For instance, she said, "Dinner," meaning, I suppose, that she wanted some. Except it was morning: the sun coming through the window clearly said so.

"You mean breakfast," I said.

"I'm not all right, Calvin," my aunt said in that same

suspiciously wheedling tone she'd used when she'd convinced me to accompany her into the Boston airport. She turned to face me, at full height now. And in her more cheerful, normal voice she said, "And I mean dinner."

59.

My mind kept returning to my aunt's description of my house in Congress: "the house of horrors," she'd called it. That was surely an exaggeration. But it was true that I often felt lonely in that house, and never lonelier than at dinner. My father's teams usually practiced or played their games during dinnertime, so mostly it was just my mother and me in the dining room, sitting across from each other at one end of a very long table. And mostly we ate root vegetables. My favorite was spaghetti squash. Although perhaps that's not a root vegetable. In any case, the spaghetti squash was not my mother's favorite. She would cook it because it was my favorite, and that is to her credit. But I think my mother regarded the spaghetti squash as an especially frivolous vegetable. As I got older I became aware that whenever I scraped at the body of the squash and then twirled them with my fork, my mother would look away, as though I were doing something that should only be done in private.

60.

My aunt was right. It was dinnertime. I'd woken up feeling so stunned, and with the light so bright, that I'd assumed that we'd slept through the day and night and all the way until morning.

In fact, I'd seen the time on my phone but had not paid attention to the a.m. or p.m. I'd just assumed it was morning. But no, it was seven o'clock at night. I looked at my phone again and saw that it was so. The sun hadn't set and wouldn't set for another three hours.

We left our rooms, took the elevator to the lobby—which, like our rooms, seemed to have been hollowed out of an enormous block of yellow marble—and walked to the front doors. As we passed the front desk, the man working behind it noticed me and pointed in my direction, and the woman he was talking to turned and walked toward me.

She was at least six feet tall, taller than my aunt, taller than me. She was wearing a tan trench coat, and her straight, shoulder-length hair was so blonde it was almost white. Her skin was even fairer than her hair, and she wore large round red-framed glasses. The red looked like neon against her pale cheeks and forehead.

"Mr. Calvin Bledsoe," she said, and the way she said it made me wonder if I'd done something wrong. She sounded like a machine, an accusatory one, although really she sounded like a Swede speaking a very careful, halting English.

I said yes, that was my name, and she said, "It was a lie," and I felt even more accused.

"What was?"

"There are precisely none of our stoves in any of the guest rooms in this particular special hotel." I realized then who she was: she was someone from Lingonnaire, the famous Swedish pellet stove company. The company, I knew, had its headquarters right here in Stockholm. Earlier I'd been so happy to hear from them on my blog, but now I was filled with dread. People often fill professional bloggers with dread, especially when we're forced to meet them. Still, I stuck out my hand, which the woman ignored. "Why did you lie?" she still wanted to know.

This time I paused before answering. The truth was, of course, that that was part of my job as a blogger for the pellet stove industry: we lied, and then we lied to ourselves about what to call and how to think about the lying, and in any case we told ourselves that the lie was harmless, which was yet another lie. But I wasn't sure I could communicate that to someone who didn't speak English as a first language, and I wasn't sure I wanted to even if I could. And so I said, "It was a joke."

"A joke?"

"An American pellet stove industry joke," I said. "The joke is that those of us in the American pellet stove industry see pellet stoves everywhere."

The woman considered that. There was something very fuzzy about her. I didn't know why I thought that, or what the thought meant, but there seemed to be a kind of a haze around her, although maybe it was just that I was still jet-lagged. "It is not very funny," she finally said, and I admitted no, I guess it wasn't. "Is your aunt a joke, too?" she asked, and I laughed, which may have given her a false impression because her blue eyes seemed to sparkle behind her glasses, as though she, too, was preparing to laugh, possibly for the first time.

"No," I said. "She's not a joke. She's right—" And here I looked to my left, where my aunt had been, but she wasn't there. I spun around, looking toward all the lobby's compass points, but there was no sign of my aunt. When I spun back to the woman, her eyes weren't sparkling anymore. "An unfunny joke is a lie," she said, and that sounded like another accusation. But before I could defend myself, she walked away from me—without telling me her name; without telling me whether she'd complain about my lie, or my joke, to my superiors in the pellet stove industry; without telling me much of anything. Still, I was happy to see her go. I'd only known the woman for a minute, and yet I really hoped I would never see her again.

"Where have you been?" my aunt said, coming up from behind me. That, of course, was the question I wanted to ask her. I turned. There was nothing fuzzy about her: she appeared, as she had two days earlier at my mother's funeral, in sharp focus. Her massive head of dark hair, her baked face, her enormous sunglasses, her primary-colored clothes, her white white sneakers. I was happy to see her again. She'd only been gone a minute, and yet I'd really missed her.

"I was right here," I said. My aunt didn't respond to that, but I could I could sense her disappointment in my answer, crackling like electricity in the air between us. So I tried again. "An unfunny joke is a lie," I said.

"Very good, Calvin," Aunt Beatrice said. She'd obviously thought I'd come up with the saying on my own, and I didn't bother to correct her misimpression.

61.

The sun may have been bright, but it couldn't have been warmer than fifty degrees outside. Still, most of the outdoor seats at all the restaurants were full. Full of people drinking Carlsberg beer, sitting under awnings with wool blankets on their laps. Meanwhile, the heat lamps were doing their best to burn away the chill. The world smelled like salt and toast, and I found myself, automatically, lowering my head and clasping my hands underneath the table, as though someone—not me—were about to say grace.

62.

The world is remarkable. This was the title of one of my mother's sermons, and it was also the title of another of the chapters in her famous book, and this was what she said for grace before we ate dinner, and this in fact was what she said for grace during her dinner with the president. "The world is remarkable," my mother said, "and we are grateful to be given a chance to live in it." Some people, when they said grace, asked for things, but not my mother: she said grace as though there would be no denying her. The first lady and the cabinet members and even the president himself seemed scared of her: they kept their heads down long after my mother had said her piece, and the waiters began to swirl with their plates and their platters and their covered dishes.

My aunt didn't say grace. She simply ordered our food,

which started coming all at once, and then regularly. Everything was open faced. Pickles, herring, salmon, meats of some kind, cucumbers, dark bread speckled with something large and corn kernelly or nut looking. No root vegetables. Nothing I ever would have eaten at home with my mother. We drank Carlsberg, my one for my aunt's every two. I asked my aunt to teach me the language, and she made me say thank you—*tack, tack*—until I made it sound less like the thing you do with your mouth, or what you use to pin something to a board, and more like the sound a clock makes. The waitress brought over two small glasses with clear liquid in it, and I said to her, "*Tack, tack*," and she said, in excellent English, "Don't thank me quite yet." I soon discovered what she meant. "Drink that all at once, Calvin," my aunt suggested, and I did that. It was like I'd swallowed sweet kerosene, and I closed my eyes against the taste. But even after the taste mostly went away, I kept my eyes closed, because I liked hearing the sound of people's voices, and with my eyes closed I could pretend that I knew them. And since I didn't know the language, I could pretend they were talking to me. When I finally opened my eyes, I saw that my aunt was laughing at me. "Or sip it if you'd rather," she said. That's what she was doing. The reflection of the overhead lights sparkled in her dark lenses. "What are you thinking, Calvin?" she asked. No one had ever asked me that question before. No one! *That I'm happy*—that's what I wanted to say. But then I thought of one of the chapters in my mother's famous book. It was called "Against Happiness," and in it she argued that our culture's pursuit of happiness ran counter to John Calvin's insistence that we seek holiness, even though we were fated to never find it. I knew what my mother would have said had I told her that I was happy (I had never told her that I was happy), and just thinking about my mother, I felt much less happy and much more like a child again, and so I said to my aunt, "I was thinking about my mother. I wonder what she'd say if she saw the two of us together right now."

My aunt frowned, tossed back the rest of her aquavit, and said, "You're never going to grow up, Calvin, until you start saying the things you want to say and not what your mother would say. Or what she'd want you to say."

What do *I want to say?* is what I almost asked, but that would have just proved that I was never going to grow up. And besides, I knew what I wanted to say, at least right at that moment.

"I'm happy," I told my aunt, who nodded.

"That's a decent start," she said, and then ordered another round of aquavit.

63.

Already, I loved my aunt, and I believe she already loved me. This seems as good a time as any to say that. To love someone is to eventually create the conditions for betraying them. This seems as good a time as any to say that, too. Because this is a story about the things my aunt taught me, and that is one of the things she taught me.

64.

Dinner took several hours. Only when the restaurant began closing around us did we get up and begin walking. We walked by the water, and then we walked over it, on a series of stone bridges. On one of the stone bridges there was a white sock. It was darker now, and the sock seemed to glow in the dusk. Aunt Beatrice nudged the sock with her foot and said, "Whenever I see a stray piece of clothing on the street, I think that someone has been raped."

65.

I believed our walk was aimless. It felt aimless. Maybe because we kept drinking: my aunt bought two more large cans of Carlsberg and we drank them as we walked. The sun was almost down by now; the stone streets were absent of shadows, the water rippling black.

We were walking side by side, very close to each other. As was true after the funeral, I wondered if my aunt was going to loop her arm in mine. I wanted her to. No one ever had, not Dawn, not my mother. I don't mean to sound pathetic, and in fact I don't think I'd ever wanted Dawn or my mother to loop her arm through mine. But I wanted my aunt to. I felt embarrassed when she didn't. So I began asking her questions. This is why people talk so much, I believe: not because they want to know something but because they don't want to feel the thing they did before they started talking.

"When did you live here, Aunt Beatrice?"

I didn't expect her to answer directly, but she did. "From 1968 through 1972," she said.

"I was born on July 1, 1968," I pointed out. I said this because I couldn't bring myself to ask the question I wanted to ask, which was, *Were you in Congress on the day when I was born?* Because I couldn't bring myself to ask, *Were* you *there?* Aunt Beatrice looked at me sideways through her veil of hair and said, "There's a drawer somewhere, Calvin."

I waited for her to explain this remark, but she didn't, and so I asked, "How did you end up in Stockholm?"

"After I left Congress," my aunt said, "I went to New York, where I met a boy. I followed him here."

"Who was he?"

"He was no one," my aunt said, and I thought I heard a little bit of the night enter her voice. And when it did, a little bit of the night entered my mind, too—I thought of my father in his grave; I thought of my mother in *her* grave, and in her church, and in her book; I thought of Dawn in Charlotte, and in her blog; I thought of the Otises in Congress—and so to get rid of all that I blurted out, "I have never understood men." Where had this come from? It took me a few seconds to locate its origin. This was what Aunt Beatrice had said to me in response to my bald head, my unruly gray-and-white beard.

My aunt nodded in approval and said, "Those were your mother's words."

"My mother said that?"

My aunt nodded again. Then she turned and threw her beer can far into the water. I can still see it, flipping end over end, can still hear its tinny splash. When my aunt heard that splash she smiled, a wide satisfied smile, as if to say of the noise, *I made that.*

"'The house of horrors,'" my aunt said. "Those were your mother's words, too."

66.

My mother once gave a sermon (and this sermon also appeared in her famous book) that provided yet another reason for John Calvin's importance. "We cannot understand God. But we can understand John Calvin, who understands God for us."

John Calvin understands God for us. But apparently he could not understand men for my mother. Maybe because he was one.

67.

And what, after all, made our house so horrible for my mother? I didn't find out that until later either. But I will tell you now, just to prove that I can and will. It's not what you think. No one was raped. No one was hit. Yes, my mother cheated and my father cheated, and in fact everyone in this story at some point or other cheated, but that was not what was so horrible. No, the house was horrible for my mother because she was living in it with two men whom she didn't understand. The two men in it didn't understand her, or each other much either, and that was not a great feeling, and, as I said, I often felt lonely in our house, and it's possible my father did, too, but I wouldn't call the loneliness horrible, and I wouldn't call the not understanding one another horrible either. It was all right. I could live with it. Apparently my father could, too. Which made it even more horrible for my mother. Because she could not live with, and love, what she couldn't understand. Which was why she preferred John Calvin to us and, I think, even to God.

68.

"And in that drawer," my aunt said, "are forty-seven birthday cards."

I should say here that alcohol made my aunt's mind, and mouth, sharper, but it made mine duller. It took me several minutes to remember that my aunt had mentioned that there was a drawer somewhere and to realize that that drawer was imaginary and that the forty-seven birthday cards she hadn't sent me were in it.

69.

I said earlier that my aunt's and my walking seemed aimless. But it's clear to me now that my aunt had an aim and that I just didn't know what it was at the time.

We were a good distance from our hotel now, I was pretty certain. Still along the water but with fewer pedestrians. And ahead of us was an incredibly bright spot in the middle of the darkness. It was like a UFO or a highway construction site at night. Coming from the spot, I could hear human voices, not so much talking as babbling. We walked toward it. Soon I could see several light towers surrounding what looked like a parking lot. In the middle of the lot were tents, rubble, pot smoke, handmade cardboard signs advertising, I think, food for sale: the signs were in Swedish and the food was all being ladled out of vats. I got the general sense that the place was being occupied, but by several different forces. Some of the people were wearing old secondhand military garb—lots of green and gray and epaulets and even a plumed hat—while others were wearing brightly colored serapes and ponchos and rasta hats. Then there was a man sitting behind a table. We paused in front of it, and he handed me a flyer. The words on the flyer were in English, English, apparently, the language in which you advertise small-animal pornography.

Sexy Sexy! the flyer said, and under that appeared a photo of a small rodent.

I said that the man was sitting behind a table. On the table was a stack of DVDs. On the cover of the DVD was a photo of what appeared to be the same small rodent.

Other than a picture of the animal looking alert with his teeth showing, there were no other pictures. I held the flyer, flipped it over (it was blank on the other side), flipped it back over, looked at it, wondered over it.

"Do the hamsters have sex with each other or with humans?" You might think that it was my aunt who asked this question, but no, it was me, Calvin Bledsoe. And I asked the question because I really wanted to know. I glanced at my aunt who smiled at me, as if to say, *Well, of course you do*, and that's what I mean when I say that I loved her.

"Gerbils," the man said, in English. "And yes." The man looked somewhat younger than me, possibly in his late thirties. His face was tan, but as smooth as my aunt's was cracked. He had dark curly hair and a curling black mustache, and he was wearing a cream-colored thermal undershirt under his suspenders. He didn't look Swedish, although I didn't know what he did look like. If anything, he looked like a strongman in the circus.

"I guess you're wondering about the genitalia," the man said in a kind of flat, American-sounding English.

"Really small?" I said.

"Not our special gerbils," the man said.

This whole time the man had been staring. Not at me but at my aunt. I didn't like that: it was as though he were attempting to set her on fire with his eyes. I'd seen my mother look at her congregation like that. As though she were burning with the truth and wouldn't be happy until they burned also.

My aunt said something in Swedish to the small-animal pornographer. Her voice sounded softer, more whispery than usual. After she'd said whatever she'd said, she took off her glasses. Her eyes were disturbing in the klieg lights: cold blue but also runny, like melting ice.

The small-animal pornographer looked up into bleached-out sky as though in deep thought, although maybe it was just that he didn't want to look at my aunt's eyes. Meanwhile, I looked back at the gerbil on the flyer. His whiskers were at attention and

it seemed to me that he had a remarkably sensitive, alert face.
"What's the gerbil's name?" I asked the small-animal pornographer, and he looked away from the sky and at me. He seemed
startled. It was clear that no one had ever asked him that particular question before.

"Gerbie," he said to me. And then he said something to Aunt
Beatrice in his own language and she said something in return,
and they went back and forth like that for a while. Finally, he
handed her a DVD and she took it. It seemed like part of a trans-
action, and so I expected my aunt to pay the man, but instead
she did something very strange: she hugged him. Just walked
around the table and hugged him. He didn't hug her back. He
kept his arms to his side as Aunt Beatrice held him. I felt jealousy
flare up in my throat and face. And I also felt an intense dislike
for the man; that he wasn't hugging my aunt back seemed like
an insult. *Don't hug him,* I wanted to say to my aunt. *Hug her,* I
wanted to say to the small-animal pornographer. Eventually, he
did: his arms were mostly pinned by my aunt's hug, but slowly
his right arm bent at the elbow and his hand went to my aunt's
back and stayed there, for one second, then several, and I felt
my aunt had been respected, and I was even more jealous than
before.

And then my aunt let go of the man, and we walked away.

"Who was that?" I asked my aunt

"Him?" my aunt said, and I could hear the shrug in her voice.
"He's no one."

"All right," I said, trying to make my shrug audible, too. But in truth, I was happy to hear Aunt Beatrice say he was no one. It is easier to feel like you're someone if you know someone else is no one.

70.

Aunt Beatrice bought yet two more Carlsbergs, warm, from another man sitting behind another table, and we drank them as we left the encampment, if that's what it was, and walked back toward the hotel. Now that we were out from under the klieg lights, we could better see the stars, the deep blackness of the sky around them. There were more people, all of them seemingly in groups, laughing. In front of us a ferry sounded its horn—a long blast and then a shorter one—and then began backing out of its berth. Passengers leaned against the railings and waved. We seemed to pass through the air the way the boat seemed to pass through the water. The air felt light around us, is what I'm saying.

My aunt handed me the DVD, and with it I beat a happy tune against my thigh as we walked.

"Again and again," she said thoughtfully, "we look for a better way, a deeper truth, and instead we find vulgarity, we find irony, we find cheapness, we find jokes. We should want what is high, which is difficult, and instead we settle for what is low, which is easy."

This was a quote, of course, from my mother's famous book. I can't say at that moment that I was happy to hear it. Suddenly my mother's face appeared before me. I saw her seeing me holding a large can of beer in one hand, the pornographic gerbil DVD in the other. *Calvin*, she said, her voice full of judgment and disappointment, and I waited, full of dread, to hear what she would say next, but she didn't say anything next and then disappeared.

"Nola makes a fair point," Aunt Beatrice said. "But then, it's probably a mistake to think that it was easy for the gerbil."

71.

It must have been after midnight by the time we reentered the hotel. The lobby was empty, intensely so. It reminded me of mother's church—not during one of my mother's services but when I was there during off-hours, alone, up in the choir loft. I remembered during those moments feeling a sense of expectation. Nothing is happening, I always thought, in my mother's empty church, but something is about to happen. Although usually the only thing that was about to happen was that I was about to write one of my blog posts.

"He was my son," my aunt said. Her voice was quieter than usual, but still, it bounced around the empty lobby.

"Who was?" I said. Aunt Beatrice didn't answer, but she didn't have to: I knew she was talking about the small-animal pornographer. I noted that she spoke about him in the past tense, just as I'd noted earlier that she'd said he was no one. And I thought that said a great deal about the seriousness of their estrangement. And I really hoped she would never end up speaking about me like that.

72.

Our rooms were connected, but they had separate doors to access our separate rooms from the hallway. My aunt entered hers, and I entered mine. With my left hand I flicked the light switch and then with my right hand tossed the gerbil DVD onto the couch that was to the right of the door. The DVD landed faceup. And next to it, I saw, was a copy of my mother's famous book. It was a hardback copy, facedown. On the back cover was a photo of my mother in her church, standing at her pulpit. The way the DVD and the book were positioned, next to each other on the couch, it looked as though my mother and Gerbie were having a conversation about John Calvin.

73.

"When I was a child I read John Calvin," my mother writes at the beginning of her famous book, "and to read John Calvin as a child is to be made aware of all the great mysteries of this world, and one of the great mysteries of this world is why more children don't read John Calvin."

74.

It is a strange thing, having a mother who has written a famous book. But it is an even stranger thing being in that famous book. I looked at the back cover of that book and saw myself at age four, in chapter 4, being asked by my mother while being pushed on the swing what the difference was between theism and the new atheistic science. I saw myself in chapter 7, ten years old, in the emergency room in the hospital in the next town over, after I'd accidentally fallen and broken my arm while reading John Calvin while walking down the stairs in my house, about which my mother wrote, "My son went to John Calvin for salvation and to Bangor for X-rays." I saw myself in chapter 11, sixteen years old, not going to the prom, and my mother telling me that it was necessary to be alone because to be alone is to find yourself in close proximity to the sacred.

75.

My mother's acolytes read her famous book and saw me as lucky. Dawn read the book and saw me as a loser. I wondered how the person who'd left the book on my couch saw me.

76.

I knocked on the door between my aunt's part of the suite and my own, and my aunt told me the door was unlocked, to come in. She was sitting on her bed, feet dangling. Her room smelled faintly of dirty laundry, and it occurred to me that neither my aunt nor I had changed clothes since we left Congress because we hadn't brought a change of clothes.

Anyway, I showed her the book, explained how I'd found it on the couch next to the gerbil DVD. The book wasn't mine, I told her, and she told me it wasn't hers either: that meant that someone else had left it there. Aunt Beatrice seemed to be thinking, thinking, thinking—she adjusted her glasses many times over the course of many seconds—until, through the closed window, there came the muted blast of a ferry horn, and then my aunt stood up and said that it was time to leave.

"The hotel?" I said.

"Stockholm," she said, walking out of the room and then calling over her shoulder, "Make sure to bring your cousin's film." Cousin! It's odd how that hadn't occurred to me immediately. I had a cousin! Big deal, you say, but it was a big deal for someone like me, who for so long had only a mother and a father. I could feel the world filling in around me. Anyway, I picked up my cousin's gerbil film, then also picked up the copy of my mother's famous book, looked at her stern face, her open mouth (the picture had been taken midsermon), her alive eyes. They seemed to be seeking me out, and I flipped the book over and tossed it back on the couch, where it bounced off the cushion and fell to the floor. I left it there and in doing so felt like I'd taken another small step toward growing up and leaving my mother behind. Although it turned out that there would be plenty of copies of my mother's famous book in my future anyway.

Seven

77.

"Never travel by car or truck," Aunt Beatrice was telling me,
"unless they're stolen."

We were on the ferry to Copenhagen, on the upper deck,
looking at, well, nothing: the world was made of fog. And the
fog let nothing else in. Not even seagulls or seagull noise. There
was just the churn of the ferry's engine and the wet of the fog
on our faces.

My aunt was telling me the best way to flee, if I had to flee.
I had my phone out, taking notes. Later, when I consulted these
notes, I noticed that my aunt rarely told me the reasons behind
her rules. Just that she had them and that I should have them, too.

"And the train . . ." My aunt kept her mouth open, as though she were prepared to finish her sentence, but then didn't, as though she felt there had been too much said about the train already.

"No, it's best to travel by boat, ship, ferry. The water route," my aunt continued with satisfaction. There had been a women's clothing store in the ferry terminal, and she'd had just enough time to buy new clothes: bright blue pants, a white turtleneck sweater. She wore the same white sneakers. She looked nautical, and her clipper ship necklace made her look even more so: it dangled over the lip of her white turtleneck, like my mother's silver cross always hung on the outside of her gray turtleneck. Finally, a detail from my last conversation with Dawn fell into my head: the name of the real estate company that had listed my under-contract house in Congress.

"Admiralty Realty," I said, and my aunt smiled. There was something bashful about this smile. She looked down as she smiled and adjusted her glasses. For the first time, I had that sense that the sunglasses could be a shield for my aunt and not just a weapon.

"My house isn't really under contract, is it?" I asked.

"It is according to Admiralty Realty," Aunt Beatrice said.

"Admiralty Realty isn't really a real estate agency, is it?" I asked.

"It is according to its website," Aunt Beatrice said.

"But you made the website," I said.

"Well, I had the right," my aunt said, and she smiled bashfully again. "After all, I am the Admiral."

But before I could ask my aunt what made her the Admiral, whether it was an actual rank that she'd actually earned or whether it was a nickname, and if it was the latter, who'd given it to her, or why she'd made the fake website in the first place, our conversation moved to who had placed the copy of my mother's book in my hotel room, and why.

"And how," I added. My aunt didn't respond to that, so I elaborated: "I mean, who even knew we were in Stockholm in the first place?"

"Your Dawn knew," my aunt said, and I remembered she was standing right next to me in the Boston airport when I told Dawn on the phone where Aunt Beatrice and I were going on our trip. She'd said, "Your Dawn knew" in her usual bright voice, but still I felt like there was an accusation in it, which made me want to defend myself, and this was another thing I learned from my aunt: Never defend yourself. Never say you're sorry. Never admit you've done anything wrong, especially when it's obvious that you have.

"Why would Dawn leave a copy of my mother's book in my hotel room?" I asked, and then immediately sensed that this was the wrong tack. Because I knew why Dawn would do such a thing: to torment me. "Besides, how would she have known the hotel we were staying in?"

My aunt looked at me, adjusted her glasses, adjusted her glasses, then reached into her purse, and pulled out her phone. I hadn't seen it since the Boston airport. By now I'd stopped being surprised by anything my aunt did or said or had done. But still, the phone did something strange to me. It made me want to own it so I could then worship it. John Calvin once wrote, "Man's nature, so to speak, is a perpetual factory of idols," and I think he was right about that.

My aunt pressed her right thumb to the phone surface, and it read her thumbprint and then made a zipping sound to indicate that she'd successfully unlocked it. My aunt said into the phone "Calvin," looked at the screen for a second longer, then handed it to me. I held the phone like it was something delicate and precious—a robin's egg, a newborn baby, a human soul, or something of that sort.

On the phone was my blog, its history. I had to go through only the two recent posts to understand what my aunt was trying to show me. I'd mentioned her in the post written right after my mother's funeral. And I'd mentioned that Aunt Beatrice and I were staying at the hotel in Stockholm, too.

I handed her back the phone, feeling guilty, feeling even more justly accused. My aunt seemed serene enough. Still, I had the sense that she thought me pitiful, that she was disappointed in me. But that was the thing about my aunt: she was sometimes difficult to read, and so you were forced to assume that she was feeling about you what you were feeling about yourself.

"You did lie, Calvin," my aunt said, and it was true: in both blog posts I had lied—about my aunt staying with me in Congress and about our hotel being equipped with Lingonnaire stoves—and I knew how fond she was of lies and thought that perhaps I hadn't disappointed her as much as I'd thought.

"A woman from Lingonnaire even came to the hotel," I said. "She called me a liar, too." But my aunt didn't react to this news, and I wondered if she already knew. The hotel lobby had been full of marble pillars, and I could picture my aunt hiding behind one, watching me trying to convince the woman from Lingonnaire that my lie was a joke.

"But you lied very poorly," Aunt Beatrice continued. "Perhaps you should stop mentioning me in your blog, or writing it at all, until you learn to become a better liar." My aunt took off her glasses. Her blue eyes looked dangerous and murky, like radioactive rocks at the bottom of a pond. "Learn to become a better liar. You should write that down, too, Calvin."

I did not write that down. Instead, I said that I had to use the bathroom and went below deck. But instead of going to the bathroom, I sat on a bench against the wall. Everyone around me was sleeping. The ferry fell and rose in the waves, and the gray metal walls dripped with condensation. There was something sticking into my back. I reached around and pulled the gerbil DVD out of the back of my pants. I must have stuck it there, like a waiter does his pad, when I boarded the ferry. That gerbil, with his whiskers and his steady little eyes: I wanted to say to him, *You shouldn't judge me, Gerbie.* And for the first time since I'd gotten on the plane from Boston to Stockholm I wanted to be home, wanted to be in my parents' house, which was now my house, in Congress, alone.

78.

Why did I become a blogger for the pellet stove industry? Because of moments like these. These terrible, inward, unwanted idle moments. If you are a blogger, then there are no unwanted idle moments. If you are a blogger, then you can fill them, at any time, from any place, by just doing your job, by just being who you are. And because that is so, then there is no need or reason or chance to wonder who you are or to wonder whether you should be someone else.

So I sat down to write my blog. But I found that if I couldn't mention my aunt, then I had nothing much to say. I couldn't think of a lie, not even a bad one. I may have been Calvin Bledsoe, but for perhaps the first time ever I wondered what it meant to be him.

But this is why blogs exist. Even if you don't know who you are, then you can get on someone else's blog to see how they know who they are.

79.

Readers Vote!

Good Monday morning, dear readers! The days grow longer, and the nights grow warmer. Sad, sad times for those of us who love our pellet stoves! But be grateful at least that you are not your backward neighbors, with their "conventional woodstoves." Because for them spring means not the arrival of flowers but instead the arrival of a fat slob driving a dump truck who dumps several hundred pounds of firewood onto their driveways, where it then sits to "season" until September, which is when your neighbors spend days and days dealing with spiders and splinters while they stack the wood, which will then barely heat their homes and cost them a small fortune until, come next May, when these poor saps will have to do it all over again!

Anyway, I know my pellet stove posse looks forward to my Monday stories of weekend parties. But I didn't really feel like "partying" this weekend. Posse, I'll get right to it: I'm being ignored, deceived, lied to. By whom? Oh, you know him. Do I love him? I want to. Does he love me? I thought so. What do I do now? Give him one last chance? Or leave him and take my revenge? I'll be doing my dealer-recommended annual easy three-step owners' maintenance of my Dingus XX while I'm waiting for your votes!

80.

Dawn's posse was as large as mine, and so there was no doubt that the blog was meant to be read by me, not them. I knew why she was mad: by now, she'd discovered that there was no such thing as Admiralty Realty and that my house was not under contract. No doubt she'd assumed that that was why I hadn't texted her back. I didn't really believe that she'd left the copy, or was somehow responsible for someone else leaving the copy, of my mother's famous book in my hotel room. But I wondered about the revenge, in what form it would come, if it would come. Mostly, though, I wondered why the blog made me feel the way it did: it made me feel lonely, for her and for me. This is why we'd gotten married in the first place: because we were lonely. I said earlier that we got divorced because Dawn wanted me to move to Charlotte and I wouldn't. But really, we got divorced because we were still lonely and Dawn thought Charlotte would change that and I thought that it wouldn't. And I wondered if this was true for other people: that they got married and divorced for the very same reason.

81.

The ferry's horn sounded and its engines made a new noise, and so I stood and tucked the gerbil DVD into the back of my pants and then went back up top to join my aunt. She was where I left her, leaning against the railing.

"Stockholm is justifiably proud of its light," my aunt said to me, and I thought of the light streaming into our hotel room windows and also of her son, my cousin, and the overhead klieg lights shining on his DVDs, "but in general I prefer the gloom."

I knew why she was saying this. We were just now pulling into Copenhagen harbor. It was nine in the morning, the sun was up, but we could not see it. Everything was gray. The clouds, the water, the docks and slips. On the other side of water, opposite the port, there were row houses, pink and green and yellow, but somehow they were gray, too, as though they'd been dusted with soot. A raw wind tossed my aunt's hair and goose-bumped my bald head. We had traveled south, but the weather had gone north.

82.

Fifteen minutes later, we were standing in a plaza, a round cobblestone plaza, eating hot dogs. Traffic was whizzing around us. My head felt thick from the travel and from the lack of sleep and from the liquor I'd consumed the night before. But my aunt Beatrice seemed energized. She was on her third hot dog. She was also drinking Carlsberg out of a large paper cup. I was already becoming wary of her appetites. By this, I mean that I was worried that she would insist on making them my appetites, too. When I'd said that it was too early for me to be drinking a beer and that two hot dogs were plenty for me, she'd replied with these words by John Calvin: "We are insatiable pits, monsters in spite of nature."

I knew the quote. My mother had used it herself, in many a sermon, usually around the major holidays. For my mother, they were words of caution. But my aunt had said them in her usual happy way, as though being an insatiable pit were a preferred state.

83.

I mentioned the traffic. The traffic was almost no cars, almost all bicycles. It was as though the Great Jailer had released all the beautiful people in northern Europe at once and told them that the conditions of their parole mandated that they go to Copenhagen and put on their most stylish, form-fitting but still water-resistant clothes and ride three-speed bicycles.

And for the second time in the last hour, I felt that I'd made the wrong choice coming with my aunt. It was the beauty of the cyclists that made me feel that way. It can be very demeaning being among beautiful people. I suddenly missed Congress, where no adults rode bicycles unless they'd lost their licenses from drunk driving and where it was seen as acceptable to wear bulky lined flannel shirts all year-round (I was wearing a lined flannel shirt), even to church, and where I was only one of many men whose best idea of self-improvement was to shave his head and grow out his beard.

Meanwhile, the beautiful people pedaled and pedaled by, and I felt their clothes were judging me, and I also wanted badly to see what was underneath them.

"Flesh," my aunt said, as though reading my mind. We were now walking along the water, which was no longer an ocean, a bay, or a harbor, but was narrower: a river or a canal. Those yellow, blue, and pink row homes were even closer now, even dirtier looking in the murk.

"They're all right," I admitted, thinking my aunt was talking about the beautiful cyclists. They were still among us, so many of them that I felt like I was being swarmed, although swarmed in orderly way, as they never seemed to leave their designated lanes.

"Who are?" my aunt said. I gestured toward the bicyclists, and she frowned and said, "Adults should not be allowed to ride bikes unless they happen to be very fat adults."

I waited to hear more. Without explanation, it seemed only like an arbitrarily mean thing to say about fat people. But of course my aunt never explained anything. Which meant the comment could only be understood as meanness. And so I repeated something I'd heard my mother say many times—at home, at church, in the car, and, of course, in her famous book: "John Calvin says we should honor everyone and I have never been in a situation where I felt this instruction was inappropriate."

Aunt Beatrice nodded. "I had sex with your father on a chaise lounge in the picnic area of the public beach on Lake Congress," she said as though in response to my mother saying that John Calvin said that we should honor everyone.

"You did what?" I said.

"Copenhagen always makes me think of flesh," my aunt said wistfully, and I thought of her son and his DVDs, and now of my father, and I wondered if there was a place that didn't make my aunt think of flesh. We were at another roundabout. There was a don't-walk light in front of us and a button that we were supposed to push in order to change the sign, but my aunt ignored both and walked out into the street. I trotted after her, apologizing to the bikers, who dinged their bells at us. By the time I got to the other side of the street, I was so angry at the bikers and their bells, and of course I was also angry at my aunt and at my father.

"I thought you said my father was a *good guy*," I said to my aunt.

"He *was* a good guy," my aunt said. "Which is why he eventually told your mother." She paused to take a drink from her paper cup and then continued. "This was on a Sunday. Your mother was at church, leading her service. This was before she'd written her famous book, but already she was thinking about it. She had always been on fire for John Calvin. I liked to tease her about it. I sometimes would try to shame her into talking about Martin Luther in one of her sermons. 'At least mention the name of the most important man in Protestant Christendom,' I once told her, and she assured me that, as always, for the love of John Calvin, she would pretend that Martin Luther didn't exist. Your mother pretended that she was teasing me back. But in fact, she was serious about ignoring Luther out of love for Calvin. If you love someone, you must pretend that someone else other people love doesn't exist. That was your mother's theory, although I don't believe she mentioned it in her famous book. Your father and I had sex because we wanted to, Calvin. The chaise lounge was merely the nearest bedlike surface. It was September and the beach was deserted. It may have been officially closed, but I like being in places that are officially closed. It was eleven in the morning, and your father and I had already been drinking. All the best and worst things happen when you've been drinking during the morning." She paused again, this time to toast me with her paper cup of beer, which she then drank down, crumpled the cup, dropped it onto the cobblestones, and finished her story. "The lake was full of sailboats. I remember their colorful sheets. It was very windy. Your father had some hair then, and it, like the boats, was in full sail. I doubt the sailors noticed your father and me, so consumed were they by their jibs and their tacking and their constant coming about. The sex was very sweet, Calvin, but also very sad. We both knew what it meant. That your father would eventually tell your mother and that your mother would tell me that she never wanted to see me again. And that was exactly what happened: your father told her, not long after you were born, and your mother said she never wanted to see me again. And except for one time, she never did."

84.

I've often thought of what it must have been like for my father to tell my mother that he'd had sex with her sister and what it must have been like for my mother to hear that, and then what it must have been like for my mother to tell my aunt to go away forever and for my aunt to hear *that*. It must have felt like the end. But what does the end feel like? As John Calvin says, "The mind is never seriously aroused to desire and ponder the life to come unless it be previously imbued with contempt for the present life."

85.

And in any case, it wasn't the end, not for any of them, not for a while at least, and it still wasn't the end for my aunt because there I was, with her, in Copenhagen.

"Honor everyone how?" my aunt was saying. This, I realized, was in response to John Calvin, and then my mother, and then me, claiming that we should honor everyone. "Should we honor everyone the same way? In what way should we honor them? Is there only one way to honor? Can one not honor through dishonor? *Look!*" she said loudly, with emphasis. *"A very fat woman on a bicycle!"* Aunt Beatrice pointed to my right, and there, as she'd announced, was a very fat woman riding a bicycle. The bicycle was too small for the woman. It looked as though she were crushing it: its tires were dangerously deflated, and the chain complained as the woman shifted gears, and the woman's knees stuck out to the sides as she pedaled. She wore flapping gray sweatpants, and an enormous orange hooded sweatshirt that seemed to ripple over her torso like lava, and a helmet that was much too small and sat on the top of her head like a dollop of something. Her face was red. From her pedaling certainly but also because of what my aunt had said. I'm sure the woman heard it. Her cheeks were red and huge and mostly swallowed up her tiny black eyes, but still, I could see them well enough, I can still see them well enough, can still see them burning as she stared at us and then at the beautiful sleek cyclists of Copenhagen as they so effortlessly passed her by.

86.

My aunt took a right turn, away from the water and toward a complex of ancient-looking fortress- or castle- or palace-type buildings. I'm sorry I can't be more specific about what the buildings looked like. It can be overwhelming having to describe a place, especially if you haven't been to many places yet and especially if you don't know what the place is called or what you're doing there. My aunt looked at the building, adjusted her glasses, adjusted them again, then took out her cell phone and typed something into it. The phone hummed as information passed out of it. It was rumored that the humming was supposed to replicate the sound we humans make as we pass through time and that the phone makers had known that was the sound we human beings make as we pass through time because they had created a phone omniscient enough to tell them so. A moment later the phone hummed again as it received information. My aunt put the phone back in her purse and walked up to the building. The building had front doors, of course, which were enormous, heavy looking, gilt around the edges. But we went instead around the side of the building, where there was a much smaller door, windowless, made of dark, splintered wood. My aunt was serious when she claimed to like being in places that were officially closed. But if she had to be in a place that was officially open, then it made her feel better to at least enter the building through an unauthorized entrance. I heard a dull thump, as though something heavy were being raised and then lowered. We waited a moment, several moments, and then my aunt opened the door and we walked in.

There was no one on the other side of this door. My aunt held it open, then closed it behind me. We were in a dark room—a cellar, it seemed, with a dim light somewhere in front of us. We walked toward the light. The floor was uneven in places, and several times I tripped over something hard—bricks or stones or human bones, all those seemed possible, it was too dark to see what they were, and in any case, my aunt was moving fast, clearly not interested in what was at our feet. Finally, we got to the light.

It was an overhead light but barely overhead: the ceiling was no more than six feet high. My aunt had gotten to the area first and was leaning over a Plexiglas barrier. I joined her there, looked at what she was looking at. It looked like ruins: a crumbled stone wall or foundation, the footprint and remains of a cobblestone road, several pillars that broke off halfway to the ceilings. The barrier went away from us, I couldn't tell how far; only the part in front of us was lit. But clearly we were looking at the remains of something, some city, some world, very old, and long gone. There is something humbling about seeing something ruined. Once, when walking in the woods as a child, I came across a brick chimney, just the chimney, the ruins of a house or cabin at its feet. I felt very humbled then, and very small, and when I got home, I told my mother about what I saw and what I had felt, and she nodded and said, quoting John Calvin, "Our true wisdom is to embrace with meek docility."

My aunt's phone hummed again. She took it out of her purse, glanced at it, returned it to her purse, then took one final long look at the ruins, and said, "Lost civilizations are fundamentally groups of people who just didn't try very hard."

And then we moved on into the rest of the museum.

87.

Because that's what it was: a museum. We found a set of stairs, spiral stairs, that led us away from the ruins into a room that was full of suits of armor, also behind glass, with signs in English

telling us who wore the armor, and when, and how each sub-
sequent kind of armor marked an improvement over the next
oldest kind of armor, leading up to the present-day body armor.
Other than us and the armor, that room was empty. But the
next room was full of people, schoolchildren mostly, and also
cannons. Hundreds of cannons, some the size of toys, some full
sized and very real looking. The cannons were lined up on either
side of the room, and the children were having a good time
standing between the rows of cannons and making concussive
noises with their mouths, some of the children pretending to be
shot and dead. My aunt, and then I, stepped over a couple of
their pretend corpses on the way to the next room.

The next room was full of guns. Machine guns, shotguns,
hunting rifles, rifles with bayonets attached, military handguns,
and more ancient and less practical pistols with bejeweled grips.
All these weapons were either in glass cases or mounted on the
walls. This room was full of children, too. These children seemed
the same age as the others, but these children were more subdued
than those in the cannon room. There was an almost religious
hush in the room as the children, hands clasped in front of them
or behind their backs, peered at the guns on the walls and underneath the glass.

"What are all these children doing here?" I asked my aunt.
She was walking ahead of me and said over her shoulder in her
loud happy way, "They're learning about the civilizations that
tried very hard."

88.

Knives and swords. The next room was full of knives and swords. Here we stopped. There was a large display case in the middle of the room. The case was, like the one holding the guns, covered with glass, and underneath the glass on what looked like a bed of velvet were maybe twenty of the most beautiful knives. Some of them were sharp and straight, like daggers, and some of them were curved, like miniature scimitars, but all their handles were encrusted with stones—rubies, emeralds, diamonds—and gleamed expensively under the glass.

My aunt tapped the glass with her right forefinger, and immediately a man came over to us. He was clearly a museum employee: he was wearing a green uniform and a name tag that said CARL. Carl was young, in his twenties, and tall, stoop shouldered. His hair was red and covered his head like a wispy bowl. He seemed to be sizing up my aunt. Finally, he said in English, "You mustn't touch the glass. That's inappropriate."

My aunt grinned wolfishly, I think in response to what he'd said. I'm guessing her least favorite words were "that's inappropriate," the way Dawn's were "all right." She responded in what I supposed was Danish, rapid-fire Danish, and Carl seemed surprised. I couldn't tell if he was surprised by the fact that she'd spoken Danish or by what she'd said in that language. He took a step back, then straightened his shoulders, took a step forward.

"Excuse me!" a woman's voice called out in English. I looked to my right. There was a woman, about my aunt's age. She was built like a bulldog, short, squat, with a bulldog's many-folded face. But she was wearing the sleek, fashionable, weather-appropriate gear that the bicyclists had been wearing. And so I judged her Danish. Although her English was perfect. And it occurred to me to wonder why, if she was Danish and in a Danish museum, she was speaking English. And if this was a Danish museum, why were all the signs in English, too? And why was Carl speaking in that language?

"I want my Indian war club," she said in English to Carl. "It has bear claws, you bash people with it." The woman's voice sounded as though she was a smoker. She raised both hands above her hand, clasped them, and then in a jerking motion made menacing gestures with her imaginary club. "They told me it was here."

"Check with Indigenous Peoples," Carl said. "It wouldn't be here, in Blades. That would be inappropriate. Miss, *keep your hands off the glass.*" This last he said to my aunt, whose hands, I noticed, were still, or once again, on the glass. I mean, both of them were on the glass, not the palms, not the fingers, just the fingertips, and with them she was putting some definite pressure on the glass. I know this because when she removed her fingers, the finger marks were visible on the glass, and they seemed to beat there, like a pulse, for a moment or two, before disappearing.

Aunt Beatrice said something to Carl in Danish again, and then smiled again, showing the space where her tooth should have been. I could tell that Carl had just noticed it, because he took another step back and sort of cocked his head, as though to get a better glimpse of the tooth that wasn't there.

"Are you sure you don't know where my Indian war club is?" said the woman to Carl, who turned away from my aunt and back toward the woman. Her hands were still clasped above her head and her rain jacket revealed a white strip of her thick belly, and I wondered if Carl had noticed it, if he would have thought it inappropriate. "Indigenous Peoples," he said again, pointing toward another room. The woman said something under her breath and then walked away, grumbling, and a few moments later I could hear her voice from another room, explaining, "You bash people with it. Like this."

89.

By this time, I'd completely forgotten that my aunt and my father had had sex. I would not forget it forever, but I'd forgotten it for now. Because for every moment in which my aunt told me something that had happened in her past, there was another that made me forget the past because I was too busy wondering what was happening in our present and what might yet happen in our future.

90.

Carl turned back to us. My aunt was behind me, but I could tell from Carl's expression that her hands were on the glass again.

"*Schtop day!*" he said. At least, that's what it sounded like to me. But I was pretty sure he was telling her in Danish to stop it. I turned to face Aunt Beatrice, and she was smiling broadly, so broadly that I wondered if it hurt her mouth, her face.

"I'm sorry," she said brightly in English, "but I don't speak Danish!" And I noticed, in any case, that her hands were still on the glass. "Such beautiful knives!" she said, and she removed her right forefinger from the glass and then tapped it again.

91.

Carl. For the rest of my life, whenever I meet a person in charge who refuses to recognize or admit that he is not actually in charge, I will think of that person as Carl. But then, I suspect my aunt's life had been full of such people, and they had had many names and that she'd made them. That is, that they had not been a Carl until she had made them, or revealed them to be, a Carl.

92.

Carl opened his mouth—to speak, I suppose, but nothing came out of it. I wondered if he didn't know what to say or what language to say it in. He closed his mouth, gave my aunt a knowing, superior look, then dropped his right hand to his belt. Hitched to his belt was not a knife or a gun, but a walkie-talkie. He unhitched it, raised it to his mouth.

And then from another room came a roaring sound, a roaring sound that got steadily louder and louder, and I turned toward it, and so did Carl, and so, I imagine, did pretty much everyone else in that room and possibly the whole museum. The roaring was that loud. It was not a series of roars, with pauses in between, but one roar, sustained. It sounded like a bear's roar, which was apt since a moment later the woman who'd been looking for the Indian club with which you bashed things came running out of Indigenous Peoples into Blades. She was holding, above her head, a club, an enormous dark wooden club with a thin handle and a fat barrel, and the barrel was studded with bear claws. The woman ran right up to Carl, poor Carl, who was now holding his walkie-talkie in front of him, like a shield. The woman roared, right in his face, and I could see her teeth, and she had all of them, and they were yellowed, and she roared and shook her club and she shook it and I saw her arms jiggle in her sleek rain jacket, and then she stopped roaring and lowered her club and presented it to Carl so that, it seemed, he might have a better look at it, and said hoarsely, "This is what I was talking about. How you could not know about this Indian war club?" And then she leaned closer to Carl and said in a confidential way, although loud enough for at least me to hear it, "Do you know where the parking lot is? I don't know where I left my car."

I turned away from the woman and toward where my aunt had been and saw her walking briskly away. I trotted after her, past the guns, the cannons, the armor, through the cellar, past the ruins of whatever lost civilization, through that wooden door and out into the world again. To my surprise, the woman from the museum was standing there in a parking lot to the right of the door. She wasn't holding the Indian war club any-more. Instead, she was holding her purse in front of her with her left hand, like an old lady certain she was about to be robbed. In her right hand was a lit cigarette. She saw us and raised the cigarette to her mouth, and her folded cheeks collapsed as she drew powerfully on the cigarette, smoked the whole thing down, then flicked it onto the parking lot.

"You shouldn't roar like that in a museum," Aunt Beatrice said to the woman, and I was surprised by how prim she sounded.

The woman nodded. "It was inappropriate," she said, and then they both laughed.

After the laugh, I expected them to embrace—they seemed clearly to be old friends, the kind who finished each other's thoughts and sentences—but they didn't. Instead, the woman frowned, creating folds within her face folds, and said to my aunt, "Admiral, are you ill?"

"Yes," Aunt Beatrice said in that unconvincingly pathetic way she'd said back in Boston that an old lady likes to be escorted into the airport. Although it was true: she didn't look good— still very tan but also, somehow, pale and diminished, like one of the brightly painted buildings that were being rained on.

The woman looked at me and then said, "Should I trust her, Calvin?" It made me feel pleased and bold that this woman knew my name even though I still didn't know hers. "Probably not," I admitted, and my aunt laughed barkingly, which made me happy even though it didn't seem to have the same effect on the woman, who was still frowning.

"Clear sailing?" the woman asked, and I recognized the words from the phone call I'd gotten in the middle of the night after my mother's funeral and after the Otises had woken me up while shooting the skunk.

Now it was my aunt's turn to frown. "*Dansk*," she said to the woman, and then they began talking in another language. I assumed it was Danish. It sounded like the language my aunt had been speaking earlier, to Carl, and also like Swedish but even slurrier. The day before, in Sweden, I'd felt helpless in the face of a language I didn't understand. Now, I felt frustrated. Because clearly, they were speaking Danish because they didn't want me to understand what they were saying. The conversation was animated, too, even frantic, as though the two of them couldn't swallow and spit the vowels and consonants fast enough.

93.

It may seem as though there were no difference between not understanding Swedish one day and not understanding Danish the next. But I felt helpless one day and frustrated the next, and that is a difference. That is progress. As John Calvin himself said, "No one can travel so far that he does not make some progress each day. So let us never give up."

94.

I took out my phone. It is common knowledge that this is one of the main functions of the cell phone: to give you something to do when you have nothing else to do or when other people are doing something and haven't invited you to be a part of it.

Aunt Beatrice and her friend had very definitely not invited me to be a part of their conversation. I began touching my phone randomly, resentfully. But there was nothing on the phone I was interested in. Bored, bored, I felt like a child again, when I was either bored by reading John Calvin or when I was bored when I wasn't reading John Calvin and then made the mistake of telling my mother, and she'd said, If you're so bored, why don't you read some John Calvin? *Stop being bored*, I told myself. *Stop being a child. Grow up! Grow up!* I fiddled with my phone some more and noticed under Tools a function I'd never used. Record. I touched the word with my index finger, and my phone began recording Aunt Beatrice and her friend's conversation. As it recorded, I held my phone out in front of me, pointed in their direction, and pretended to read something long and important on it until, finally, there was a pause in the conversation. I'd seen this happen with the Otises in the middle of their dusk-time fights, when they would pause as though trying to decide whether to keep on fighting or to forgive, if not forget.

And then the woman said one last thing in Danish and then, in English, added, "You never got a new tooth." My aunt smiled, giving proof that she never did get one.

"New teeth are expensive," my aunt said.

"You weren't waiting for *me* to pay for it," the woman said, and she was smiling again now, too.

"Well," my aunt said, "you *were* the one who knocked it out."

And then I stopped recording. Now, at least, I knew who had knocked out my aunt's tooth, but before I could learn when and why, a car alarm went off, and my aunt and I turned in the direction of the noise and saw the car, a dark blue BMW, its headlights flashing, and also saw a cyclist lying on the street, the bike still between his legs, the front wheel still spinning. He must have been riding past the car when the alarm went off, must have been so startled that he'd fallen off his bike. The man got up, noticed that the back wheel of his bike had been damaged in the fall, and then bent over and noticed a rip at the knee in his expensive-looking pants, and then he began kicking the car's passenger's-side door. Other cyclists gathered around, cheering the man on, and the whole scene was as mob-like and tribal as any of my father's high school football games. Then the alarm quit and the crowd dispersed, and the man pushed his broken bike away, and when we turned back to the woman, she was gone.

95.

The woman's disappearance seemed to make my aunt happy. She began to walk so quickly and so happily that she might as well have been skipping. "Wrong Way Connie!" she said, clapping her hands.

"What's that mean?" I asked.

"I don't mean to brag," my aunt said, bragging, "but we were the best rare metals and antiquities thieves in all of northern Europe. Never caught. Never suspected. Partners in crime! Best friends! Wrong Way Connie!" she repeated. "Because she makes people—"

"Look the wrong way," I finished for her, and my aunt clapped her hands again. Of course I knew she was talking about the woman who'd just disappeared. Aunt Beatrice then patted her pocketbook, and of course I knew one of those beautiful knives was in there, that my aunt had stolen it when Wrong Way Connie had distracted Carl with her Indian club, and I was afraid Aunt Beatrice was going to pull out the knife and show it to me right there, only blocks away from the museum she'd just stolen it from, and to distract her from that I said, "But where did Wrong Way Connie get that club?"

"Oh, there are always Indian clubs lying around that museum. No one keeps track of them, so obsessed are they with their shiny suits of armor and cannons and guns and . . ." And then she patted her purse again.

"And why did she knock out your tooth?" I asked, not expecting an immediate answer and in fact not getting one. My aunt continued walking, in the opposite direction from which we'd come earlier, although her pace had slowed and her breathing was labored, jagged, as though it were getting caught on something sharp on the way from her lungs to her mouth. And I thought about what Connie had said about Aunt Beatrice looking ill. And then my aunt said, breathing hard, "I'd really like to sit quietly in a church right now, Calvin."

So we found a church and sat in it quietly. There were no parishioners in the church. They were no tourists in it either. It was not the kind of church you'd seek out: it was not baroque or simple enough to satisfy those who valued either of those things. I believe the church was Lutheran. Martin Luther: John Calvin's more famous rival. It made me feel seditious just sitting there. The church was made of dark wood and dark stone, and it was quiet and cold, and the only people inside the church besides my aunt and me were two old women and an old man, shuffling around, shelving hymnals in the pew pockets, and whispering to one another as they walked up and down the aisles. It was like a library for people who believed in God.

"Do you believe in God?" I asked my aunt in a whisper, and she responded, not in a whisper, "People believe in God because they're too frightened not to."

This kind of argument, I knew, had always infuriated my mother. "Cynicism," she had said in one of her sermons and had also written in her famous book, "has failed to bring us closer to the truth and instead has only further estranged us from goodness and from God."

"Does that mean you do or you don't believe in God?" I asked my aunt, thinking I knew the answer. But my aunt surprised me.

"Oh, I do," Aunt Beatrice said.

"Me, too," I said. And that was the first and last thing we ever said on the subject.

96.

"Now, Calvin," my aunt said. "Tell me what you've learned today."

I'd been quizzed enough times by my mother on what I'd learned from reading John Calvin to not be surprised by the request. But I never answered her the way I was about to answer my aunt. Maybe it was the spirit of Calvin's rival, Martin Luther, or maybe it was the spirit of my mother's rival, my aunt, or maybe it was my own spirit, which I was in the process of trying to find. And as I knew very well, if you really wanted to find your spirit, you needed commandments to guide you. I consulted my phone and said, "Thou shall never travel by car or truck unless they're stolen. Thou shall lie, but only if thou lies well. Thou shall honor through dishonor. Thou shall have sex with thy sister's husband because thou wants to. If thou loves someone, then thou shall pretend that someone else other people love doesn't exist. Thou shall betray the ones thou loves the most. Thou shall drink in the morning even though thou shall probably regret it. Thou shall try very hard. Thou shall steal while thy partner distracts. Thou shall not obey those people who tell thou that what thou is doing is inappropriate. Thou shall expect to get punched in the face for thine inappropriate acts. Thou shall not apologize to the person who has punched thou, nor should thou expect an apology. Thou shall believe in God, even, or especially, if thou doesn't believe in acting godly." Then I paused, and when I did, I became aware that I was panting. Learning lessons is like hard exercise, especially if the lessons you're learning are the opposite of the lessons you've already learned. Still, I managed to quiet my panting, looked at my aunt in what I hoped was a bold manner, and added, "Thou shall learn many languages, not so thou may communicate with as many people as possible but so thou may speak freely in front of people who don't speak those languages."

When I said that, my aunt smiled hugely and clapped, like a pleased child. Aunt Beatrice loved it when you told her that you knew she was up to something. Although of course that didn't mean that she would then tell you what she was up to.

My aunt's phone buzzed, and she removed it from her purse, looked at it, returned it to her purse, and then stood up abruptly. "God orders what we cannot do," my aunt announced, quoting John Calvin, "that we may know what we ought to ask of him." Then she ran out of the church and into the street, and it took me a few moments to catch up with her.

"What ought we ask of him?" I asked, still breathing hard, harder than my aunt, I noticed. It seemed that our time in church had restored her, just as her sister, my mother, had always insisted it was predestined to do.

"That he delay our train," my aunt said.

"Train?" I said, because that had been one of the commandments I'd forgotten to recite—"Thou shall not speak of traveling by train, let alone travel by train"—and besides I hadn't known that there was one and that my aunt was intending for us to catch it. But there was the train station, right in front of us, its PA system summoning us out of the fog. And there was our train, waiting for us at platform 12, even though it was fifteen minutes past its departure time. And we did catch it, and only after we took our seats did my aunt say, "Because I betrayed her brother, who was also my husband," and it wasn't until after the train pulled out of the station that I understood that Aunt Beatrice was telling me why Wrong Way Connie had knocked out her tooth.

Eight

97.

Our tickets were for Madrid, but Aunt Beatrice said to never mind about that, that she and Morten (who was my aunt's husband and Connie's brother) had taken hundreds of trains and not once had they ended up in the place where they were supposed to go.

98.

Aunt Beatrice and I were on the train in her sleeper room, an hour outside of Copenhagen by now. I'd asked her why we'd left Copenhagen so quickly. "Oh, I was there to steal the knife," she said. There were two couches in the room: one that was permanently a couch and one that folded out into a bed. My aunt was slumped on the one that folded out into a bed, but her mentioning the stolen knife seemed to remind her of something, because she sat up and said suddenly, "Calvin! The film." I didn't understand, and this seemed to agitate her. "The film!" she said. "The gerbil! Zhow's gerbil film!" It took me a minute to understand what she was saying and that Zhow was her son's name. It was an odd name; I couldn't imagine my aunt choosing it. But I decided not to say that. Instead, I reached around, pulled the DVD out of my waistband, showed it to her, then placed it next to me on my couch. My aunt snatched up the DVD and stuffed it into her purse, where, presumably, the knife still was. There was already quite a collection of illicit objects in there, I thought.

Anyway, after my aunt had put the DVD in her purse, she slumped back on her couch. I pressed her to tell me more about Morten and she said, "Morten loved trains." And I understood why my aunt and he had been on so many of them and, if she'd betrayed him, and had had a good reason to betray him, why she was less than fond of them herself. "And he hated Copenhagen."

"Where was he from?"

"Copenhagen," my aunt said. "We lived there from 1973 to 1975. And Morten tolerated it. Because I was happy and because our business with Connie was so profitable. But it was too cold for Morten. He always wanted to live somewhere where he could wear shorts." My aunt paused, transparently thinking of Morten and his shorts, and of course I thought of Dawn, wearing her shorts in Charlotte, and I wondered when Dawn would come into my life again or if she would come into my life again. "Morten had excellent legs," my aunt continued.

"How did you betray him?" I asked.

"Of course, Morten was a smuggler. Smugglers in general have good legs," Aunt Beatrice said. "I don't know why it's true, but it is. Gun smugglers have the very best legs, as a rule. Then, in descending order, art. Jewels and diamonds. Pornography. Human traffickers—"

"What did Morten smuggle?" I interrupted, not wanting to hear what was lower than human trafficking, and my aunt smiled broadly again, and I saw the space formerly occupied by the tooth that Connie had knocked out, and I suspected the answer was, Everything.

99.

I excused myself to go the corridor bathroom (our rooms had sinks but no toilets). Once in it, I didn't use the toilet except to sit on it while I listened to the recording I'd made earlier of Connie and Aunt Beatrice. Of course, they were speaking in Danish, and I didn't understand any of it. But my phone had another function I'd never used before—Translate—and my phone could translate anything it had recorded into English. Maybe that's why all the signs in the Copenhagen museum had been in English and why Carl had spoken English, too, knowing, inevitably, that everything would be translated into English.

Anyway, I translated the conversation into English. The miracle of technology: not just the translation but that my aunt's voice and Connie's voice when translated into English actually sounded like their voices. I'd assumed that their voices would come out sounding automated. Like the voice on my phone back in Congress, telling me it was "clear sailing." Either that person had wanted to obscure his voice, or he'd been working with some outdated technology.

". . . the knife?" Connie said in midsentence because I'd started recording midsentence.

"Among other things," my aunt said.

"Clear sailing," Connie repeated. "You think that was my brother. So you're wandering around Europe, gathering and stealing things, hoping you'll find him, or that he finds you, and then you'll give him these things." My aunt didn't respond to that. I could picture her, fiddling with her glasses.

"I'm sorry, Admiral," Connie said, and I could tell by her voice that she really was sorry. "But I think he's dead."

"Probably," my aunt said, although I couldn't tell by her cheerful voice whether she thought he was or wasn't.

"You killed him," Connie said.

"Only figuratively," my aunt said.

"Does Calvin know what you're doing here?"

"He doesn't know anything."

"You should tell him."

"It's better that he doesn't know anything."

"I still hate you," Connie said.

"That's because you know everything," Aunt Beatrice said.

Then there was a pause, after which Wrong Way Connie said,

translated from the original Danish, "He should know at least something." And then she pointed out in English that my aunt had never gotten her tooth replaced, and then I stopped playing the recording and put away my phone.

100.

Up until this point, I hadn't been able to figure out a sense of purpose to our trip. Up until this point, it had seemed as though my aunt, as she'd announced earlier, really did just want to show me some of her old haunts. And that the things she'd been given, and stolen, were trinkets, keepsakes. Only when I listened to the recording did it occur to me that they might be meant as gifts for someone. Only when I listened to the recording did it occur to me that we might be looking for someone. What Connie had said made sense. After all, I was running away from my Dawn; why shouldn't my aunt be running toward her Morten?

101.

I left the bathroom and returned to my aunt's room. She was sitting on her bed, looking at the gerbil DVD. I don't mean she was watching the film itself. Because of course she didn't have proper technology. Because of course the proper technology was obsolete. Her phone, and my phone, had made it so. No, Aunt Beatrice was looking at the DVD case, looking at the gerbil on the front, then flipping it over and looking at the gerbil on the back. I could tell how frustrated she was. She was actually grinding her teeth, so badly did she want to watch that film.

"We'll have to find a DVD player," I said to my aunt, and this startled her, as she fumbled with and nearly dropped the DVD. Which pleased me. It made me feel like I was starting to get somewhere. If to be grown up was to have the ability to startle, then maybe I really was starting to grow up.

"Yes," she said, returning the DVD to her purse. "A mother does like to see what her children have been up to."

I didn't say anything after that. I was thinking of how to tell Aunt Beatrice that I knew who we were looking for. But I didn't want to let on that I'd recorded and translated her conversation because I suspected I'd have occasion to do so again. So I sat there and I sat there as if I were mulling over some great puzzle, and then, as if thunderstruck, I said, "Clear sailing!" My aunt stared at me, sitting on her bed, her legs crossed at her ankles. I wondered if she was onto me, if my epiphany sounded as phony to her ears as her claims of feebleness sounded to mine. But I continued. "You think that was Morten. Telling you that all's forgiven. Telling you to come find him if you want to. And you want to. That's why you got Zhow's DVD. That's why you stole the knife. They're presents to give to Morten once we find him."

Of course, Connie had come up with this theory, not I. But this was another commandment I learned during my time with Aunt Beatrice: "Thou shall record other people's conversations and pass off their ideas as thine own."

My aunt took off her glasses at that, swung them by the stem with her gnarled, veiny right hand while she considered me. I said earlier that her eyes were like marbles, but they were also like brains: red lined and rutted and oddly discolored, and frankly gross and totally beyond me. "Why would he call you and not me?" she asked, and I could tell she was testing me. But I'd already thought of this.

"Because people are still looking for him," I said. "Whatever he did, and whomever you betrayed him to, those people are still looking for him. And if people are looking for him, they're probably looking for him to contact you. But they wouldn't be looking for him to contact me." I didn't bother to mention how he knew to contact me. Because he'd read my blog. My blog! It seems I had quite a readership after all, although I don't know how likely it is that any of these readers ended up buying a pellet stove. "And so that's what you need to do," I added. "You need to find him before these other people do."

Aunt Beatrice put her glasses back on. "Very good, Calvin," she said, and her voice went even higher than usual, and her approval was like the sun, finally burning off the cold and wet of Copenhagen.

102.

I still wanted to know how and why my aunt had betrayed Morten. But I'd already asked her that question, and I knew that if I asked her again that might even further delay my getting the answer. And so I asked her something else. This is yet another thing my aunt taught me. You're more likely to get an answer to a question that isn't important than one that is. Which then might end up being more important than you thought it was.

"What's Morten's nickname?" I asked. Because there was no doubt in my mind that he had one.

"The Sociologist," my aunt said. I waited for more, but there was no more. From college, of course, I knew that sociology was a discipline, a course of study, a major, but I had no idea what it really was or what a sociologist really did.

"What is a sociologist?" I asked.

"A sociologist," my aunt said, "is someone who likes to say things that sound profound until you think about them and realize that they're mostly just obvious."

"But why was he called that?"

"Because before he was a smuggler, he was a sociologist." I didn't say anything to that, and my aunt must have taken my silence for disapproval because she shrugged and admitted, "Some nicknames are better than others."

103.

We were on the subject of romantic failure and betrayal now, and apparently my aunt wanted to stay on that subject. She asked me, "Why did you and Dawn get divorced?" I hadn't mentioned that Dawn and I had been married, let alone divorced, but by this point I'd stopped wondering how my aunt knew things I hadn't told her. By now, I just assumed she knew.

"I was lonely," I told my aunt, and she shook her head. Not out of sadness or dismay; no, she shook her head because she thought that was the wrong answer.

"Dawn cheated on you," my aunt said.

"No!" I said, and I was surprised at how loudly I said this and how badly I wanted what my aunt had said not to be true. Not because Dawn's infidelity would have hurt so much but because I was certain I knew Dawn and that was not what I was certain I knew about her. Where did I learn to be this certain about women? From men, of course, including the theologian John Calvin, who was certain that "undoubtedly the dress of a virtuous and godly woman must differ from that of a strumpet."

"No, you're right," my aunt said. She fiddled with her sunglasses. The train blew its horn and I turned and looked out the window, and another train was rattling past us, a freight train so close that I could imagine reaching out and touching the graffitied cars.

"Say you had a baby," my aunt said.

"All right," I said. I thought she was speaking merely hypothetically, but then I realized that she really wanted me to say that.

"I had a baby," I said.

"Give the baby a sex, Calvin," Aunt Beatrice said. "And an age."

I had no idea my aunt was doing, but I wanted to find out. "A boy," I said, maybe because I'd been one. "One year old."

"A one-year-old baby boy named . . ." Aunt Beatrice said, and then quickly, before I could respond, she added, "No. You don't like to think about his name. It's too awful."

"Because he died," I guessed, and I immediately felt that I had said something true, even though what I'd said was false. And then I understood what my aunt was up to. She was teaching me how to lie, how to be a better liar.

"Of cancer," I said, warming to the assignment, and my aunt winced, as though my answer had caused her real physical pain.

"Cancer," she repeated flatly. "Please, Calvin. You have to try harder than that."

It is terrible to disappoint the person you love; if you disappoint the person you love, what hope do you have of doing better with the people you don't? So I tried harder to find a better way of dying for my son. My life, after all, had recently been emptied by death. My father. My mother. But I didn't think a child could die of a heart attack. And it seemed too implausible that another family member would be struck by a train, even though I was on one. Meanwhile, my aunt was growing impatient. She was fiddling with the strap of her purse, fiddled with her glasses, her purse strap, and I felt an urgent need to please her and also a strong sense that I would fail to do what I urgently needed to do. "Kidney stones!" I finally blurted out, and my aunt smiled.

"Rarely fatal," she said, nodding, "and almost never in children unless left untreated for a long time. Pain. Neglect. Shame. Bewilderment. Denial. Death. *Kidney stones.* Very good, Calvin."

We didn't say anything after that, not for a little while. I hadn't met the Sociologist, and at this point I barely knew anything about him, but still, I thought I understood his fondness for train travel. My aunt's room was toward the back of the train, and I had the strong sense that there was a long life in front of me and a short life behind.

"Yes, my son died of kidney stones," I repeated, wanting to stay in the moment, the occasion of my first good lie. "And after that Dawn and I were never the same."

104.

After we talked about my fake son, my thoughts turned to my aunt's real one.

"What kind of name is Zhow?" I asked.

"A Portuguese one," my aunt said.

"Why does he have a Portuguese name?"

"Zhow's father is the Sociologist," she said. Which didn't answer the question of why he'd been given a Portuguese name. But it did answer my next question, which was going to be, And why are you and Zhow so estranged?

Neither of us said anything for a while after that. The cabin grew dark, but neither my aunt nor I turned on the lights. It was pleasant, to not have to do anything, to have something else move you through the darkness. But my mind was moving through the darkness, too. There was something nagging at it, and me, something my aunt had said earlier: "A mother does like to see what her children have been up to."

"How many children do you have?" I asked my aunt.

"Enough," my aunt said quickly. She looked away from me and toward the door, like she very much wanted to be on the other side of it.

105.

And was *this* the moment when I began to suspect that my aunt was really my mother? Possibly. Because I came away from this conversation—about my marriage and divorce, and the fake death of my fake son, and the existence of my aunt's real son—anxious, impatient, desperate for the rest of the long life in front of me to get started. As though I already had wasted so much time.

Nine

- - - - -

106.

I left my aunt's room, went back to my own. The train stopped
when it reached the German border, and I grew tired waiting for
it to start moving again, and I fell asleep. I dreamt no dreams.
When I woke up, it was around five o'clock. I looked out the
window. The scene outside the train was flat, dreary, depressed:
rain-soaked parking lots, rain-soaked backs of buildings, rain-
soaked fields. The weather had gone bad inside the train, too.
Maybe it was something my aunt and I had talked about before
she'd left and before I'd fallen asleep. The terrible fate of my
imaginary son seemed to hang there in the room, like a blanket
over a lamp, and I suddenly felt a kind of longing for his mother.

107.

Hostile Territory

My dear readers, thank you for all your helpful hints about how I might handle heartbreak. Smear campaign! Identity theft! Maiming! Murder! A new pellet stove! And in fact, I *have* had my eye on Casco's newest Lilac model, ideal for those moments when you want your energy-efficient, environmentally healthy primary heat source to do double duty as a potpourri dispenser.

But I'm going to say something shocking, posse: there is some warmth even a pellet stove cannot give. Which is why I'm thinking of leaving my house here in Charlotte and going on a trip, to Europe. At first, I thought I'd travel to Sweden, but then I thought no, maybe I'd visit Denmark. But now I've decided that I'd like to see Germany and that I'd like to see it by train. Germany is hostile territory, as you know: that country is the black sooty heart of the international industrial "conventional woodstove" syndicate. Which is why I don't want to travel by myself. But I've gotten word of an old friend in those parts, an old friend who became a new enemy but who I hope will become a friend again. These are my questions for my old friend: Can we forgive, and forget? Will you travel with me? Will you let me travel with you? As soon I hear from him, I'll be on my way. Wish me luck, posse, and expect further reports from the road—or the rails!

108.

I read this post several times. I was disturbed, of course, that Dawn seemed to know exactly where I was. But I was also disturbed by Dawn's conciliatory tone: I'd never heard her use the expression "forgive and forget," nor did I think her capable of forgiving and forgetting. Which is why, maybe, it seemed like she might be up to something. But it was also true that since I'd met my aunt, it seemed like everyone might be up to something.

Anyway, after I'd read and reread the post, I went to my aunt's room, which was next to my own. I raised my hand to knock on the door, but before I could actually knock I heard my aunt say in her high warbly voice, "All I could think when I felt the bullet going through me was, I hope that's not the femoral artery."

And then another voice, a woman's, younger but also more gravelly, said, "Can I tell you about the time right after my divorce when I was all alone in my awful new apartment with no furniture and no utensils and I saved myself from choking on an unmicrowaved microwavable chicken burrito by ramming a Slim Jim down my throat?"

"Come in, Calvin," my aunt said, even though I still hadn't knocked. I opened the door. My aunt's room was the same as mine. On one side was a couch. On the other was the sleeper bed that folded up into a couch. But it was unfolded now, and its sheets were mussed up. My aunt was sitting on it, her shoes off, and holding a plastic cup of red wine, mostly gone. On the floor, at her ankle-socked feet, was a large bottle of red wine, half-empty. And sitting on the other couch was the woman who,

I guessed, had said that strange thing about saving herself with the Slim Jim. Her hair was short, pixieish, and gray, but her face was much younger than her hair: unlined, round cheeked, tanned, lightly freckled. She was wearing a slim tan skirt and a long-sleeved light blue blouse buttoned to the second to last button, and there was a tan blazer rumpled on the couch next to her, and there was a red bandanna knotted around her neck, and on the floor next to her bare feet were shoes, tan shoes, no heels, flat, soft looking, rounded toe, more slippers than shoes. She looked like a woman who was going on a job interview who then decided to go to the rodeo who then decided to be in a ballet. Her brown eyes were big and seemed to have a hard time settling on something: they darted from my face, to the cell phone in my hand, to the bottle of wine, to the corridor behind me, to my aunt, to my face again. She was also holding a plastic cup of wine, and, as with my aunt, she'd mostly finished hers. And then she did finish it, and my aunt picked up the bottle and refilled the woman's cup and then her own, and then said, "Calvin, this is my neighbor."

"One oh eight," the woman said, and when she saw how this confused me, her eyes darted to the door, which opened inward, and I saw the number 107 there and realized that her room was next to my aunt's. "Caroline," she said, then smiled, the kind of smile that showed no teeth but with the lifting of the corners of the mouth seemed to elevate the rest of the face.

"Caroline and I were just swapping war stories," my aunt said. She then paused. I knew I was supposed to say something but suddenly felt incapable. My aunt let me hang there for a moment, adjusted her glasses, and then said, "You seem momentarily very stupid, Calvin. Was there something you wanted?"

In truth, I'd forgotten by now what I wanted, which was to tell my aunt about Dawn's post, and about how she was coming to Germany, and about how she seemed to know that I was on this train. "I was just checking in on you to see if you were all right," I said, which was just as stupid as my silence: if anyone didn't need checking in on, it was my aunt. And then I told Caroline it was nice to meet her and then backed out of the room. I noticed that the train was slowing again. I passed a porter in the corridor and asked him why, and he said that we were pulling into Hamburg, where we would be stopped for an hour and a half.

109.

I have mentioned my head and how I'd shaved it. But of course I used to have hair. And oddly enough, my hair, when I had it, was like Dawn's: curly, coarse, wild but also, in places, matted down as though slept on, although it looked that way even when I hadn't slept on it. And they called me Geeker. I'm thinking of when I was a teenager, fifteen years old, and I had glasses, and I also had braces. But I think it was mostly my hair that caused Charles Otis and some of the other boys I went to school with to call me Geeker. I say "some of the other boys," but really most of the boys called me this. Several girls also. None of my teachers, as far as I knew.

110.

I mention this, about my nickname and my hair, because I hadn't shaved my head in four days now, and I could feel the hair sprouting, but only in patches and, with it, the return of my past and my nickname. And then, too, I'd been wearing the same clothes—jeans, flannel shirt, running shoes—since we left Congress. And while I'd brushed my teeth in the Stockholm hotel (they'd given me the brush), I'd left it in the room when we'd fled. Up until now, this hadn't bothered me: the professional blogger is rarely bothered by his appearance, as people rarely see him. But now that Caroline had seen me, I was bothered. And so when the train stopped in Hamburg, I got off to see if I could buy any of these things—a razor, some clothes, some toiletries. The train station seemed like it was made of glass, and within the glass there were stalls and stores, and many of those were made of glass, too, and in some of those stalls and stores were the things—a razor, some clothes, some toiletries—that I needed, and I bought them with my credit card, and while I didn't see anything else of Hamburg before I got back on the train, if it's anything like its train station, then it's a bright place, full of the things you need, especially if you need the things I needed, and I highly recommend it.

111.

But before I got back onto the train, let me tell you what happened to me in the men's clothing store. I had already decided on a pair of brown leather ankle boots and a shiny blue-collared shirt, and socks, and underwear, and now I was trying on a pair of jeans. The jeans were expensive. Also, they were said by their tag to be distressed (everything else on the tag was in German except for the English word "distressed"), and it did, in fact, look as though something terrible had happened to the jeans—they were bleached and holey in spots and frayed in the pockets and at the cuffs—and of course when you think of something terrible happening in Germany, you think of the Holocaust, and when I when I realized that the jeans would always remind me of the Holocaust, I didn't really want jeans anymore and was just about to return to the dressing room to take them off when I saw behind me, reflected in the full-length mirror, someone I knew. He was turned sideways, pretending to be just another shopper, flipping through a rack of shiny jackets. I couldn't really see his face, but I recognized him anyway, from his terrible posture: he was the flat-voiced minister who I'd seen sitting with my mother in her church many years ago and then two days earlier in the Boston airport.

112.

Before I met my aunt, I would have pretended that I hadn't seen the flat-voiced minister; I would have kept my head down, averted my eyes, walked in the other direction, avoided conflict. But this was another thing she'd taught me, another commandment: "Thou shall avoid conflict unless the other person wishes to avoid conflict, and in that case thou shall pursue it." I walked right up to the flat-voiced minister. It was the most aggressive thing I'd ever done up to that point. It felt good. Although I was conscious of the tag identifying the jeans as *distressed*. It drifted and flapped at my hip as I walked.

Once the flat-voiced minister noticed me walking toward him, he momentarily sank deeper into the rack of coats but then must have realized there was no hiding from me. He righted himself. Turned to face me. Adjusted his hat—the gray, crown-dented, flat-brimmed hat I remembered from before. He was still wearing that gray suit, too. Before, I'd thought of his clothes as funereal and ministerial. But now that I knew my aunt was looking for the Sociologist, and that other people were looking for him, too, the man also looked like someone who might be looking for someone else. He looked like a spy, in other words, in addition to looking like a minister. Because this was another thing my aunt taught me: that someone is always also someone else, or at least has the capacity to be someone else, if someone else is indeed what he wants to be.

"Who are you?" I asked the man.

"You know who I am," the man said, and from the way he said that, I could tell he was offended. "I am the Reverend John Lawrence, from Hebron, Iowa."

I didn't recognize the name or the place. "Never heard of you," I said. I could tell this surprised him. I wondered if my mother had told him that she'd told me about him. The Reverend John Lawrence's shoulders went back. Not all the way back. He just became a slightly less perfect question mark. He took off his hat, regarded it, made sure the crown was properly dented, and ran his fingers along the brim, composing himself. I imagined his sermons. There would be plenty of pauses. I imagined his church. There would be plenty of empty pews. And then I pictured the pew that he and my mother had been sitting in those many years ago. And then the Reverend John Lawrence returned the hat to his head and said in a slightly less flat, more hopeful, more desperate voice, "Where's your mother?"

This, of course, surprised me. Because now that I was thinking that he might be a spy, I'd half expected him to ask where the Sociologist was. But also because the Reverend John Lawrence knew as well as I did where my mother was.

"My mother isn't anywhere," I said, and that sounded terrible, and so I amended it: "My mother is dead." Which, oddly enough, sounded much better. "She was pulverized by a train." That sounded better yet. The Reverend John Lawrence winced when I said "pulverized." And I knew I would be saying that for the entirety of our relationship, however long that ended up being.

113.

Back when I'd first spotted the Reverend John Lawrence sitting with my mother in the pew in her church, I thought he was more or less her age. But I realized now he was much younger, in his midfifties at most. Like Caroline, his face was younger than his hair and his posture. His clothes, on the other hand, looked as though they'd been worn forever. That before he'd worn them his father had worn them, and before his father had worn them his grandfather had worn them. I knew what these clothes were trying to communicate, because my mother's clothes had tried to communicate the same thing. The Reverend John Lawrence was someone who had renounced all worldly things and wanted to announce to the world that he'd renounced all worldly things. And when I realized that, I decided I would be buying those distressed jeans after all.

114.

The Reverend John Lawrence. John. I knew, without him telling me, which Protestant theologian he'd been named after.

115.

When the Reverend John Lawrence asked where my mother was and then winced when I'd said she'd been pulverized, I had an inkling that my mother had been something more to him than just the author of a famous book about John Calvin; I had an inkling that while he probably wasn't a spy, he might have been my mother's illicit lover (because that was another thing my aunt taught me: pretty much everyone in my life had an illicit lover). Which was why I set out to punish the Reverend John Lawrence, but cheerfully, as my aunt might have done. "Wait, do you think my mother wasn't *pulverized* by that train?" I asked, making sure my voice went up at the end of the sentence as though it were my aunt talking and not me. Odd: each time I said the word "pulverized" my mother seemed more alive to me even though the word was meant to suggest how very dead she was. "*Pulverized*," I said again, and the Reverend John Lawrence winced again, and then a furious look took over his face and he clenched his fists. He took a step forward and I thought, for a moment, that he was going to hit me. But then he stopped to fiddle with his hat. The Reverend John Lawrence's hat to him was what my aunt's sunglasses were to her.

"I loved Nola," the Reverend John Lawrence said, and the simple unadorned way he said this made me want to murder him, which remained the case for the rest of our time together.

"You loved her book," I corrected, and then when this didn't seem to have affected him, I added, "and you loved John Calvin."

"That was who she was," he said. "She was her book, and she was John Calvin." The Reverend John Lawrence paused and looked at me squarely. "And she loved me," he said in that same simple, unadorned way, and I knew that he really believed it was true, and that maybe it actually was true, and I realized I couldn't have said with the same certainty that my father had loved her or that she had loved him, or that I had loved my mother or that she had loved me.

"I doubt it," I said. And then, again, with emphasis: "*Pulverized.*"

"The volunteer firemen said they'd never seen anything like it," the Reverend John Lawrence said. His voice sounded paranoid. I could imagine him sitting in a darkened room, thinking these middle-of-the-night thoughts.

"You think the volunteer firemen lied," I said.

"They didn't lie," the Reverend John Lawrence said. "They

were good, honest men." I wondered how he knew this, except that maybe, in his cosmology, volunteer firemen were always good, honest men. I wondered if he'd still think this if he'd met the Otises. Unless he'd already met them. I had no idea, I realized, how much and for how long his world and my world had been the same world. "Your mother fooled them."

"Into thinking she'd been *pulverized*," I said.

"We were supposed to go a cruise together," he said simply, and I remembered what my mother said at my father's burial about not wanting to go on cruises alone, or maybe at all, and I believed that the Reverend John Lawrence was telling me the truth about that, too.

"I want to understand this," I said. "You believe my mother faked her own death. You believe that my aunt and I also believe that my mother faked her death. And that we know where she is. And that we're going to find her. And that by following us, you're going to find her, too." I paused to let him hear the ridiculousness of his beliefs, but he just looked at me sternly, and I knew that he'd do anything to prove his quest wasn't foolish or futile. I wondered if it had been he who'd told Dawn that I was on a train in Germany. And I also wondered if it had been he who'd left the copy of my mother's famous book on the couch in my hotel room in Stockholm. But I didn't want to stop to ask just then. I figured I would have another opportunity later, and I was right about that. "My mother loved you," I continued. "But she pretended to be *pulverized* by a train. Just so she wouldn't have to go on a cruise with you."

And the Reverend John Lawrence's hands went to his head, and he fiddled with his hat for a few moments, and I could tell that this was a problem for him, that this was a snarl in his belief system that he could not quite untangle.

"I love her. We're supposed to go on a cruise together," he insisted, except this time he was talking about my mother and their cruise in the present tense. I felt sorry for him, and although I still wanted to murder him, I also wanted to help him understand the depth of his delusion. Although to force a person to understand the depth of his delusion is also a kind of murder.

"Hero-worship," I said, quoting John Calvin, "is innate to human nature, and it is founded on some of our noblest feelings—gratitude, love, and admiration—but which, like all other feelings, when uncontrolled by principle and reason, may easily degenerate into the wildest exaggerations, and lead to most dangerous consequences."

The Reverend John Lawrence didn't say anything to that at first. His hands went once again to his hat. He took it off, fiddled with it for a few moments, put it back on again, and then said, "You're traveling by *train*. Nola was killed by a *train*. And do you know who loved *trains*?" I suspected he was talking about my mother, but I didn't want to give him the satisfaction of telling me another thing about her that I should have known but didn't. "The Sociologist," I said instead. The Reverend John Lawrence looked at me, baffled, for one beat and then another, and then said flatly, "No, the Conductor." And then he turned and fled the store.

Ten

116.

The Reverend John Lawrence had presumably returned to the train, but before I could follow him, I had to first retrieve my old clothes, my wallet, my passport, and my train ticket from the dressing room, then pay for my new clothes (I wore the distressed jeans out of the store), and then run to the train, which I barely caught before it pulled out of the Hamburg station.

I went first to my room, where I deposited my bag. I half expected to find the Reverend John Lawrence waiting for me there. He was crazy, my mother was dead, but if he were not crazy, and my mother really had faked her death, then I wondered if it was because she saw the future, and in it, no matter where she was, the Reverend John Lawrence would always be waiting for her. Because that was how I saw Dawn—that no matter where I was, no matter whether we were married or divorced, whether she was in Charlotte and I was in Congress, or Europe, that she would be waiting for me, that she was fated to be in my life forever, because that's what I deserved. And for that matter, until she died: that was how I felt about my mother and John Calvin, too.

117.

My aunt was sitting on the bed, drying her hands with a bathroom towel. On the bed next to her was the knife. It looked like she was cleaning up after a murder.

Caroline wasn't in the room. There was no sign that she'd ever been there. Even the bottle of wine, even the plastic cups, were gone.

It's hard to tell if a person wearing sunglasses is tired. This, I'm sure, was yet another reason my aunt wore them. But still, the way she raised her head slowly to look at me, the way she wearily dried and dried her hands with that towel, communicated to me how very tired she was. But then I remembered the missing bottle of wine, which was probably an empty bottle of wine, and I thought I'd located the reason for her fatigue.

Anyway, I told Aunt Beatrice about how I'd confronted the Reverend John Lawrence in the clothing store, and how he'd apparently loved my mother and said she loved him, and how they were supposed to go on a cruise together, and how he believed my mother had faked her death, and how he believed we were somehow in on the deception, and how we were taking this train to meet her, and he was clearly deluded, he was clearly crazy, but he also mentioned something about the train that had hit my mother, and also the train we, and presumably he, were on, and also "the Conductor," and what was *that* about? What was "the Conductor" supposed to mean?

Meanwhile my aunt dried her hands and dried her hands until the drying of her hands began to take on a religious aspect. Finally, she stopped drying her hands, then lay down on her bed and placed the towel over her face, like a veil, or a shroud, and then *that* took on a religious aspect also.

"Why do you think he's crazy?" Aunt Beatrice finally asked, and the towel puffed up with each word.

"You think he's not?"

"I think he's in love."

I hadn't really argued with my aunt up until now. Maybe up until now I hadn't wanted to start an argument because I hadn't thought I'd win the argument. But I really did believe I was in the right this time. So I repeated the facts, as I understood them, and then said, "That's not love. That's delusion."

My aunt didn't respond right away. She was quiet for so long that I wondered if she'd fallen asleep. Her breathing was so shallow, it didn't even disturb the cloth. And only then, right before my aunt spoke, did I realize that my aunt believed the Sociologist was alive, just as the Reverend John Lawrence believed my mother was alive, and so when I said he was deluded, I might as well have been saying my aunt was deluded, too.

"You can be so stupid, Calvin," Aunt Beatrice finally said. It was the second time in as many hours that she'd called me stupid. And though she said it in her normal bright tone, I could feel and hear how much she really meant it.

"Did I hurt your feelings, Calvin?" my aunt said in that same tone, her face still underneath the cloth.

I admitted that she had and then waited for her to apologize. She didn't, of course. She did remove the cloth, though, so that maybe I could better see and hear how sorry she wasn't.

"Good," Aunt Beatrice said, and then added, "I said what I said because it was true. And because I wanted to."

Fuck you is what I wanted to say and is what I should have said because it was what I wanted to say, and that was the lesson here: say what you want to say. "Just because you say something is true," I said instead, trying to control my voice, trying to keep the pain out of it, "and just because you say what you want, doesn't mean it doesn't hurt."

My aunt nodded. "If it doesn't hurt," she said, "then you're not doing it right."

118.

I left my aunt's room without saying goodbye. But then I didn't know where to go. Home, I thought. It was early afternoon there. My house would be empty. The dog had probably run off by now. The green would be empty, too. It would be too early in the day for the Otises to commence one of their public battles. It would be peaceful, empty, and I would be alone, and there would be no one there to point out my stupidity. I missed it suddenly, and desperately, the way you do a place that you can't get to as soon as you need to. I could go to my sleeper room on the train, of course. But to do what? I wasn't tired. I could write my blog, but my aunt had told me not to. She'd told me I didn't know anything about lying, and now she'd told me I didn't know anything about love either. Well, *fuck her* again that was my thought, a thought that didn't seem suitable for a blog post or a sermon or my house or even my room. And so I went to the train's bar car.

119.

If you need proof of how thoroughly Aunt Beatrice was in my life, and my head, by now: I went to the bar car in flight from my aunt, and when I got to the bar car, my first thought was how much my aunt would hate it.

Because the bar car wasn't gloomy. It was brightly lit—not as brightly lit as the place where we'd been given the gerbil film but not far from it. On my left as I walked into the car was a counter, and at that counter you ordered your drinks and also your food if you wanted some. I couldn't imagine wanting some: the car smelled like long-suffering meat, and there was something bubbling on the stovetop behind the bar and something being overcooked in the microwave above the stovetop.

Which was fine. I wasn't there to eat. I ordered two Carlsbergs from the bartender. I wasn't expecting anyone to show up to drink the second one—not my aunt, not the Reverend John

Lawrence. No, I planned on drinking them both, fast. And then ordering two more, and then two more, as needed.

The bartender gave me the cans of beer, and I paid him and then turned to face the rest of the car. On my right were three booths. They were filled with happy beer drinkers, four people to a booth. On the left was a tiny high-top table bolted to the wall and floor, and next to the table, two stools. The stools' seats were covered with a bright, busily patterned fabric that reminded me of the smocks dental hygienists wear. The stools were bolted to the floor, too. They were close enough to the table for you to put your drink on it but too far away to lean on. There was no footrest on the stools themselves, and so you either had to let your feet dangle or to prop your feet on the wall-length baseboard radiator, which was blasting very hot air. I did that, and the hot air seemed to immediately saturate my distressed jeans. I leaned forward and tried to look out the windows— that side of the car was mostly windows—but the bar was so bright that all I could see outside was darkness. From behind me I could hear the Germans in the booths laughing. I knew they were Germans because I could understand a few random German words—mainly *ja* and *nein*—and that I could understand a few words, whereas before I could understand nothing in Swedish or Danish, might have seemed like further progress, it wasn't: because these were words that even a child, even a non-German-speaking child, would know, and I'd known them as a child, and I'd felt lonely as a child, and I felt even lonelier now. And that was not progress. I looked out the windows into the dark nothing, listened to the laughter behind me, finished one beer, then started drinking the other, and I decided that once I finished that beer I would kill myself.

And I must have said out loud, "I'm going to kill myself!" because Caroline sat down on the stool next to mine and wanted to know more about it. Now when or why, but how.

"Booze," she said, her eyes going to my Carlsberg. "No, that'd take too long. Knife," she said, her eyes going to the counter, but the knives there were only plastic. "Self-inflicted gunshot? But you don't look like you'd own a gun. *Or* know how to fire one."

"I could throw myself under the train," I suggested, and Caroline seemed to like that idea. She sipped her glass of red wine and nodded thoughtfully. I wondered if my aunt had told her how my mother had died. And I also wondered how it had never occurred to me until that moment that maybe my mother's death hadn't been accidental, that maybe she had driven her car on the tracks on purpose, that my hypothetical suicide had been her actual one.

120.

Now that Caroline was there, I didn't want her to leave, and I wanted to say something to keep her here, but I didn't know what, and so I asked Caroline to tell me the story she'd been telling my aunt earlier. She nodded grimly, and her eyes went to the top of her head as though she were trying to remember where she'd left off.

"Can I tell you what Ron liked to eat?" she asked. I said she could, and she said, "Ron liked to eat kale," and she said "kale" like Dawn said "conventional woodstove." "So after we got divorced I decided I wanted to eat the opposite of kale. I wanted the most disgusting food I could find. A microwavable chicken burrito and a Slim Jim from the Red E Mart. I brought the food back to my new apartment. It was the kind of apartment in a building off the interstate with a billboard saying if you'd lived there you'd be home by now."

She paused to see if I was following her. In fact, I had never seen one of those signs, but I still said, "You know, by the time I see those signs, I've already passed the exit."

Caroline nodded. "The apartment was not as convenient as it first seemed. Can I tell you what it smelled like?"

"All right," I said, as was habit by now. Dawn would have hated me for saying that and would have said so, but Caroline didn't seem to notice.

"It smelled like chemicals, like dry cleaning. Let me remind you that I had no plates, no utensils, no furniture."

"It sounds wonderful."

"I let Ron take everything. I wanted to start over. I had no money, no health insurance. All I had was the apartment, the Slim Jim, the microwavable chicken burrito. Junk food. Isolation. Deprivation. I wanted to live like I did in college."

"I never lived like that in college," I admitted.

"I didn't either. I wanted to live like other people lived in college. I was really looking forward to sticking that burrito in the microwave and then forty-five to sixty seconds later hearing that *ding*."

"So you did have a microwave."

"I did not have a microwave. I'd unwrapped the burrito, stuck it in the cardboard sleeve and then stood there, in front of the counter, where the microwave would have been in a normal kitchen. I stood there for minutes, just coming to the slow understanding that I did not have a microwave. I don't know for certain, but I must have been slack jawed. Can I tell you how I felt?"

I'd noticed by now that Caroline liked to ask if she could tell you something, and so as an experiment I said, "No." She smiled at that, her mouth once again elevating her face, although she then went ahead and told me how she felt anyway.

"Bereft. Like something essential had been taken from me. Because you know who had a microwave?"

"The Red E Mart?"

Caroline didn't respond right away. The Germans were still in their booths but were quiet, as though they, too, were listening to Caroline's story. The lights had dimmed in the bar car. It felt more like a place my aunt might like. Outside the bar car's windows I could see the outlines of trees and then a house, dark, except for one light on upstairs.

"You know," Caroline finally said. "The Red E Mart probably did have a microwave. And had I thought of that, then that would have probably changed the trajectory of this story. But no, not the Red E Mart. It was Ron. Ron had my microwave.

This is what the jerk had done to me, Calvin." Caroline sounded tired, as though she'd lost her enthusiasm for the story. It was the way my mother had sounded when she'd delivered my father's eulogy. It was the way I felt when thinking about Dawn, and the end of our marriage, and also the beginning and middle of our marriage. But I didn't want the story to end, by which I mean I didn't want her to stop talking to me, and so I tried to encourage her by saying, "He stole your heart and then he stole your microwave."

"Well, actually, it was Ron's microwave. From before the marriage."

"Oh," I said, and Caroline nodded, her eyes on the ceiling now, and I waited for her to finish telling the story until it became clear to me that she wasn't going to finish telling the story.

121.

This was one of things Caroline and my aunt had in common. They rarely told you the whole story. My aunt never told you the whole story because she wanted you to figure out the rest for yourself; Caroline didn't tell you the whole story because she often hadn't yet figured out how the story she was telling was supposed to end.

122.

I said earlier that Caroline's eyes were always in motion. They were moving now. They seemed to operate almost independently from the rest of her face. They flitted to me, to the window, to her almost empty glass of wine, to the bar, to the window, to me, to the ceiling.

Look at me! is what I wanted to say. But I was afraid that would sound stupid. And I didn't want to sound stupid anymore. I wanted to say something that Caroline would remember, but I did not want her to remember how stupid I sounded. But how would I do that? What would I say? Suddenly, one of my aunt's commandments came into my head: "Thou shall lie, but only if thou lies well." And so I said, "I was married once. To a woman named Dawn. We had a son. It's still too painful to even say his name. To even think it. Because when he was a year old, he died. Of kidney stones. And after that, Dawn and I were never the same."

And Caroline looked at me, and then kept looking at me! That's what I remember. That she looked at me, straight at me, her large brown eyes, slightly threaded with red. That she looked at me and kept looking at me for a very long time.

123.

The rest of the night was like a dream if your definition of a dream includes getting very drunk in the bar car while hurtling through the German night before having sex with a strange woman in her room on a train, which is next to your elderly aunt's room and then, afterward, trying to organize your feelings while one of the *Lord of the Rings* movies is playing with the sound off on the strange woman's laptop computer.

"This is the one where someone's always looking off into the distance, hoping for the arrival of the wizard and his cavalry and whatnot," Caroline said.

Caroline, it turns out, was from Sheboygan, Wisconsin. She told me that she'd been in Copenhagen for an international convention of seafood processors and that she was taking the train to another international convention of seafood processors in Marseille.

"There's a seafood processor in Sheboygan, Wisconsin?"

"Lake and river fish processor," she explained. "Seafood's just a catchall. And here they come." On the laptop many riders with long spears crested a hill, surveying the enemy below and shaking their long spears, celebrating in advance. Caroline and I were lying side by side, back down in bed. I was naked except for my new unbuttoned shiny blue German shirt, Caroline except for her ballet slippers.

124.

An hour later, when the movie was over, Caroline closed her laptop, looked at me squarely, and said, "We had some good sex." Which is more than Dawn, or John Calvin, or my mother in her famous book, ever said on the subject.

125.

The sentence "We had some good sex" will make you gabby. I immediately told Caroline about my job, and my parents and their deaths, and my aunt's appearance, and our trip, and the places we'd been and the people we'd met and the things we'd done, which included stealing the knife. I worried about this last—worried that Caroline would think less of my aunt and, by association, less of me—but it didn't seem to bother her, or even surprise her much. She nodded and listened and sipped from a plastic cup of red wine (this was another thing she and my aunt seemed to have in common: there always seemed to be alcohol around, and she always seemed to be drinking it, and it didn't seem to affect her much), and when I was done telling her my story, she drained her cup, put it on the bedside table, and then asked, "Why do you keep saying 'my mother's famous book'?"

"Because it is," I said, and I was surprised to hear how defensive I sounded.

Caroline shrugged and said, "Well, *I've* never heard of it." And then she turned off the lights, and we went to sleep.

Eleven

126.

When I woke up it was seven in the morning. It was the morning of my third day in Europe. I rolled over to kiss Caroline good morning, but she wasn't there. She'd left a note saying she had to make some work calls and didn't want to wake me and that she'd see me later! That was her exclamation point, and it made me glad. I went back to my own room, feeling triumphant. After having sex with Dawn, I'd always felt unworthy: not unworthy of Dawn but unworthy of the act that so many people who were not John Calvin and my mother had thought and written and talked so much about. But now, I felt different. I had had sex and it was *good*, and now I wanted to tell someone about it.

127.

It Was *Good*

Dear readers, I don't know if you've ever made love on a train, but I highly recommend it. A train doesn't move so much as it *chugs*, sort of *bucks*, but smoothly, as it proceeds toward its next station.

128.

And then I stopped. Because I was thinking of my mother—not only what she would think about the subject but also how it was written. I'd eavesdropped on many of her conversations with her acolytes, had heard her make a case against the elaborate metaphor, especially when writing about God. "One does not do justice to God," she wrote in her famous book, "by turning him into a metaphor." I don't know if that's true about God, but I thought it might be true about sex and trains. In any case, I decided to start again.

129.

It Was *Good*

Dear readers, there is no pellet stove in this blog post. There is just one hard cock and one wet pussy and . . .

130.

And then I stopped again. Not because of John Calvin or my mother but because I pictured the people who at that moment

I cared about the most. Which is to say, I pictured my aunt and now Caroline and then thought of them reading the post, and suddenly I did not want to finish it or publish it, which is why most professional bloggers spend most of their professional lives trying to avoid having that thought, or picturing those people, or having those people in their lives in the first place

131.

I put my phone in my pocket and went to see my aunt.

She was sitting on her folded-up bed in her room, drinking a cup of coffee. On the floor next to her was a silver tray. On the tray, a silver pot, steam drifting out of the spout, and next to the pot, also on the tray, a white mug identical to my aunt's except that it was empty. She poured coffee into the mug and handed it to me, and I sat on the couch and we drank in silence. The weather was just as foul outside—low-hanging steely clouds and rain speckling the train windows—but my inner weather had improved. I thought of my aunt and my father, and what they had done, and then of my mother and the Reverend John Lawrence, and what *they'd* apparently done, and I felt more generous toward them than I had before, which apparently is what good sex will do to you, and I also felt superior to them, which also, apparently, is what good sex will do to you.

"Remember, thou shall never apologize, Calvin," my aunt finally said, reciting one of her commandments. It occurred to me that Caroline and I had had sex in the next room over and that it might have been loud, might have kept her up. Was she talking about that? Or was she talking about the previous night, when I'd said what I'd said about love and delusion, and she'd said that I was stupid?

"Apologize for what?" I said, and my aunt said, "Exactly." And then she said, "Caroline," and when she said Caroline's name, my penis throbbed as a reminder. But one of the things that it reminded me of was how my penis throbbed when I'd had kidney stones. And how easily it is that good things are ruined by the bad things they so closely resemble.

"I had sex with her, and she said it was good," I said before I could stop myself. And just saying that felt like an accomplishment, like another step away from who I'd been and toward who I wanted to be. Although the news didn't seem to surprise my aunt at all. "Good for you," she said, sipping from her cup. "I like Caroline. Even though she's Interpol."

I didn't respond to this. I didn't want to admit that I didn't know what it meant to be Interpol, or what Interpol even was. Just as I hadn't wanted to admit to Caroline the night before that I had never watched *The Lord of the Rings* or read the books the movies were made from. When you are made to read John Calvin as a child, you aren't exactly encouraged to read or watch or learn the things that other people are reading or watching or learning as children instead of reading John Calvin. And then, when I was an adult, and was supposedly free to do what I want and had access to the technology that would supposedly allow me to catch up on all the things I'd missed, there was too much, much too much, and I would always be behind, and so I decided to write about pellet stoves and selectively quote the John Calvin

I had read as a child and selectively quote from the famous book that my mother had written about reading and making me read John Calvin, and that was it.

"Interpol," Aunt Beatrice said. "The international police. Although more of a spy agency than law enforcement proper."

I thought that was ridiculous and I said so. In response, my aunt said, "Doesn't Caroline remind you of someone." It wasn't a question. Which meant she thought I should know the answer. I thought about it, but no, Caroline hadn't reminded me of anyone. "Not even," my aunt said, "that lovely young ice maiden you spoke to in Stockholm."

I knew now Aunt Beatrice was talking about the tall, pale woman from the Swedish pellet stove company who accosted me in the hotel lobby and told me that unfunny jokes were lies. This was even more ridiculous: she and Caroline had looked nothing alike. She'd had blonde hair, and Caroline's was gray; she'd had blue eyes, and Caroline's were brown; she'd worn glasses, and Caroline did not. Plus, I pointed out, that woman worked for Lingonnaire, the pellet stove manufacturer, whereas Caroline was a seafood processor. When I said that Caroline was a seafood processor, it sounded only slightly less ridiculous than my aunt saying that she was a pellet stove manufacturer in addition to being a policewoman who was also spy. Still, I persisted. "Caroline's from Sheboygan, Wisconsin," I said.

"That's how I know she's Interpol," my aunt said. "If she were really from Wisconsin, she'd be from Racine."

I had no idea what this was supposed to mean, but before

I could pursue it further the train came a stop. I looked outside the window and saw that we'd pulled into the Paris station.
Sometime during the night, we'd crossed into France, and I'd
not realized it. I felt an odd sense of accomplishment. I know
now that it's the sense of accomplishment a traveler feels when
he's entered a new country. *I did it!* a traveler feels, even though
the traveler hasn't done anything. I looked back to my aunt, to
see if she was feeling what I was feeling. She wasn't in the room
anymore. "Calvin," she said from the hallway, and I followed
her voice, and then her, and moments later we were off the train
and in Paris.

132.

Two weeks before there had been a terrorist attack in Paris, and
in fact the train station itself had been bombed, and several plat-
forms were still closed, and there was still a whiff of cordite in
the air, although that was probably just my imagination, since
I'd never, to my knowledge, actually smelled cordite. There were
police everywhere in the station, and they were all holding guns,
huge black automatic rifles slung over their shoulders and across
their chests, where everyone could see them. The police and their
guns made me nervous—after all, who knew what kind of stolen
things my aunt had in her purse or on her person—and so I kept
my head down as we walked through the station until my aunt
stopped, elbowed me, and gestured with her head toward a high
table near one of the kiosks in the station. There on the table

was a cell phone, and next to that was a machine gun with the muzzle pointed toward me. A black policewoman was sitting at the table. She was wearing a balaclava, not over her face (which was why I could see that she was black) but instead pulled down beneath her chin, bunched up like a turtleneck, and she was holding, and in fact was smiling at, but had not yet begun to eat or lick, the most enormous ice cream cone I have ever seen.

133.

From the train station we took a subway, and after several minutes we got off the subway. When we exited the station, I'd had hopes of seeing Paris, the Paris one always hears that one should see. But I saw no Eiffel Tower, no Louvre, no Orsay, no Montmarte, no arrondissements of note. Instead, we walked past many unbeautiful buildings. Gray-and-black concrete and dirty tinted glass, and brutal angles and graffiti everywhere. Most of the graffiti lacked brightness and was simply a different drab color than the drab-colored building it happened to be painted on.

I mentioned to my aunt my disappointment, and she said, "I've never liked Paris." I thought she was talking about the Paris we were walking through, but no. "I don't like great cities," she said. "Or great countries."

When she said that, I thought of my mother. One of the things that had made her famous book so popular was that it had an odd nationalist bent. In her book, she'd argued that America, for all its faults, was the best country in the world. It was also, she argued, the most Calvinist country. Which was what, I suppose, made it the best. "Like John Calvin," my mother wrote in her famous book, "the people of the United States have been much concerned with the rule of law, and there is much evidence in the counter-experiences of other countries to suggest he, and we, have been right to be thus concerned."

But I didn't say this to my aunt. Instead, I said, "America is number one." This had been the campaign slogan of the man who would eventually become our president. Charles Otis, my old classmate and neighbor, was one of his supporters and had taken to wearing a red mesh baseball hat with that slogan on its face, although on Charles's hat the symbol was on the wrong side of the number: AMERICA IS 1#.

My aunt repeated the slogan and said, "It's true. That's why I don't like it."

"But you lived in Ohio," I pointed out.

"For thirty-six years," my aunt. "Ending five days ago." Which meant that she'd lived in Ohio right up until she'd come to her sister's funeral. Which meant she'd lived in the same time zone as me for most of my life and had not even bothered to see me or contact me. Why? That's what I wanted to ask, and in fact that's what I did ask, but Aunt Beatrice misunderstood the question.

"No one thinks Ohio is great," my aunt said. "Not even Ohioans. That's why I wanted to live there."

134.

"You seem very aware of dark people, Calvin," my aunt said as we walked. It was true there were dark people everywhere. Darker people who I assumed were from Africa. Somewhat darker lighter people who I assumed were from the Middle East or from northern Africa. These people were wearing clothes, of course, and I'm sure they were of different height and weight and so on. But basically I noticed how many of them there were and that their skin color was different from mine. My aunt was right that I was aware of them. The police—who, like the policewoman in the station, had their balaclavas bunched around their necks, but who, unlike the policewoman in the station, all seemed to be white—seemed equally aware of them. Every time they passed a dark person or a dark person passed them, the gendarmes' hands went to their guns and pushed them out from their chests, as though inviting the dark people to show them their guns, too.

"No," I said. Because this is how white Americans, even, or especially, white Americans in a very white place like Congress, are taught to talk about race: to deny that they are aware of it. In fact, our future president had been elected because he said he was not aware of it. "Yes," I said. "I'm sorry." Because this is the other way white Americans are taught to talk about race: to admit that yes, they are aware of it and that they're sorry. And in fact this was another reason our future president had been elected: because, unlike those white people he thought were weak for saying they were sorry, he refused to say he was sorry, or that he was even aware that there were reasons for him to *be* sorry, let alone for him to *say* he was sorry, which, sorry, he was not going to do. "I'm sorry," I said again.

"Don't be," my aunt said loudly, cheerfully. "They're aware of you, too."

135.

The weather started to clear, the sun peeking out from behind the clouds. I rolled up the sleeves of my shiny new German shirt and could feel sweat beading around my hair buds.

"Most of the dark people I know are criminals," my aunt said in her same loud, cheerful voice, and several dark people looked in her direction, and several police did, too, and I wondered if they were just responding to the tone and volume of her voice or whether they understood English. I really hoped they didn't speak English. Aunt Beatrice had told Caroline the day before about the time she'd been shot and hoped the bullet wouldn't hit her femoral artery, wherever or whatever that was. It wasn't hard to imagine why someone would shoot her.

"I'm guessing that most of the white people you know are criminals, too," I pointed out.

My aunt nodded and said, "When your mother and I were sixteen years old, we stole a safe."

"What?" I said, but it was as though I'd said, *Whose?*

"It was our father's," Aunt Beatrice said. "Or at least his church's. It was where he kept the offerings, the tithes, the rainy-day funds, the church improvement funds. Your mother and I didn't need the money. We just wanted to see if we could steal it. I say 'we,' but of course it was my idea. Nola just tagged along reluctantly. The safe was very heavy. The two of us managed to drag it out of the church in the middle of the night. There, I thought, we'd stolen it. Or at least moved it. And after that, we wanted to see if we could open it. We rolled it down the hill. Square things roll wrong, Calvin. The safe left large punctures and dents in the hill, and all the way down I could heard the change inside the safe rattling and clanging. The safe came to rest at the bottom of the hill, near the train tracks. We ran to see if we'd done it, but we hadn't done it: the safe was still unopened. I didn't know what to do. I was ready to give up. But your mother had lost her reluctance. The sight of that rolling safe had inspired her. She had an idea. She heard the train coming and suggested we roll the safe onto the tracks. I suppose your mother thought the train would crack it open and then pass over the wreckage. But no, the safe lodged under the train and stayed lodged. We could see it throw sparks, could hear its terrible scrapes and cries as the train headed toward Quebec. I say 'terrible.' But your mother didn't think it was terrible. She laughed when she realized what had happened and then ran to catch up with the train. I don't think she wanted to be there when the safe opened, and as far as either of us knew, it never did open. No, she just liked the sparks, the noise. She ran after the train, managed to jump onto the steps that lead to the caboose, and holding on to the railing with one hand, she waved to me with the other, looking just like—"

"A conductor," I said. Because I knew why my aunt was telling me this story: my mother's nickname was the Conductor, and the Reverend John Lawrence knew it; and her nickname, and the fact that she'd supposedly been killed by a train, and the fact that we were traveling by train were his proof that she was still alive.

136.

The Conductor. For days and days afterward, I thought about my aunt's story about my mother and the safe and the train and her nickname. I wished my mother had told me that story when I was a child, or even when I was an adult. Because I would have loved her if I'd known that in addition to her being my mother and the author of a famous book on John Calvin, she was also the Conductor. But maybe she felt that she couldn't tell me the story and still be the kind of mother that, it turns out, I didn't want her to be.

137.

As was true in Stockholm and Copenhagen, I had the sense that Aunt Beatrice and I were wandering through Paris with no purpose or destination, but in fact there was a purpose, and there was a destination.

After thirty minutes of walking, we stopped in front of a warehouse. That is, it looked like it had been warehouse, a warehouse that seemed to be a remnant from a former architectural era. It was brick with elaborate detailing on the face and French words etched into the cornice. Whereas surrounding it were parking lots and the piled brick remnants of the buildings that I supposed had been destroyed to make the parking lots, and then new buildings, mostly glass and steel, one or two stories, not residences but businesses: a grocery store, a pet store, a place that seemed to manufacture chocolate and candy, a Renault car dealership. There were people in the businesses, I could see them looking out through the huge windows, clearly wondering what would happen when the world came in. I knew the feeling. It was the feeling I had when I first met my aunt and all the moments I spent with her afterward.

138.

"For instance, the Butcher," my aunt said. We were inside the building now. Which looked as though it'd been abandoned, condemned. There was yellow caution tape everywhere. Several signs, in French, and they were warning of danger. I knew this not from the words, which I could not understand, but the illustration of a man with rocks falling onto his head. For good reason: the interior and walls and ceilings were crumbling, scatterings of brick and plaster pieces on the floor. The place smelled like dust and mice. Other than the wreckage, and the signs and tape warning you of the wreckage, there seemed to be nothing in the building at all.

"So called," my aunt said, "because she preferred to cut off limbs and digits and so on rather than treat them. No one ever confused the Butcher with a conventional healer. I watched her cauterize stomach wounds with her cigarette lighter. My bullet wound, she dug out the bullet with a steak knife from the restaurant I'd been shot in. Once, she conducted an abortion in a life raft. She could have performed the procedure on dry land, but no, she preferred the raft. Not once did a patient die on her," Aunt Beatrice said, and of course by now I realized the Butcher was a doctor, and then my aunt added, "unless the Butcher wanted him to die.

"Hello!" my aunt then yelled, and waited for a response. I wondered whom she was summoning; I wondered if it was the Sociologist, and if soon a man with good legs would materialize from the building's jumbled innards. But no one materialized, and no one yelled back. My aunt then yelled some words in a language I recognized as French. She again waited for a response. The words did nothing. It was as though they left her mouth, hung in the air for a moment, and then chased one another down a deep hole.

It was the first time on our trip that Aunt Beatrice seemed confounded by something. She walked outside the building, stood in the middle of the street, looked at the building. It was noon by now, the sun high and blasting the already scorched-looking bricks. The building's second-story windows were boarded up. The third-story windows were covered with plastic, but the plastic was ripped, and its tendrils were waving at us in the breeze.

"Maybe it's the wrong place," I suggested.

"It's the right place," my aunt said, and she turned toward the new glassy buildings. "But it's possible the Butcher is in the wrong one."

139.

The Butcher's real name was Monique Belknap. Her name—Docteur Monique Belknap—was etched on the glass door that led to the waiting room and, inside the waiting room behind a high counter, a pale-faced receptionist. My aunt reacted to each of these things—the etched name, the glass door, the waiting room, the receptionist—as though they were impossibilities, wonders, miracles, but unwanted ones. When the reception-ist said "Can I help you?" or "Do you have an appointment?" (she spoke in French, but I'm guessing she said one of those two things), my aunt once again took off her glasses and looked at the woman in astonishment, the way I must have looked at Gerbie back in Stockholm.

"I am here," my aunt said in English, and it was a kind of harsh, barking English—as though it were not my aunt speaking but the dog she'd stolen and then abandoned in Congress—"to see *Dr.* Belknap."

It was the kind of voice that seemed to rule out even the possibility of disagreement, and indeed I don't think my aunt expected any, because she began to head for the door to the right of the counter, a door that seemed to lead into another, more inner room.

But the receptionist managed to disagree anyway. She

walked out from behind the counter, and I could see by her clothes—loose green V-neck shirt, matching green drawstringed pants—and by her manner—brisk, officious—that she wasn't a receptionist or wasn't only a receptionist: she was also a nurse. "First," she said, in halting but firm English, "you are weighed and . . ." Here she paused, possibly to think of the right English word. "Measured," she finally said. My aunt seemed about to once again object, but the nurse said, "Everyone is weighed and measured."

That seemed to do something strange to my aunt. She became, at that moment, a patient. She consented to being weighed and measured. The scale and whatever you call the apparatus that measures your height were right there in the waiting room, which also served as the examining room. I don't know how tall Aunt Beatrice was and how much she weighed—the nurse delivered the information in French, and besides, I'm sure the units of measure were in meters and grams and not pounds and inches—but no one is ever the height and weight they wish they were, and my aunt seemed to shrink at the news. The nurse then asked her to sit in one of the two chairs in the room, and my aunt did. Between the chairs there was a low table, but there were no magazines on it. The nurse said something in French, and my aunt offered her arm. And then the nurse said something else in French, and my aunt pushed up the sleeve of her sweater. Forearm and a swath of bicep. The skin was white as my aunt's face was brown, white like a fish belly, laced with raised blue veins. It looked like an arm that had spent its long life in a cave.

The nurse wrapped a thick black strap around my aunt's bicep, took up the black ball, pressed it and pressed it, then allowed the device to depress. She read the blood pressure on the gauge, announced the reading to my aunt, then announced something else. My aunt opened her mouth dutifully, and the nurse put a thermometer in it, and a minute later she removed the thermometer and announced that reading. Then she looked at my aunt for one long second and said something else in French, and my aunt nodded meekly.

140.

To be a patient is to be diminished. This is a universal truth, one so obvious that even my mother, even John Calvin, never saw the need to make a larger theological or cultural point about it. But I mention it because it was the first time I saw my aunt in a position that we've all been in and act like the rest of us. She looked so resigned, so lost, so scared. She looked like you or me.

It was the receptionist who was also a nurse who'd made Aunt Beatrice look this way, of course. And I had the strong desire to avenge my aunt's diminishment. My mother had written in her famous book, "As John Calvin teaches us, the only vengeance that matters is God's. Compared to God's vengeance, all human vengeance is petty, feeble, and not worth considering, let alone pursuing." And I'd believed that was so until I met my aunt. I was next to the high counter, across the room from where the woman was attending to my aunt; on the other side of the counter was the receptionist's desk, and on that desk was a computer. It was a bulky desktop, some years old, and I knew its weakness: like a dog or a child, or really most of us, it surrendered and shut down when faced with contradictory commands. I reached across the counter, and with my left thumb and forefinger, hit Control X, and with my right thumb and forefinger hit Control P. The computer stopped humming, and its screen went black. I turned around. The receptionist who was also a nurse said one last thing to my aunt, then turned, walked across the room behind the counter, and sat down at her desk. I went to sit by my aunt. And we watched and listened as the woman struck keys and pushed buttons and swore in French at her computer and, then, in an act of final frustration, slapped the keyboard with both hands. When she did that, my aunt, very gently, very briefly, placed her left hand on my right, and I knew then that she knew what I'd done, and that I'd done it for her, and that it had made her happy.

141.

A minute later the door to the right of the counter opened, and in the doorway appeared a black woman. Trim, wearing slim white pants and a light blue long-sleeved button-down shirt with the sleeves rolled up to the elbows. There was a ballpoint pen sticking out of the top of her shirt pocket, and a stethoscope was hooked around her neck. Closely shorn curly white hair. She looked like a runner to my aunt's basketball player; her face was thin, nearly gaunt, with high cheekbones, and her skin, unlike my aunt's, was smooth, maintained. I thought I could see the sheen of face cream on her forehead.

My aunt stood up. She seemed somewhat restored. "*Dr.* Belknap," she said in her usual bright way, again with ironic emphasis on the title.

But if that were bait, the Butcher, so called, didn't rise to it. She said something in French, and my aunt started to say in English, "Butcher—," but the Butcher interrupted.

"Docteur Belknap," she said with no emphasis. I'd only just met the woman, but she was clearly right about that: whatever had made her the Butcher had clearly been erased, drained, excised, amputated.

My aunt stared at her for three beats, and then continued. "This is my nephew, Calvin." I waved at the Butcher, but the Butcher didn't wave back. She said something to my aunt in French. My aunt then walked toward her and the open door. I made to follow, but my aunt said, "Please wait for me here, Calvin."

This confused and then annoyed me. Why, I wanted to know, did my aunt drag me off the train and through Paris and to the doctor's office only then to sit in the room outside the doctor's office? Aunt Beatrice must have sensed my annoyance because she said, in that uncharacteristically meek, patient-like way, "An old lady does like being accompanied to the doctor's office." And then she followed the Butcher through the doorway and shut the door behind her.

142.

I remembered that my aunt had said something similar when she asked me to accompany her into the Boston airport, and I felt sure I was being manipulated then, and I felt sure I was being manipulated now, too. Whatever subject being discussed inside that office, I felt sure that it wasn't health related. No, I felt sure that it had something to do with the Sociologist: where he was, who else was looking for him, how Aunt Beatrice might find him before they did.

143.

To kill time, I once again took out my phone. I looked at it for twenty minutes. There was nothing on it worth reporting. The only reason I mention it now is that right as Aunt Beatrice and the Butcher emerged through that door, I remembered that the Butcher had spoken French to my aunt, and then I remembered the Record function on my phone, and then I touched Record.

144.

My aunt walked out first, a little unsteadily, I thought, clutching her purse with both hands. She nodded at me and I followed her to the main office door. But before I left the room I noticed the Butcher standing in the doorway to her inner office. She was small, but her presence seemed to fill the doorway and the rest of the room, too. I recognized that: it was the way my aunt usually seemed to me. It was the way everyone who knows something important seems to everyone who doesn't. Doctor Belknap's whole face was shining now, not just her forehead.

"Beatrice," she shouted out to my aunt. My aunt stopped and looked at the Butcher. And then the Butcher said many French words that I didn't recognize and that my aunt seemed not to acknowledge. When the Butcher stopped talking, Aunt Beatrice turned her back and continued on her way, and I then stopped recording and followed her out of the office.

145.

"When people pretend to be from somewhere in America," my aunt said once we were out on the street, "they always say they're from Sheboygan, Wisconsin." It took a moment for me to realize that my aunt was telling me why she thought Caroline was Interpol. And it says a good deal about how much my aunt had changed my way of thinking that this made even a little bit of sense to me.

146.

We retraced our steps back toward the train station. My aunt seemed to have recovered somewhat from being a patient, but still, there was something thoughtful and melancholy about her. I wanted to ask her about what the Butcher had said, but I knew she wouldn't answer my question. And I didn't need to, because I had the recording and a way to translate it. All I needed now was the time and space and privacy to listen to it.

"The Butcher," my aunt finally said. "I almost didn't recognize her."

"Has she changed much?" I asked, and when Aunt Beatrice nodded, I asked, "How?" and my aunt said, "She's stopped trying to get away with something."

147.

"Our cultural moment is dominated by people whose loftiest goal is to get away with something. As John Calvin teaches us, none of us ever gets to heaven on the basis of what we've gotten away with." This is a passage from my mother's famous book. I'm certain, after spending this time with my aunt, that those words were directed at her as much as they were directed at our cultural moment.

Although I knew now it wasn't as though my mother *hadn't* tried to get away with something. That safe, for instance, that my mother and my aunt had stolen from their father's church. It had been heavy. It had taken the two of them to steal it.

148.

My aunt abruptly stopped walking, right in front of a pharmacy. She reached into her bag and first pulled out a skull. It gleamed white in the sun, and I thought I saw something like eternity in its gaping mouth and eye sockets. "Where'd you get that?" I asked, but I knew it had come from the Butcher's office. I was sure that the Butcher had not given it to my aunt; I was sure my aunt had stolen it. She returned the skull to her purse and pulled out a prescription pad. My aunt took out a pen, filled out and then signed one of the prescriptions, tore it off the pad. Then she smiled at me, proudly gap toothed, restored, and walked into the pharmacy.

"Take these," Aunt Beatrice said when she came out of the pharmacy. She was holding a pill bottle, and out of it she shook four tiny white pills and popped two in her mouth and then handed me the other two.

"What are they?"

"Painkillers."

"But I'm not in pain," I said.

"Not yet, at least," my aunt said in her way, and I wondered what she meant by that, if anything. Nevertheless, I didn't take them but instead put them in the pocket of my shiny blue German shirt.

Then we continued walking. The streets were still full of dark people, but I wasn't as aware of them, and I was proud of that; I'd felt like, again, I'd made some progress. But then I became aware of my relative lack of awareness and wondered how that could ever be any kind of progress. And in any case how, if I were still aware that the streets were still full of dark people, could I really be not as aware of them? It was though as I'd already taken the painkillers. My thoughts were looping around, loops within loops. I needed something to straighten them out, something to focus on. There, in the distance, not far from the subway station, I saw an enormous man, his back to me, and on the back of his enormous black T-shirt were these words, in large white block letters: IM DIFFICULT TO KIDNAP.

"T-shirts have more to say about our cultural moment than movies or TV or books," I said, thinking that this was the kind of generalization my aunt would make, or like made.

"Oh, Calvin," my aunt said. She sounded dismayed, and I thought at first she was referring to the quality of my generalization. I turned to face her and saw that she had stopped walking and was now looking at her phone. She handed it to me. On it was the homepage of Congress's local paper. And on the homepage was news that our house—hers and mine, and my father's, and mother's, and her parents before her—was gone. It wasn't an article that told us so. Our local paper had no articles. It had photos with captions. The caption said that our house had burned to the ground two days earlier, that it had been the house of the revered high school sports coach, Roger Bledsoe, and the world-famous writer, Reverend Nola Bledsoe, both recently deceased. The current owner, their son, Calvin Bledsoe, had yet to be located. The caption said that the volunteer firemen were considering the fire suspicious. Congress had six volunteer firemen. In the photo, four of them were holding the hose, which was spraying the smoky ruin with water, but apparently not enough and apparently too late. Charles Otis wasn't in the picture, but to the left of the hose bearers was his father, Leland Otis, a toothpick sticking out of the corner of his mouth, not doing anything except facing the camera and holding an ax across his chest, the way the Paris gendarmes were holding their automatic weapons.

149.

I didn't cry when my father died or when my mother died, but I cried when I learned that my house had burned down. Cried as we descended into the subway, and cried on the subway, and cried as we exited the subway, and cried as I entered into the train station, where I still cried, loudly, heavily, under the arrivals and departures board. I didn't care who saw me crying, and whoever saw me didn't seem to care either: people just kept walking past me, to and from their trains. My aunt did nothing to stop me or console me. She just let me cry until I felt empty. Which was how I'd often felt when I was in my house: empty. Which was really why I'd been crying. And my aunt must have realized that because when I finally stopped crying she said, "It's okay, Calvin. You weren't really using that life anyway."

And then she tapped me on my shirt pocket, and I was reminded of those painkillers, of how she'd said I might yet need to take them, and then I took them. And then she shook two more out of her bottle and dropped them in my open palm, and then I took those pills, too.

Twelve

150.

I woke to the grinding of brakes, the whooshing of air through open car windows.

To my left was my aunt. She was gripping the steering wheel with her left hand. Not even gripping, and not even with the whole hand, just her index and middle fingers gently touching the bottom of the wheel. Her hair was blowing so wildly that I could barely see her face, and I wondered how she could see the road clearly enough to drive on it.

"We're in a car," I said sleepily. Aunt Beatrice didn't seem inclined to respond to that. The air coming through my open window was wet and heavy, and through the windshield I could see dark gray clouds against light gray sky. "We're in a car," I said again, somewhat more awake now, and when I sat up and leaned forward I became aware that I wasn't wearing a seatbelt. And then I went to strap mine on and became aware that there wasn't a seatbelt.

"I feel like I've been drugged," I said.

"In a sense, you have been drugged, Calvin," my aunt said through her hair and the roar of traffic and the wind. "Penoxalian. Part of the barbiturate family. Five hundred milligrams is the recommended dosage for humans. You ingested something closer to the recommended dosage for horses."

Aunt Beatrice's tone was full of authority. It sounded as though she were in a lab, or at least a drugstore, wrangling pills with her tiny knife. I could picture her behind a high counter wearing a white smock. I was about to ask her how she'd come to know so much about pharmacology when a man's voice, a man's very flat voice, came from the backseat, quoting John Calvin, "Knowledge of the sciences is so much smoke apart from the heavenly science of Christ."

I turned around. There was the Reverend John Lawrence, sitting in the middle of the backseat. He was holding his hat at chest level, as a mourner would at a funeral, although if I'd been the dearly departed, I doubted the Reverend John Lawrence would much mourn me.

I noticed the Reverend John Lawrence wasn't belted in either. Behind him was a cargo area and, at the end of that, a long window, and by that I understood that we were riding in a station wagon.

I turned and faced my aunt again. "Is this what it's like to be dead?" I asked. That wasn't the question I wanted to ask: I wanted to ask how long had I been asleep, where were we, where was Caroline, what was the Reverend John Lawrence doing in the backseat of this station wagon, where had we gotten the station wagon. But the drugs were still in my system and wouldn't let me. They seemed to have made my mind their mind. Or rather, their mind was between me and where I wanted my mind to go. But where did my mind want to go? It wanted to return to the moments before I woke up in the station wagon but after I took the drugs. But the drugs were sitting there between those moments and this one. And I wondered if this was what it was like to be dead: to remember that there were things to be remembered without being able to remember them.

Or to only selectively remember them. Because a moment later I remembered that my house in Congress had been burned to the ground. And then I thought, why would anyone do such a thing? And then I thought: revenge. And then I thought: Dawn.

"Dawn burned down my house!" I shouted.

"That does make sense," my aunt admitted, running her fingers along the bottom of the steering wheel like a piano.

Meanwhile, from the backseat came a long, low groan. Such a sad sick sound. It made me wonder if the Reverend John Lawrence had known the house, how well he had known it, in what capacity, whether he'd been inside it with my mother when my father was alive, whether he'd dreamt of being inside it on a more permanent basis after my father had died.

151.

"I was in the process of stealing this station wagon from just outside the train station," my aunt said, "when the Reverend came up from behind and introduced himself. He said that he knew that I knew where poor Nola was, and I couldn't disagree. And then he said that I would take him to her or that he'd alert the Paris gendarmes to my grand theft, and I told him that I'd do my best."

This was definitely a threat: my mother was dead, my aunt was saying, and if the Reverend John Lawrence wanted to go where she was, well, then my aunt was happy to take him there. I wondered if the Reverend John Lawrence had heard the same thing I'd heard. I doubted it; it seemed likely that he'd heard something hopeful instead. Aunt Beatrice pulled the curtain of her hair aside and grinned at me. Sometimes her missing tooth made her look comical, but now it made her look cruel, and then she allowed her hair to hide her face from me again.

"What about Caroline?" I said.

"Oh, there wasn't time to say goodbye, Calvin," Aunt Beatrice said through her hair.

"All right," I said. It was ridiculous, I had only just met Caroline, we had had sex only once, but I almost cried again and would have if not for the drugs still in my system and the Reverend John Lawrence in the backseat.

"Caroline," my aunt said, glancing at the Reverend John Lawrence in the rearview, "was Calvin's lovely friend from the train. She hails, I believe she said, from Sheboygan, Wisconsin."

I felt that this reference to Caroline's supposed place of origin was a taunt, directed at me. This was the thing about my aunt's cruelty: it was indiscriminate. This isn't to say that she couldn't control it but that she chose not to.

"Odd," the Reverend John Lawrence said. "Several of my most troubled parishioners have claimed to be from Sheboygan." He paused, and I could feel the old station wagon buck and shudder as my aunt pushed it to an unsafe high speed. "But that has always turned out to be a lie," the Reverend John Lawrence said. I felt like he, too, was trying to be cruel, although he probably felt like he was just being truthful. As though the truth couldn't be just as cruel as a lie.

"You know you weren't her only lover," I said to the Reverend John Lawrence. I didn't even bother to turn to address him. I simply faced forward as I talked, as though he weren't important enough for me to bother using my neck. "You weren't even the only one from Iowa." And then I began to list my mother's imaginary lovers. The ministers, they were from all over: Iowa, Missouri, South Carolina, Texas, Rhode Island, Washington State, Washington, DC. I was always alerted to their presence by their rental cars, parked outside the church. After they left, I'd ask her where they were from, and she told me." I paused to see if any of this was sticking, and sure enough, I heard angry, tortured breathing coming from the backseat. "She was very forthcoming," I told the Reverend John Lawrence. "She told me that she liked to have sex with her ministers in the church: sometimes in a pew, sometimes behind the altar, sometimes up in the choir loft, up against the organ. I once asked her if this didn't seem blasphemous to her, and she said no, because when she had sex with a minister in her church, she imagined she was having sex with John Calvin instead." I paused again, then added, "But she'd basically have sex with anyone. It didn't have to be minister; it didn't have to be one of her acolytes. My father's colleagues. Other coaches. Even assistant coaches. Men on the county road crew. Once, a plumber. Once, an electrician." I paused for a third time, because I was running out of people and professions. But then I remembered how the Reverend John Lawrence had said the volunteer firemen who'd found my mother's burning car were good, honest men, and also that I'd seen a picture of Leland Otis in the newspaper, holding his ax and facing away from my burning house. "Several volunteer firemen," I said. "Once, I walked into our house and my mother was kissing one of them, our ancient grizzled neighbor, Leland Otis, right there in the entryway. Leland Otis: the man always has a toothpick in his mouth. Even when he was kissing my mother, I could see the pick in the corner of his mouth, bobbing, as they went at each other. My mother and I laughed about it afterward." Here I paused, for a fourth time, glanced over at my aunt, who was grinning, and bouncing her head up and down, like she was listening to some really good music. I said earlier that my aunt's cruelty was indiscriminate. But it was also contagious, and inspiring. She was so good at it, and I wanted to prove that I could be good at it, too. And I could! I was! I then returned my eyes to the windshield. The wind and the road blasted in from the open windows, but still I could hear the Reverend John Lawrence breathing fiercely from the backseat. I kept waiting for him to put his hands around my neck from behind, but it's to his credit, I suppose, that he didn't. "Yes, my mother told me about all of them, every single man," I said, still facing forward but saying it extra loud and extra slow to make the Reverend John Lawrence could hear every word. "Funny, though, that she never mentioned you."

152.

After that, a sort of peace or truce settled over the station wagon. The landscape changed, became less industrial, more pastoral: I saw sheep, men tending them on horses and tractors and on foot. On our left, lakes—at first isolated and distant and mist shrouded, but then soon the landscape was thick with them, one after the other. Gradually the weather cleared; the gray clouds disappeared and then there was nothing but baby blue sky. And as the bad weather burned off, so did the effect of the pills. My mind came back to me. Or at least it started doing what I wanted it to do. For instance, wondering why this station wagon didn't have any seatbelts.

"You might also wonder," Aunt Beatrice said, "why it doesn't have working heat or brake lights, or why it refuses to shift into reverse."

I remembered the truck my aunt had stolen, how beat up it was, how its speedometer didn't even work, and I asked her why she stole such terrible old cars.

"An old car is a burden," Aunt Beatrice said. "The owners rarely report them stolen. They *want* them stolen." Before I could remind her that the last vehicle she'd stolen had come with a dog and had the dog's owner wanted the dog to be stolen, too, my aunt added, "There are obviously exceptions, Calvin."

My phone then buzzed in my right pants pocket. I took it out and saw a text from Caroline. *Hey, where'd you go?*

I wanted to text her back, of course, but didn't feel like I could do so without my aunt catching me at it. So I returned my phone to my pants pocket. I thought all this had been done slyly enough, but Aunt Beatrice asked, "Who was that on the phone, Calvin?"

"Dawn," I said. Why this was better than saying "Caroline," I don't know, except that my aunt seemed to know everything and I seemed to know nothing, but at least now I knew that it had been Caroline who'd texted me, whereas my aunt had thought it was Dawn. It was a pointless lie, in other words. Although as I knew by now, there is no such thing as a pointless lie. A lie is always born with a point.

"What'd she want?" Her tone was as chipper as usual. I couldn't hear any suspicion in it.

"She wanted to know where I was."

"Why didn't you tell her?"

"Because she burned down my house," I said, and then added, "and because I don't know where we are."

My aunt didn't respond for a long time. Her silence now seemed sullen to me, and I wondered if she knew, after all, that

I'd lied to her. But no, she was waiting for the moment, an hour into her silence, when she could simply point out the windshield and at the large sign that welcomed us to Geneva, Switzerland.

153.

"Imagine," my mother wrote in her famous book. "Imagine the moment when John Calvin first entered the city of Geneva, Switzerland, in 1536. He'd had no intention of going to Geneva; he'd been traveling from Paris to his home in Strasbourg. But war in France forced him to seek haven in Geneva. John Calvin was twenty-seven years old. That is difficult to imagine in our contemporary culture; in our contemporary culture many twenty-seven-year-old men and women still live at home with their parents; in our contemporary culture many men and women are essentially seen as and treated like and indeed act like children. I would want these twenty-seven-year-old children to imagine themselves otherwise. I would want them to imagine themselves as young John Calvin. Imagine being forced to flee to a city that doesn't know you, or you it. Imagine feeling not as though this were a tragedy but an opportunity. Imagine coming to a place that needs you even more than you need it."

154.

Once I heard where we were going—or rather, where we already were—I turned around in my seat to get a look at the Reverend John Lawrence. Surely, as a student of my mother's, and of John Calvin's, he knew the significance of Geneva; surely he knew that John Calvin had preached in that city's St. Peter's church and would see something—hope, probably—in our going there. He was sitting in the middle of the bench seat and had put his hat back on his head, as though expecting imminent departure. And he was grinning crazily. The grin looked all wrong on his gaunt face: it made him look less like a minister and more like a child. But then, he was riding in the backseat, and people who ride in the backseat always look like children.

155.

Why did I hate the Reverend John Lawrence? It wasn't because he was in love with my mother, or even that he'd had sex with her, if he had had sex with her. It was that crazy grin. When I saw it on his face, I could also picture it on mine. When he was imagining the moment he would reunite with my mother who in his mind was not really dead, I was imagining the moment when my aunt would reveal to me that she was really my mother. He was a fool. But I couldn't think that without thinking that I was probably a fool, too. I saw myself in him, and him in me, and that's why I hated him, and that's why I wanted him gone.

156.

"You left behind a copy of my mother's famous book in my hotel room in Stockholm," I said. It was a theory, but I said it as a fact, hoping that would make it one.

But it wasn't. The Reverend John Lawrence stopped smiling, cocked his head to one side, scowled. He clearly didn't know what

I was talking about. Which infuriated me. Because that meant I was wrong about him leaving that book in my Stockholm hotel room. Which meant I was riding in the backseat, too, still. And I was tired of that. You could not grow up while riding in the backseat. Which was why I persisted.

"And," I added, "you've been telling Dawn where I am."

"Dawn?" he asked, scowling. Again, clearly, he hadn't done any of the things I'd accused him of doing. "Your scowling ex-wife?"

I turned to my aunt. She nodded and said, "Yes, Calvin, I understand what you understand. The Reverend didn't do either of those things. And we still don't know who did." She said this in her normal, chipper voice, but something in it made me think that she did know, and I was right about that.

157.

Not long afterward, the car slowed in traffic as it passed over a bridge. There were hundreds of sailboats in their slips although none out on Lake Geneva itself. The mountains in the distance were still flecked with white, and the sky was blue and the lake bluer yet. Off to the right there was a fountain shooting and arcing out of the lake, looking not like water out of a lake but like water out of a hose, and of course I thought of the volunteer firemen and of my house in Congress.

After we'd crossed the bridge my aunt pulled out her own phone and said into it, "St. Peter's Cathedral, Geneva,

Switzerland." The phone whirred. And as it did, the Reverend John Lawrence said flatly from the backseat, "I find that technology dehumanizes us."

"I hope so," my aunt said. The phone stopped whirring and my aunt placed it on the dashboard, and an automated man's voice told her to take a left in sixty meters. "Because most people I know could stand to be less human."

158.

There was no legal parking in front of St. Peter's, but nonetheless my aunt parked in front of St. Peter's, pulled right up over the curb and onto the cobblestone plaza in front of the church. Aunt Beatrice got out of the station wagon and began walking toward the church. The Reverend John Lawrence and I did the same. I noticed my aunt was limping, leaning to her right, like a woman in need of a cane. But then, we'd been in the station wagon for several hours, and the drive had made me feel stiff, too. "Are you allowed to park there?" I asked when I caught up with her.

"No."

"Won't you get a ticket or towed?"

"I doubt it."

"Why?"

"Because if you park in a place you're so obviously not permitted to park in," my aunt said, "then people assume you have some special permission to park there."

159.

St. Peter's was much bigger than my mother's church: you could have comfortably fit ten of my mother's church inside. And it was made of stone and not wood. As in my mother's church, there was nothing on the walls, no icons or murals or tale-telling stained glass. I knew from my mother's famous book that St. Peter's had once been Roman Catholic and that John Calvin had attempted to strip the building of anything that smacked of ornamentation and idolatry. But it hadn't worked. The walls were bare, but they looked wrong; their bareness just served to remind you that they hadn't always been bare. It had been over four hundred years since John Calvin had remodeled, but still, his church looked like a man who has just shaved off his mustache.

160.

I felt a presence. It wasn't John Calvin. It was my mother. There, in front of me, was a pulpit. And I could picture her behind it. I could hear her voice, in all its authority, in all its certainty. Ridiculous to think that a voice like that could ever be silenced, even by a train. *The Conductor*, I thought. And for a moment, I wondered if the Reverend John Lawrence wasn't deluded after all.

And then I noticed my aunt, scanning the church, from one side to the other, pew to nave, her head on a swivel. I wondered if she was looking for the Sociologist, or for whomever else was looking for the Sociologist. I wondered if she felt a presence, too.

161.

It was a Tuesday. Midafternoon. There was no service. But the church was crowded. Loud with murmurs. People in groups, milling around. Single people, sitting in the pews. Three women next to me, looking at the arched ceiling. They were Italian. I knew this not because they were speaking Italian, but because they were holding copies of the Italian-language edition of my mother's famous book.

162.

My mother's famous book was published in twenty-seven languages. In forty-three countries. Many of those countries were majority Protestant. But some were Roman Catholic, and some were Orthodox. Some were Hindu. Buddhist. Muslim. Animist. Some were nothing. Some didn't know what they were. The book had been on the hardcover best-seller lists in thirty of those countries, and then, after two years of being in hardcover, it was finally published in paperback and then it was a best seller in thirty-five countries. It became more than a book in many of those places. In Israel it was made into a radio program, aired once a week; one week a chapter was read in Hebrew by an ultra-Orthodox settler and then the next week in Arabic by a Palestinian. In Argentina it was made into a stage play, a musical, in which my mother, a Calvinist Eva Perón, sang her praise songs to John Calvin from a balcony. And a small filmmaking studio in Finland had made the book into a movie, a movie in which my mother was a character, and I was a character, and

John Calvin was a character, a character whom my mother and I are looking for and whom we find living near the Arctic Circle with the Sámi. John Calvin was bearded down to the sternum and up to just below his eyes. This bearded John Calvin is wearing a tracksuit under his parka, and in the final frame the three of us—me, my mother, John Calvin—are seen from the back, riding north through the snowy woods on our snowmobiles.

163.

And why was my mother's famous book so famous? I don't think it was that her readers cared so much about John Calvin or believed in his ideas. I think that they cared that my mother cared; they believed because she believed. They could tell, no matter what language the book was in, how truly my mother believed in John Calvin. They wanted to believe in something the way my mother believed in John Calvin. It wasn't necessarily that they wanted to believe in what she believed. They wanted to believe how she believed.

164.

It wasn't just the three Italian women: nearly every person in that church, dozens and dozens of them, was holding a copy of my mother's famous book.

"Do you know what else your mother was afraid of?" my aunt asked me. We were standing toward the back of the church. The Reverend John Lawrence had wandered to the front, and for a moment I'd lost him in the crowd of my mother's fans.

"What?"

"The religious crazies," she said in her normal voice, which echoed and bounced around the church. A few people turned and looked at us. Their expressions were hostile, deranged even, and I thought I understood what my aunt meant.

"She was afraid that the religious crazies might hurt her?"

"She was afraid," my aunt said, "that people might think she was one of them."

165.

A few moments later my aunt said, "You'll be wanting to know how I betrayed the Sociologist." This seemed to come out of nowhere and to be out of context, but by now I'd learned that the only context that mattered when it came to my aunt's stories was that she told them when she felt like it was time to tell them. She spoke loudly, as though she didn't care who heard. And in fact, the religious crazies didn't seem to care about what she was saying. They ignored us, fixated as they were on John Calvin's church and on their copies of my mother's famous book, not understanding, I suppose, that their hero, my mother, was in my aunt's story, too. "It was 1979. Your mother came to visit the Sociologist and me. This was eleven years after our estrangement."

I didn't even bother asking her where this had happened. I figured I'd eventually learn. I said, instead, for the sake of clarity, "By 'eleven years after our estrangement,' you really mean, eleven years after you had sex with my father and my mother said she never wanted to see you again." For this was one of the lessons I'd learned from my aunt: you have an obligation to be clear, especially when it comes to other people's crimes.

But Aunt Beatrice didn't seem to mind, or even notice. "The Sociologist," she continued, "was by now mostly smuggling weapons. Real weapons, not decorative ones. Guns, not knives. Occasionally, he smuggled into the country the people to whom he then sold the smuggled weapons. More occasionally, he smuggled out of the country the political leaders who had been overthrown by the people whom he'd smuggled into the country and to whom he'd sold the smuggled weapons. It was a happy time for both of us. For all of us, I should say. Zhow was of course with us. He was already quite interested in animals, although I assumed his interest was more zoological than carnal. Connie was there, too. She and I were already anticipating our future. In it, we would no longer be smuggling or stealing objects. Those are not crimes for old people, Calvin. Technology is not a weapon. Technology is a crutch. We knew we couldn't steal antiquities forever. Old things are heavy things. But information, we could steal and sell. The Sociologist was there to sell weapons. But Connie and I were there to work on the technology. As long as we had the technology, we could be in wheelchairs and still steal and sell what people wanted most."

"And fifteen years later you were slapping women in Ohio," I reminded her. I did this not out of cruelty but because at that moment she looked and sounded old and tired, and I wanted to remind her that she was not done then so that she would believe she was not done now either.

"There is no work, however vile or sordid, that does not glisten before God," my aunt quoted, which was the quote that my mother had used to defend my blogging from the disapproval of the Reverend John Lawrence. "I was so happy when I heard from your mother and that she said she wanted to see me. I'd missed her, Calvin. You may be surprised to hear that, but it's true. I said earlier that Connie was my best friend. That was fine. But I would have given up my best friend in exchange for my sister. I wanted her back in my life again. I wanted her to meet the Sociologist. I wanted her to visit us. Although of course I also wanted to know why she wanted to visit us. I was afraid she'd want an apology. And as you know, I couldn't give her that. But no, at first all it seemed she wanted was to walk on the beach and talk about Congress. Her church. The house. 'The house of horrors.' She was terrified of you, Calvin. She admitted that to me. She didn't understand you. She said you didn't seem to care about John Calvin, or anything, and I said that you sounded wonderful! Your mother laughed at that. She did! I was so glad she was back in my life, Calvin."

My aunt paused. I now recognize the pause. It was the pause you take before you remember some pain you felt, some pain you caused.

"And I was glad that she liked the Sociologist. And that he liked her. They had a lot in common. They were very compatible."

It pained me to hear Aunt Beatrice speak so euphemistically, and so I said, "They had sex," and my aunt nodded.

"I was actually proud of your mother, Calvin. Because she had done it to hurt me. That was her intention. I drove her to the airport, walked her to the gate, and right as she was about to board the plane back to Boston, she told me what she and the Sociologist had done, days earlier, while Connie and I were working. I didn't have to ask her why, but she told me anyway: 'I wanted to hurt you,' she said. And then she walked down the gangway and I never saw her again. I admired everything about that. But the Sociologist, *Morten*, was different. Because he had known it would hurt me, and he did not want to hurt me, but he went ahead and did it anyway." I didn't bother to point out to my aunt that she knew that having sex with my father would hurt my mother, and that presumably she had not wanted to hurt my mother, but she'd done it anyway. As John Calvin once said, "When the same qualities which we admire in ourselves are seen in others, even though they be superior . . . we maliciously lower and carp at them."

"I called Interpol," my aunt continued. "I called the CIA, I called everyone I could think of, and told them who the Sociologist was, and what he had done, and where they could find him, and then Connie punched me in the face, for betraying her brother, and for ruining our business, and then the Sociologist went on the run, and I told Zhow his father was dead, which was exactly how I felt about him, and so not exactly a lie, and then Zhow and I moved to Ohio, and then when Zhow was eighteen I told him that I'd betrayed his father and that it was possible he wasn't dead, and then Zhow left me, and then . . ." My aunt didn't finish the sentence; it just sort of trailed off, and I tried to follow it, in my head, as it led from Ohio, briefly back to Congress, and then Stockholm, and then Copenhagen, and then Paris, and now here.

"I'm sorry, Calvin," my aunt said.

"It's all right," I said. Because I assumed my aunt was apologizing for telling me something about my mother that I didn't want to know. But she needn't have apologized for that. Didn't she realize that the more I learned about my mother's sins, the more I loved her?

Although of course my aunt realized that. And anyway, that's not what she was apologizing for.

My aunt regarded me for a moment. She looked piratical, with her missing tooth and her hair swept over one eye, and her silver ship necklace humming in the soft church light. Then she grabbed my upper arms. It was as close as she'd ever come to hugging me. I felt like something was about to be revealed to me. My aunt's lips were pursed, her skin furrowed and creased, all lines leading toward her mouth. *Tell me*, I wanted to say, and I might have actually said it, because my aunt nodded ruefully as though to indicate that I had asked for it, and girlishly, Americanly, *loudly*, in a voice no one in the church could have missed, she said, "Oh my Gawd! You're Nola Bledsoe's son!"

166.

John Calvin said, "The pastor ought to have two voices: one, for gathering the sheep; and another, for warding off and driving away wolves and thieves."

I tried both voices. When I was surrounded (and I was surrounded immediately, from all sides, by my mother's fans, her acolytes; they were five deep around me, and some of them were hyperventilating, and their breathlessness became my breathlessness), I said, "Yes, I am Calvin Bledsoe." I said this calmly, soothingly, but it did not calm them. It did not soothe them. The gang pressed even closer to me. Many of them had their copies of my mother's famous book in their hands, waving the books over their heads. And I said, somewhat less calmly, that there was no need to push, that it was wonderful to meet them, so good of them to come, what a great surprise, what a beautiful church, so good to see so many people with their copies of my mother's famous book, would anyone like me to sign their copy, I'd be happy to sign their copy, I just needed some space, and a pen, could everyone give me some space, and does anyone have a pen?

I had no idea what I was saying, obviously. I was scared, obviously. And in any case, they weren't listening. I wasn't what they wanted. They wanted my mother. I knew how they felt; at that moment, I wanted my mother, too.

I wasn't what they wanted, but they pushed closer anyway. Their bodies oppressed me. So did their mouths, and the many languages I didn't understand coming out of them. I reached for my phone, so I could translate them. I didn't know what else to do. But there was no room for me to even reach for my phone. The crowd was that close. And I hated them. And I wondered if my mother had ever hated them, too—hated them even though she had made them. Or especially since she had made them.

"Go away!" I screamed, in a voice even louder and more girlish than my aunt's had been. "My mother's dead! You didn't know her! I didn't know her! She didn't know John Calvin! She was the Conductor! She was pulverized by a train! She's gone! What else do you want! You already have her famous book! There's nothing more of her to have!"

This, as John Calvin had recommended, was the voice to ward away the wolves. It worked, for a moment. The people backed up respectfully, as one does when faced with a crazy person. When they did, I could finally see over the top of them. I'd lost my aunt after she'd said what she'd said, but now I spotted her. She was at the front of the church, talking with the Reverend John Lawrence, who was sitting in John Calvin's chair. I knew it was John Calvin's chair because there was a green sign next to it that read CHAISE DE CALVIN. The chair was made of wood, dark wood, although I couldn't see much more of the chair because, of course, the Reverend John Lawrence was sitting in it. No, he wasn't sitting in it; he was one with it. His back was against its back; his arms were over its arms. My aunt didn't seem happy about it. Her back was to me, and I couldn't see her face, but she was waving her arms, gesturing toward the Reverend John Lawrence, the chair, the church, him, the chair. This didn't seem to affect him much, though. The Reverend John Lawrence just sat there, with this beatific look on his face, as though preparing to be transported. Or already in the process of being transported. His eyes were far away, and I knew he was seeing the person he wanted to see—my mother—at the end of his journey. My aunt put her right hand on the back of the chair and seemed to try to pull it, tug it, wobble it, but that had no effect on the Reverend John Lawrence, although it had an effect on me. Because I remembered one of the commandments—"Thou shall steal while thy partner distracts"—and realized why she'd announced my presence: I was the distraction she'd created so that she could then steal John Calvin's chair.

167.

The crowd soon recovered. It began to advance on me again. And it was my fear of them, more than anything—more than wanting to help out my aunt, more than wanting to hurt the Reverend John Lawrence (although I did want to hurt him)—that caused me to do what I did next.

"Hey!" I shouted. That word sounded so American, so out of place in that Swiss house of God, which was also the house of John Calvin. "Who does that guy think he is, sitting in John Calvin's chair?"

168.

I won't describe what happened next, except to say that it was swift and brutal, and that the Reverend John Lawrence was wounded during it, and that while it was his fault that he'd sat in John Calvin's chair, it was my fault that he was hurt being removed from it. It was the first time something I'd said had caused someone to be physically hurt, although it wouldn't be the last time, or the worst wounding.

And then he was gone. The crowd had taken him away, to somewhere else in the church. I could hear them shouting. Their voices sounded like pitchforks. My aunt was gone, too. Meanwhile, there was John Calvin's chair, tipped over. I righted it. Admired it. Swept the church with my eyes to make sure that no one was around. And there wasn't. Because I'd done it! I'd created the distraction that would allow me to steal the chair! And so I stole it.

Thirteen

169.

My aunt was waiting for me outside St. Peter's. As she'd promised, the station wagon hadn't been ticketed or towed. She was in the driver's seat. The station wagon's long back door was swung way open. And it occurred to me that my aunt didn't just steal old vehicles. She stole old vehicles with large cargo areas, perfect for stowing large stolen objects. I stuffed John Calvin's chair into the wayback, slammed the door, and got into the station wagon, and then we drove off.

170.

I'd expected Aunt Beatrice to be happy that I'd stolen John Calvin's chair for her, but no.

"That was unnecessary," she said, and her voice was flat—as flat as the Reverend John Lawrence's. I wondered where he was at that moment. If there were a cell or a torture chamber or a morgue in St. Peter's, it would not have surprised me if he were in it.

"What was?"

"Why did you steal the chair?" my aunt asked, and her voice wasn't flat anymore. I could hear the puzzled hurt in it.

"Didn't you want it stolen?" I asked, and my aunt frowned.

"No, Calvin," she said. "I didn't want it *stolen*."

My aunt didn't say more. She just sat at the wheel, fuming. For the first time, I fully understood that verb. It was though her anger was a gas, and I could smell the fumes. How had I so badly misread her intentions? I went back in time to picture the scene. There was the Reverend John Lawrence in John Calvin's chair. There was Aunt Beatrice, standing over him, berating him, pleading with him. What had she wanted, if she hadn't wanted him to get out of the chair so she could steal it? Whatever she wanted, he wasn't moving. I could see him clearly. He wasn't moving, no matter what my aunt said or did. That chair had given him power. My aunt, I pictured her, in the church: she looked hunched over, ancient, diminished. Like a supplicant who'd failed to move the powerful man in the chair she'd wanted to steal. And then I had moved him, or had had him moved. And then I'd stolen it. And that was why she was so disturbed.

"You wanted to steal the chair yourself," I guessed.

My aunt in the past had said, "Very good, Calvin," when I'd

made a good guess about something about her past or our present. But this time, fuming, she said nothing.

171.

What do you do when the person you love most in the world—
and my aunt was the person I loved most in the world—is feeling
weak, vulnerable, defensive? You press your advantage.

"Are you going to steal anything else?" I asked. When she
didn't answer that question, I asked, more forcefully, "Do you
even know where the Sociologist is?" And when my aunt didn't
answer *that* question, I demanded, "*Where are we going?*"

"It's best not to know everything, Calvin," my aunt said
calmly, brightly. She already seemed back to normal. And just
like that, over the course of three sentences, my advantage had
disappeared. We pulled onto the highway, picked up speed. The
wind blew through the windows, and my aunt's hair whipped
around her face, and I bounced around without my seatbelt and
began to think that this was going to be a perpetual way of being
for me, and for us.

"Is it best to know *nothing*?" I shouted out of desperation and
over the wind sounds.

"For some people, yes," my aunt said, and before I could
object, she quoted John Calvin and said, "There is no worse
screen to block out the Spirit than confidence in our own
intelligence."

"That's the third time you've called me stupid," I pointed out.

"I didn't call you anything, Calvin," my aunt said. "I was only quoting John Calvin."

After that, there didn't seem to be much to say. I curled toward the door, away from my aunt, and took out my phone. There was the last message on my phone, from Caroline, wondering where I'd gone. I texted her back: *Sorry! An emergency trip to Geneva.* And then in another text I typed, *I'm thinking of you.* Almost immediately I received a text back from her: *Me, too! Come meet me in Marseille!* And then I turned to my aunt and said, "I'm going to travel on my own for a while."

My aunt didn't respond right away, and didn't look at me either. She just faced forward and continued driving, fingers drumming against the steering wheel. The station wagon hit a bump, and John Calvin's chair rattled around in the wayback and then settled again.

"Do you think that's a good idea, Calvin?" Aunt Beatrice finally asked.

It was a parental question, one equipped with its own answer: "It is not a good idea." And then it occurred to me, as it should have long before, that in order to grow up I would not only have to stop listening to my mother but to my aunt also.

"I do," I said. "It is."

"But why?"

"Because you won't tell me the truth," I said, telling her the truth because I wanted to. "And because I'm starting to hate you for that."

My aunt's fingers stopped drumming when I said that. With her left hand, she reached up, touched her sunglasses, and I thought she going to take them off, but she didn't. She opened her mouth, and I thought she was going to speak, but she didn't do that either. Aunt Beatrice seemed, suddenly, like someone who didn't know what to do or say. But she didn't do or say anything else to dissuade me from doing what I wanted to do either. Instead, she took the first exit to Lyon and dropped me off at the train station there. I got out of the station wagon, walked around to the driver's side. My aunt had taken off her glasses, hooked them behind her ears and onto the top of her head. Her blue eyes looked shiny, wet, full of deep, tender feeling. "I hope I see you again, Calvin," she said in the same wheedling, sad-sack way that she'd said that an old lady likes to be seen off at the airport or taken to the doctor. Which made me even more determined to get away from her.

"Of course you will," I said. "Let's talk in a few days."

My aunt nodded, unhooked her sunglasses, placed them over her eyes again. "You'll need my number," she said, and in the next moment my phone started buzzing in my pants' pocket. I took it out. It was a number I didn't recognize, and I assumed (and still assume) that it was my aunt's. I silenced my phone. By the time I looked back to my aunt, she was already driving away.

172.

According to the train schedule, I would be seeing Caroline in three hours and forty-two minutes. I texted Caroline my arrival time, and she texted me back immediately, saying that she'd meet me at the station. Then I boarded the train. I didn't have a private compartment this time; the trip was too short to need one. And anyway, the train was mostly empty, and I had a whole row of seats to myself. I stretched out on the seats, feeling happy, feeling accomplished: because I'd finally said and got what I wanted, and as a result, I felt confident that I would continue to say and get what I wanted.

But in the meantime, I had three hours and forty-two minutes to kill. So, first, I checked Dawn's blog. There were no new posts from the road, no new updates. Not that she needed to. Arson is its own kind of update. Out of all the things I'd felt for and about her during all our years together, I'd never once felt angry. Dawn had always been angry enough for the both of us. Well, I was angry now, too, and (and I suppose this is true of most angry people) I began entertaining lots of vague thoughts about how I'd express my anger if I ever saw her again.

173.

Next, I checked my own blog. Why, I don't know: I hadn't posted anything and so had given no one anything to respond to. Although it turned out I had, and they had.

It Was *Good*

Dear readers, I don't know if you've ever had sex on a train, but I highly recommend it. A train doesn't move so much as it *chugs*, sort of *bucks*, but smoothly, as it proceeds toward its next station. I hope my posse doesn't mind my kissing and telling, but last night, I got *fucked*! The woman I was with—let's call her C—said she wanted to *fuck* me, and I let her, and fucked back, too. There is no pellet stove in this blog post. There was no pellet stove in our train compartment either. There was just a forty-seven-year-old man and a who-knows-how-old woman, and the faint taste and smell of booze on our breaths, and sadness and hope and lust in our hearts, and the slow, relentless chugging of the train, and one hard cock and one wet pussy, and C chewed on my lip and I liked that, and I ran my tongue around her navel and up and down her inner thighs and she liked that, and time sort of passed, but frantically, and during our last time C was on top of me and she reached back and ran her index finger over my balls and it felt as though I'd been electrocuted and that the electrocution had saved me, religiously saved me, and I tried to explain that feeling to C, right there, while she was on top of me, moving with the train, until she asked me to please shut up and just fuck her and I did that, and in short there was a lot of fucking. And it was good, posse! You don't exist, and my father is dead, and my mother is dead, and John Calvin is dead, and my house has been burned to the ground and I feel empty, but fuck it, the house, and fuck her, the woman who burned it down, and fuck them, my parents, and fuck him, John Calvin, and fuck you, dear readers, fuck you, posse. I just wanted to write to you all this one last time and tell you that I had sex, and was worthy of it, and it was *good*!

174.

There were two comments on this blog post.

The first was from the pellet stove industry. It read, in its entirety: *You're fired!!! #industrystandards #inappropriate #wordlimit.*

Then the second comment. The pellet stove industry had never figured out a way to draw readers or responders to its blog posts, but it *had* figured out a way to identify the readers if they did respond and also to determine the location from which they were responding. The second comment was written by Dawn Probst (Probst was her last name), who was writing from the Charlotte Douglas International Airport. Dawn's comment read, in its entirety, *Who are you?!?*

You know who I am. I'm Calvin Bledsoe, I'd responded. Although of course I hadn't been the one who'd responded.

175.

John Calvin once described "that dread and amazement with which . . . holy men were struck and overwhelmed whenever they beheld the presence of God."

Which is the way I felt when I beheld the presence of the blog post I hadn't written.

I did a number of things in quick succession and then repeatedly over the course of the train trip to Marseille.

First, I tried to delete the post. But apparently, upon my firing, I'd been denied access to the blog. Although why the industry itself hadn't deleted the blog, why it hadn't just gotten rid of the whole thing, was a mystery to me.

Second, I tried to respond to the post, denying that I'd written it. But for the second time, I was denied access.

Third, I texted the industry, and in that text I denied having written the post. The industry texted back and pointed out that I was the only one who had access to the account. I texted back and pointed out that the industry had access to the account. And the industry texted back and asked, why would the industry write and publish such a post? And then I texted back and asked, why would I write and publish such a post? And then the industry texted back and said, who knows why, maybe I was a sick fuck. A sick fuck who had not only written a sick post but who had also somehow found a way to prevent the industry from taking the sick post down. And then before I could text back that no, I wasn't a sick fuck, and no, I hadn't figured out a way to do that, the industry texted again and said that it was blocking my texts, beginning immediately. And then I texted back and asked them not to do that. But then my text failed to send, and so clearly they'd done that.

Fourth, I asked myself, was I a sick fuck? Because after all, a few of those words were mine—I hadn't posted them, but I had written them—and all those thoughts were mine, and if they weren't the thoughts of a sick fuck, then what were they?

Fifth, I asked myself, who had access to my blog? Who had

access to my thoughts, my feelings, my brain, my heart, my soul? And who had access to Caroline's sleeper on the train between Hamburg and Paris? Because the blog was a pretty accurate representation of what Caroline and I had done, what we had said.

Sixth, I thought of Caroline. She could have written the blog post. But why would she have written the blog post? There wasn't a reason for her to have done that. And there wouldn't be a reason for her to believe me when I said that I wasn't the one who'd written it either. And she would have read it, too. I'd told her what I did for a living. She would no doubt have checked up on me. This is what the internet was made for. People will tell you that the internet was made to facilitate the free flow of information. But that's just another way of saying the internet was made for people to check up on other people.

Seventh, if it wasn't Caroline, and it wasn't me, then who had written the blog post?

Eighth, it had to have been my aunt. But how? And why? Why would she do that to me? What was so offensive about my life, my livelihood, that she felt compelled to ruin it? My house had been destroyed, that was bad enough, but I felt my life being destroyed now, too. Why did my aunt hate that life so much? What had been so wrong with it? What was so wrong with me? What was so wrong with her? It hurt my head to think about all this, and so I went back to the first thing on the list and tried again to delete my blog post.

And in this way I spent the three-hour-and-forty-two minute train trip from Lyon to Marseille.

176.

By the time I reached Marseille it was ten at night. I was in something of a panic. Caroline. Caroline. I felt this terrible urgent need to see her and also an even stronger sense that after seeing her I would end up feeling something even worse than the terrible urgent need. Terror. Shame. Denial. Resignation. Futility. These feelings weighed on me—on my heart and on my head, but especially on my bladder. I'd gone to the bathroom at least six times on the train, and each time I'd felt less relief than the time before. And only after I'd gotten off the train and gone to the bathroom *again* did I realize that my kidney stones had returned.

There was a men's room on the way from the track to the Marseille station proper. I waddled into it. It was humid in there, oppressive, like a greenhouse without the vegetation. There were two urinals, both unused. I took the one on the left. Tried to conduct my business. I won't bore or disgust you with the details, except to say that my abdomen felt like it was hosting a zeppelin and that the zeppelin was armed with arrowheads, made out of shards of glass, and that the zeppelin was firing them through my urethra. Even though I knew from experience that there was nothing a doctor could do for me, that the stones had to run their course, I said out loud to my sad self, "Oh, Doctor!" and in my voice, I heard my aunt's voice, the unconvincingly pathetic one. And then I remembered that I'd never translated and then listened to the recording of what the Butcher had said to Aunt Beatrice before we'd left her office in Paris.

I finished at the urinal, zipped up, and took out my phone, but before I could listen to my recording of the Butcher, I heard the bathroom door open, then quick-approaching footsteps. The footsteps stopped at the other urinal, to my right. I looked in that direction, in clear violation of rules guiding urination in men's rooms, and saw that there was a man standing there, and he was not using the urinal, and he was wearing a black ski mask. He also was holding what looked like a black pillowcase. Without saying anything, he put the pillowcase over my head. It smelled like something that had been in a closet for too long.

This might sound strange to you, but I didn't scream or struggle—at least not right away. I didn't say anything at all. A feeling of calm fell over me. As though I'd been waiting for this to happen. As though it were predestined. For as John Calvin himself said, "Nothing, including human suffering, happens by chance."

But then the man—I assumed he was a man—removed my cell phone from my hand. Then: smashing sounds. And with those sounds I was jolted back into life. I screamed. I screamed for my phone and for all the people—my aunt, Caroline, the Unknown Caller—who wouldn't know where I was without it. When I paused in my screaming, the man—it was a man's voice, one I didn't recognize—said, "Please don't take this personally." And then he propelled my head forward, bouncing it off the top of the urinal. And that's the last thing I remember until I woke up who knows how many hours later on the SS *Antonio*.

Fourteen

177.

I didn't know how many hours and days I spent on that ship. My phone, remember, had been taken from me, destroyed, and so I had no sense or proof of time. Until the very end of the journey, I was not allowed to leave my tiny room. The room had no windows. The walls were gray; the room itself was sparsely furnished: a cot, a sink, a toilet. The door was locked. There was no mirror in the room. I was glad about that. I was afraid to see my forehead, which pulsed like it was another living thing. Once, I made the mistake of touching it, and I felt a round opening there, like a mouth, and in fact when I touched it, it seemed as though it screamed, although it was probably just me screaming.

178.

I was fed seven times. Seven times someone—I assume the man
in the ski mask—slid a tray of food under the door. I had no idea
whether the meals were supposed to be breakfast, lunch, or dinner. Each meal was the same. A large piece of salted fish, a pile
of peas. I refused to eat, out of principle, although I couldn't tell
you what I thought the principle was. I did drink, water directly
out of the tap, using my cupped hands. As for my kidney stones,
they compelled me to use the toilet often, which offered not
relief but more torment and dread.

179.

When the second tray was slid under the door, I asked quickly if
I could have something to write with. My voice was so weak and
scratchy that I doubted if anyone besides me could have heard it.
But when the third tray emerged under the door some time later,
there, next to the fish and the peas, was a blue ballpoint pen.

I took it and began writing on the walls. I wrote columns,
four of them. In the first column I wrote the names of the people
who might have had me kidnapped:

The Sociologist
Aunt Beatrice
Dawn
Caroline
The Reverend John Lawrence
The Man in the Mask

The only name I crossed out was the Man in the Mask. Of course, I knew that he'd done the kidnapping, but I had the sense that he was working for someone else, that he'd kidnapped me on someone else's behalf. I wasn't really interested in keeping anyone on the list who was doing something on somebody else's behalf.

And I wondered: Had my mother ever felt this way, about God or about John Calvin? That she wasn't really interested anymore in doing something on somebody else's behalf?

Anyway, in the second column I wrote all the names of the people who I thought might be waiting for me when the ship got to where it was going. It was the same list. I didn't cross anyone out.

In the third column I simply wrote: Aunt Beatrice. I looked at her name, looked at it. She was, of course, the key to all this, but as a fellow victim, a perpetrator, or both, I didn't know.

And then my pen ran out of ink. That was just as well. I wasn't really getting anywhere with my columns.

180.

Then, between the arrival of my fourth and fifth trays, something strange happened. I was asleep again. I shouldn't say "again": I was asleep, or in a state much like sleep, most of my time aboard that ship. It wasn't as though I was tired. But my head wound and my hunger and my loneliness and my kidney stones made being awake seem like too much work and not enough reward.

"In order to see," a man's voice said, "you must open your eyes."

I didn't recognize the man's voice. It wasn't automated, like the Unknown Caller's. It wasn't the Man in the Mask's voice either. It wasn't a voice I had heard before. It was a calm, clear voice, and it seemed to come from everywhere and nowhere.

Anyway, with my eyes still closed, I thought about what the voice had said. The message seemed clear enough, even obvious: I should open my eyes. I opened my eyes, but the room was only dark. And when I got up and turned on the overhead light, the room was only light.

181.

After that, I vowed to stay awake with the light on until the sixth tray came. I sat up in my bed, got up from my bed, walked from wall to wall, touching all four walls, just to remind myself that they, and I, were real. There were my markings on the wall. There was the defunct pen on the sink. There was my toilet. The toilet smelled. I smelled, too: my unwashed distressed German jeans, my dirty shiny shirt. I rubbed my head, being careful to avoid the wound. I'd bought a razor back in Hamburg but had never used it, had left it behind on the train. Mostly there was baldness, mostly there was nothing, but here and there I felt stubble that was more than just stubble, actual growing blades of hair, isolated patches, popping up like unconnected ideas.

By this point, I had decided I wasn't even going to try to pass my stones anymore. I was going to wait until the voice told me what to do about them. And if the voice didn't tell me what to do about them, well, I would just suffer them and keep them with me forever.

"We suffer most," the voice said, "when someone we love has caused us pain."

182.

John Calvin once wrote about his conversion from Catholicism to, well, Calvinism: "Being exceedingly alarmed at the misery into which I had fallen, and much more at that which threatened me in view of death, I, duty bound, made it my first business to betake myself to your way."

That was the way I began to feel about the voice. The more the voice told me, the more obvious the message seemed to be, the more it seemed I was not quite getting the message and the more desperate I was to get what I was not quite getting.

183.

Also, I really should have eaten something. All would have seemed less mysterious if I'd eaten at least from one tray. But hunger is like a narcotic. It prevents you from thinking clearly, sure, but you can also become addicted to it: when the seventh tray came sliding under the door, I remember feeling that I just couldn't wait not to eat what was on it.

184.

The overhead bulb went out. It fizzed liked bulbs do when they're about to quit, and then it quit, and then my room was completely dark.

"Why don't you eat, Calvin?" the voice said, and I felt lit up from within. It was the first time the voice had asked me a question, the first time it had addressed me by name. And I thought then of how my aunt often addressed me by name, and how every time she did so, it felt like she was trying to remind me of who I was, or who I could be.

"Because of my principles," I said. My voice was strange to me: it sounded thin, starved, wraithlike.

"Principles are merely rules," the voice said, "that no one but yourself says you have to follow."

"What are *your* principles?" I asked. This might strike you as a bold question for me to ask. But remember, I was in the dark now, and it's sometimes easier to ask questions you shouldn't in the dark. Also, I felt like I was ready to ask a question; the voice had made me ready, not just to be spoken to but to speak back, too. As John Calvin had said about his own conversion, "Having thus received some taste and knowledge of true godliness, I was immediately inflamed with so intense a desire to make progress therein."

Meanwhile, as I waited for the answer, I could feel the engine catch, could hear the ship groan and turn, could hear its cargo shift all around me. And that noise, that groaning and turning and shifting, must have done something to me. I lurched over to the toilet and expelled the stone. I remembered from before that feeling of great release, and then, after hearing the puny sound of my stone plinking into the water, that feeling of mild shame that something so small had caused me such great misery.

Anyway, the voice never did tell me what its principles were, because just then the door swung open. I'd been standing at the toilet, but the light coming through the doorway was so over-whelming that I staggered back and sat down on the cot again. There in the doorway was the man who kidnapped me. He was wearing a paramilitary outfit: black boots, black pants tucked into the boots, ribbed black sweater with epaulets. But he wasn't wearing the ski mask, and so I could see he was young or, at any rate, younger than I: blond, clean shaven, dimpled, a crew cut. I had never seen him before. He gestured for me to stand up and said, "We're almost there."

185.

Outside on the deck the night air was heavy and warm. The harbor lights sparkled in the distance, and farther in the distance car lights crossed a bridge, and even farther more car lights crossed another bridge. The bridges crossed a river, or a harbor, or a bay, some body of water rippling black. On both sides of the ship there were steep humped hills, the dark only occasionally dot-ted by window lights. But those few lights didn't make it seem lonely. They made it seem like this was a place where someone always stayed up to wait for you. Up on the hill to my left I saw the outline of enormous statue, a giant or a Jesus, I couldn't tell which, his arms stretched wide in what looked like welcome.

186.

It took a long time for us to ease into the dock, so long that by the time the ship finally stopped moving and the gangway was lowered, I could see the promise of daybreak beyond the hills.

The man who'd kidnapped me had disappeared for a time after releasing me from my room, but now he was back. "Ready?" he said, gesturing toward the gangway.

"Are you going to put a pillowcase over my head again?" I asked, and he nodded thoughtfully as though I'd asked a good question.

"No," he said. "We only do that when we're kidnapping someone. If you wear a ski mask and put a sack over someone's head in public, it makes anyone who sees it assume that person with the sack over his head deserves it. That he really has done something terrible."

"And if you don't put a sack over his head?" I asked, and the man said, "Then people think he's being kidnapped."

187.

Minutes later, we left the ship and were following a thin strip of concrete that ran serpentine along and across canals and boat slips, past what looked like a customs house, an old one, chipping pale pink paint on crumbling stucco. We kept walking. To the left I could see a shipyard, stacks and stacks of blue metal shipping containers; to the right, bobbing in their berths, small sailboats, five of them, with white hulls and bright sails. The man escorted me past the sailboats, veering right and then continuing to veer right alongside and across a channel of water and then right again across another channel of water. Except that it was the same channel of water, and we'd crossed it twice. In front of us now was the ship I'd just been on, the SS *Antonio*. We were headed back to it. And in that way I discovered that whatever country we were in, it wasn't an especially efficient country. It was a country that required you to do the most to accomplish the least.

Finally, we approached a plastic-covered pallet on the concrete, between an open cargo hold and an idling white van. A man was lifting up the plastic, peeking underneath, as if doing inventory. From behind I could see his black hair curling around his white shirt collar.

The kidnapper shouted something to the man in yet another language I didn't understand. What the kidnapper had said was loud but full of shushing sounds. It was as though the kidnapper was bellowing at someone to be quiet.

The man turned around. It was someone I knew. But his wasn't a name I'd thought to write on my cell wall.

"*Bom dia!*" Zhow said, arms raised, and for a moment I thought he was going to hug me, like a cousin, like a brother, but he didn't. "Welcome to Lisbon!" he said instead.

Then he stepped closer to me. Squinted, as though he weren't sure I was who he thought I was. "Ow," Zhow said, and I realized he wasn't squinting at me but at my head wound.

"He . . ." I started to say, turning to gesture at the man who'd given me the head wound. But he was gone. I really hoped I would never see him again, and I never did.

I turned back to Zhow. "How do you spell your name?" and he told me: J-o-ã-o. I thanked him and then asked him if he knew where Aunt Beatrice was. His dark face darkened. Instead of answering, he walked back to the small pallet and began removing boxes from the pallet and putting them into the back of a white van parked nearby. I stood there uselessly until João gestured with his head to help. I walked over to the pallet. I was afraid in my weakened state that I wouldn't be able to lift and carry the box, but it was surprisingly light. I peeked inside and saw stacks of DVDs.

"Are you smuggling pornography?" I asked João, and he smiled, as if to say, *Of course*. But that didn't make much sense to me. You could get pornography anywhere. On your phone, for instance, if you had one, although when I'd had one, I'd never gotten pornography there.

"But why do you bother?" I asked, and my cousin shrugged.

"I like it better when it's smuggled," he said.

Then we got into the van and drove. To our right, what I know now to be the Tagus River. To the left were faded pink, yellow, and blue houses with wrought-iron balconies off the front. Laundry—underwear, socks, even sneakers—hung from the railings. The balconies were so narrow: it didn't seem possible for a normal-sized person to fit on them. Maybe, I thought, they were there just to hang laundry.

We took a left and began switchbacking up a series of hills. The streets were narrow, barely wider than the van, and on either side of them were walls covered with gleaming sky blue tiles with thin white fleur-de-lis. I opened my window and got a whiff of citrus, and saw, above a courtyard wall, lemons and oranges hanging from branches, the shiny leaves fluttering in the wind.

João drove fast, his tires thumping against the cobblestones.

"You seem to really know where you're going," I said.

"I was born here," he said, and I knew then why he'd been given a Portuguese name.

"But you've been living in Stockholm," I said. And then I took a guess. "And before that you lived with your mother in Ohio."

"I *lived* in Ohio for sixteen years," João said. "I've *lived* in Stockholm for twenty. But I was born here." And I could tell how much that distinction really meant to him. And of course I then thought about Congress. I was born there, had lived there all my life, had never really imagined living anywhere else. But now I hoped I'd never see it again.

Suddenly there were three black poles in the middle of the street. João stopped the van, turned it off. Just left it there in the middle of the street, with the pornography still in back, and from then on we walked.

We walked up. Up a series of steep stairs that led to streets that led to more steep stairs. After about fifteen minutes of climbing we reached a point where to the right there were buildings but to the left there was nothing really. A chain-link fence. The remains of a building, what once had been a foundation, some rubble. On the other side of the rubble the land fell off steeply into a ravine filled with bricks, garbage, fallen trees. The sun was now burning off the remaining misty morning. We came to the top of our particular hill. In the distance there was another one. On top of it was a church, some cedar trees. It looked like the highest hill. But probably there was no highest hill: Lisbon seemed like a city where you would never find the highest hill. On the ship I'd wondered if we were going to sail forever. Now I wondered if we were going to climb forever. If so, I would need better shoes: I could feel the cobblestones through the thin soles of my German boots. "How much farther?" I asked João, who was a few of feet ahead of me. Two stories above his head were two black brackets, fixed to the blue-tiled wall, and hanging from the brackets were two gray tin pails, mini–palm trees in them, graffiti on the pails. Between and slightly above the brackets was a window, open. And out of that window a voice announced, "Distance is a matter of the mind and not just the map." I recognized the voice. It was the voice I'd been hearing in my room on the ship. I'd assumed, on the ship, that the voice was speaking to me, and to me alone. But no. João was looking up at the window: he'd heard the voice, too.

188.

Seconds later, a door opened onto the street. A man stepped through the open door. He had a full head of white hair, curly, and a white beard, also full, but trimmed: he hadn't allowed it to creep too far down the neck or climb too high on the cheeks. A pair of silver wire-rimmed glasses dangled by a thick strap around his neck, and when he put the glasses on to get a better look at me, I saw that they were round, scholarly. He was wearing a long-sleeved blue oxford shirt with two breast pockets, the sleeves rolled to the elbows and the shirt tucked into a pair of khaki shorts. The shorts came down to the middle of his thighs. His legs were thin, long, lightly muscled, tan, flecked with white hair. It was by them that I recognized him. My aunt was right: the Sociologist had really good legs.

Fifteen

- - - - - - -

189.

"A sociologist is someone who likes to say things that sound profound until you think about them and realize that they're mostly just obvious." That's what my aunt had said on the train, after we'd left Copenhagen, when I'd asked her what a sociologist was. And I remembered her definition when I first met the Sociologist in Lisbon. As I said, the Sociologist put on his glasses to get a better look at me, and then, once he'd seen what he needed to see, the Sociologist glanced up, at a seagull soaring over our heads from hill to hill, and said, "The gull is truly a master of flight."

When the Sociologist said that about the gull, I thought of

the similarly obvious things he'd said to me on the ship. But from where had he said them?

"There was a speaker and a microphone in the floor drain," the Sociologist said, eyes still on the gull. I hadn't even noticed a floor drain. Earlier I said that no one ever looks up, but it's possible that not enough people look down either. "A camera in the lightbulb, too," João added. All this—the speaker, the microphone, the camera—seemed like needless flourishes, which reminded me of another seemingly needless flourish, the very first one, the one that caused us to leave Congress and come to Europe in the first place.

"Unknown Caller," I said. "Clear sailing." The two of them looked at me expectantly, as though waiting for me to say more. Clearly, it wasn't them; clearly neither of them had called me in Congress the night before my aunt had taken me away from that place. So my aunt, I thought, had been wrong about that. But I didn't realize until later that in fact my aunt had never told me she thought it was the Sociologist who'd made that call: Connie had guessed that Aunt Beatrice believed the Sociologist was the Unknown Caller, and I'd passed off that hypothesis as my own, and my aunt had not told me I was wrong. But she hadn't exactly told me I was right either.

"Where's my aunt?" I wanted to know, and the Sociologist fiddled with his glasses for a moment in a way that very much reminded me of my aunt, and then he suggested we all go inside.

190.

The Sociologist's house looked like it was being remodeled. The first floor was essentially without interior walls. A vast rectangular space, like a ballroom or a basketball court. The walls had been stripped to the studs, and there were tools everywhere: hammers, crowbars, table saws, trowels, drills. Bags of plaster. Rolls of insulation. Stacks of flooring. Piles of terra-cotta. The ceilings had been ripped open, too, rusty nails sticking out of dark brown beams.

There were stairs at both ends of that large room. We took the far staircase, which was steep and narrow, open on one side, no railing. The upstairs looked more inhabited. A long carpeted hallway with five rooms on either side. At the end of the hallway there was an open door, and we walked through it. This, I realized, was the room the Sociologist had shouted from earlier. The room was large, even larger than my hotel room in Stockholm. The walls were painted bright yellow and glowed in the morning sun.

In the far corner of the room there was a heap of technology, much of it seemingly obsolete. An overlarge cumbersome-looking microphone affixed to a short bulky stand. A CB. A ham radio. A TV with knobs. A DVD player. Several ancient apparatuses I didn't recognize and couldn't name. No cell phones. No computers. Nothing of the present, only of the past.

The only piece of furniture in the room was a large comfortable-looking white wingback chair. The Sociologist sat in it. João sat on the windowsill behind him. It seemed demeaning to sit on the floor, at the Sociologist's feet, so to speak, and so I stood.

"The Admiral is missing," the Sociologist said, "but only insofar as we don't know where she is."

"The two of you split up," João said to me. It was an accusation. As though it were my fault Aunt Beatrice and I had separated back in Lyon. And I suppose it was.

"I just wanted to travel by myself for a while," I said.

"So our hired muscle had to separate, too," João said. It was interesting. João was speaking English, but it wasn't a foreign-sounding English. It sounded native, colloquial, flat, much like the Reverend John Lawrence's. He spoke English like an Ohioan, no matter where he was born. "One went with my mother, and one went with . . ." And then he nodded in my direction.

"Your hired muscle bounced my head off a urinal," I said. "He said not to take it personally."

"Our other mercenary evidently said something similar to your aunt," the Sociologist said. "But the Admiral took it personally anyway." And for the first time I saw the Sociologist smile. The smile just burst all over his face. He quickly corralled it, though, and was stoic again. But I saw it: for that brief moment I saw how happy it made him to think of the manner in which Aunt Beatrice had taken her attempted kidnapping personally.

But why? I asked the Sociologist. Why did he want to kidnap my aunt and bring her to Lisbon? Did he want reunion or revenge?

"That's a good question," the Sociologist said again, but he didn't seem like he was being evasive: I just don't think he himself had yet decided on an answer.

"But you don't need to kidnap Aunt Beatrice," I said. "She has all these gifts for you." I explained what they were and added, "She's been looking for you." This seemed to astonish the Sociologist. He took off his glasses, letting them dangle from their string while he rubbed his face. When he removed his hands, the Sociologist's face looked young, the way old faces can look when revisited by some kind of young hope, or fear.

"You know this?"

I told him I did. I told him that Aunt Beatrice had admitted she was looking for him. Although, again, I didn't realize until later that this was true only in the sense that my aunt had allowed me to believe that it was true.

191.

The Sociologist then turned to his son, who looked as astonished as his father. It was easy to picture João, thirty-odd years into the future, white haired, white bearded, long shanked, rubbing his face, wondering how so late in life he'd gotten something so fundamental so wrong. "She didn't," João began to say, then stopped himself. I could see he was wary of me listening, but the Sociologist nodded for him to go on. "She didn't even mention you."

"Tell me," the Sociologist said.

"I *already* told you."

"Please tell me again."

João did. He recounted the conversation he'd had with Aunt Beatrice in Stockholm, the one that I'd heard but not understood because it was in Swedish. He'd asked what she wanted, and she'd said, "I just wanted to spend some time with my son before I die."

"She sounded pathetic," João said to me and his father, and I heard my aunt's voice, sounding pathetic, when she'd said something similar to me back in Boston. "But there was nothing wrong with her except that she was a liar. That's what I told her. And then I told her that I wasn't her son. I told her, 'As far as you're concerned, I'm no one.'"

The Sociologist didn't say anything to that. Me neither. I couldn't believe that anyone had dared say something like that to my aunt. I had the sense that João couldn't quite believe it either. He had a look on his face I'd only seen once before, when my old classmate and neighbor, Charles Otis, had won a hot-dog-eating contest at the Congress town fair. Like Charles, then, João now looked proud, and queasy.

"That was wrong," the Sociologist finally said. His voice was even softer than normal, maybe because he was talking to himself.

"But she betrayed you," João said.

"People are betrayed," his father said in his usual solemn, obvious way. "But usually, before or after they are betrayed, they are the ones doing the betraying."

Once again no one said anything for a time. The message was

obvious enough, but the sentence had wound around it, and it took both João and I some time to untangle the cord.

"Well, shit," João finally said, and once again I could hear the state of Ohio in his voice.

192.

The Sociologist then told João what my aunt had told me in Geneva: the story of how the Sociologist and my mother had had sex, which was why my aunt had betrayed him. I knew this already, of course, but I was surprised to discover that João had not.

As I learned over the next couple of days, João was eighteen when my aunt had admitted to João that she'd betrayed his father and that the Sociologist might, in fact, still be alive. João had then fled Ohio, and had gone to Europe, where he'd found the Sociologist, because the Sociologist had allowed João to find him. And while they'd never lived together for fear of alerting Interpol to the Sociologist's existence, they'd been in close contact. In fact, João had contacted his father after we'd seen João in Stockholm, and they'd decided to have their mercenaries follow us, kidnap us, bring us to Lisbon.

But what I found most revealing about all this was that my aunt had simply told João that she was the betrayer, and not that she'd been betrayed first, and that the Sociologist had never bothered to tell his son the complete story. Until now.

Why hadn't Aunt Beatrice told João the whole truth? Because she would rather have been known as the victimizer than the victim. And why didn't the Sociologist tell João the whole truth? Because he would have rather been known as the victim than the victimizer. There are two kinds of bad people. There's my aunt, who did bad things and didn't mind if you knew about them. And there's the Sociologist, who very much minded. Although I never did learn whether he regretted having done bad things or just regretted other people's knowing about them.

193.

Anyway, now that he knew that my aunt was looking for him, the Sociologist had no choice but to tell. When he was done with the story, João asked if I would leave them alone for a moment. I stepped into the hall, and João closed the door behind me. Downstairs there were work noises—hammering, sawing, drilling. Men shouting in Portuguese over the sounds of their tools. Yes, things were starting to happen downstairs, and upstairs, too.

194.

The Sociologist opened the door a few minutes later and asked me to come back in. When I did, I noticed that João was sitting in the chair. Just like that, he'd taken his father's place. João's lips were pursed, as though he was determined not to say something. The Sociologist spoke for him.

"How can we contact the Admiral?" the Sociologist wanted to know.

"I don't suppose either of you has a cell phone," I said. But the pile of antiquated machinery in the corner told me that of course they didn't. They hadn't forsaken technology, just the theory behind it that suggested that the only thing that qualified as technology was the newest technology. Whereas the Sociologist and João only found useful the most antiquated technology. Not that I could argue with their belief system. And not that I could have done anything with their cell phone if they'd had one. I hadn't memorized my aunt's phone number. I had trusted that my cell phone, now destroyed, would keep it memorized for me.

But I did have one other idea.

195.

The three of us descended the stairs into the work zone, where there were a dozen men with their belts and their tools. The Sociologist nodded and waved and said *Bom dia!* to the men as we passed through their zone and then outside.

"You're having a lot of work done on your house," I said, and then winced at how obvious a statement that was, but the Sociologist seemed to enjoy it. He flashed and then extinguished that sudden, fleeting smile again, and said, "Oh, it's not my house."

"What do you mean?"

"It's a hotel. Or it was a hotel. It's going to be one again when they're finished renovating it."

"Is it your hotel?"

"Of course not."

"Do you have permission to stay in it?"

"Who says I need permission?"

"Did you tell the workers you have permission?"

"No."

"They why do they let you stay there?"

"Because I act like I don't need anyone's permission."

And I began to understand a little why my aunt had loved him before she betrayed him.

196.

We left the hotel and walked down the hill. After a few minutes we reached the van—it was where João had left it, still blocking the intersection that was blocked by those three black poles— climbed in it, drove to an internet cafe. We walked into the cafe, paid for our hour, sat down in front of a computer. I could see in the upper right-hand corner of the computer that it was June 15. That meant that I'd been on the ship for three days; it'd had been eight days since I'd left Congress. A lot had changed for me in those eight days. But not everything: after all, here I was, once again, staring at a screen, preparing to write yet another blog post, one that I hoped would somehow travel through the void and reach my aunt, wherever she was.

My plan was to post a comment on Dawn's blog: my aunt might not check Dawn's blog, but then, she might. In any case, it was the only thing I could think to do. But first, out of desperation, I tried my own blog. "It's probably still frozen," I warned the Sociologist and João. "Someone published a pornographic post under my name."

This seemed to galvanize João a little. How pornographic was the post? he wanted to know. I didn't answer him. I suspect he would have been disappointed in me, that the post would not for him have crossed the threshold into pornography proper. In any case, the pornographic post was gone, but my access to the blog had been mysteriously restored. There were no posts and no responses—not from Dawn, which was a relief, nor Caroline, which was a disappointment. But then, this was what I was there to do: give people something to respond to.

Journey's End

I apologize, dear readers, for my long silence. Since you last heard from me, I was impersonated, fired, assaulted, kidnapped, imprisoned, mentally tortured. Or at least that's what it feels like to be here in Lisbon, without access to a pellet stove! But fear not. I've been hired as a consultant for the Journey's End (Fim da Viagem, for my Portuguese posse!), a hotel being remodeled on Rua Costa du Castelo by the owner, who is an old friend of my aunt's and my mother's. The hotel's grand reopening is on June 18. It's going to be huge celebration, and the owner says that all are welcome. It may be too warm to fire up the Vitra 2000s (one in every room, and the Max model in the lobby), but I feel better just knowing that they'll be installed and that you'll be joining us!

197.

The party was the Sociologist's idea, and it was also his idea that it take place on June 18. The eighteenth was my aunt's birthday, he explained. But of course I knew that, because it would have been my mother's birthday, her seventy-ninth birthday, had it not been for that train.

Before I hit Send I warned the Sociologist, "If I do this, Aunt Beatrice won't be the only one who shows up. There might be lots of people." I named them: Dawn. Caroline. The Reverend John Lawrence. His sister Connie and the Butcher. "Who knows who else?" I said. Because I was sure there were other people. Other people who were reading my blog. The pellet stove industry, for instance. Other people who were looking for my aunt, and other people looking for the Sociologist himself. Interpol, for instance.

The Sociologist considered what I'd said. Nodding, nodding. I could sense something building, something huge and disappointing, the most obvious of all his obvious aphorisms. "We have the room," the Sociologist finally said instead. "After all, we do live in a hotel." I could hear it then, in his voice, and I can still hear it: the loneliness of all his years in exile. Small rooms, empty hotels, caves, boxcars. Fields, attics, cellars, penthouses. Maybe even churches. The Sociologist had been so many places. And he'd been alone in all of them. I knew what he was thinking: that anything would be better than more of that loneliness. "Please just do it, Calvin," he said. And so I did what the Sociologist asked me to do.

Sixteen

198.

After I'd posted on my blog, we spent the next two days cleaning up the hotel. The workers had quit for the weekend (it was the weekend), and the Sociologist, João, and I picked up where they'd left off. We concentrated on the ballroom: first, we patched and painted. When we were done with that we scrubbed the floor of its last carpet remnants, buffed it with the power buffer. When we were done with that João went out and came back with a long buffet table, and on it he put a pair of speakers and, in between the pair of speakers, a CD player and a receiver. When we were done it looked like a room that had seen too many parties but was somewhat recovered and ready for another one.

199.

While we worked I had two significant conversations.

The first one was with João. We were spackling the ballroom's walls. Ever since he'd found out the truth about why his mother had betrayed his father, João had been quiet, thoughtful. I knew what he was feeling: I'd felt the same way after I'd learned about my father and my aunt, and then about my mother and the Sociologist. When someone puts a new thought in your head, you want to let it stay there for a while until you're ready for it to come out of your mouth.

"I suppose she never talked about me," João said. He was referring to his mother. It was true that Aunt Beatrice had rarely mentioned João, and one of the times she had, she'd said he was no one. But I wasn't going to tell João that. No, I would tell him a lie. Because under the same circumstances, I would have wanted someone to lie to me.

"She talked about you all the time," I said.

"That's obviously a lie," he said. But I could tell he was trying not to smile.

We spackled for a while in silence, and then João asked, "You don't really believe she's dying, do you?"

"No," I said, because I didn't, but I thought of the recording I'd made of the Butcher back in Paris, and how now that my phone was destroyed, I'd never be able to listen to it, although I was wrong about that.

200.

The second conversation was with the Sociologist. It was later on that same day. João had left the house on an errand. The Sociologist was on a ladder, rewiring a chandelier, and I was steadying the ladder.

"I had sex with your mother because she wanted to, Calvin," the Sociologist said. My foot was on the bottom rung, and each hand gripped the side of the ladder, and I thought how easy it would be to just knock over the ladder and kill him. But on whose behalf? Not, I realized, on my mother's behalf, and not on my father's either. No, if I were to kill the Sociologist, it would have been on my aunt's behalf. As though she were something more than just an aunt.

I said earlier that when someone puts a new thought in your head, you want to let it stay there for a while until you're ready for it to come out of your mouth. But what happens when the new thought stays in your head for so long that it becomes an old thought? It does what all old things do. It dies. And I didn't want it to die.

"Did you ever wonder if my aunt was really my mother?" I asked the Sociologist in a rush before I could decide not to.

The Sociologist was rummaging around in the ceiling's innards and didn't answer at first, didn't answer for a while, and I thought again how easy it would be to kill him. But of course, if you have that thought twice, that means it's not so easy.

"Yes," the Sociologist finally said.

"Did she ever say so?"

"No," the Sociologist said. "But she talked about you all the time."

"That's obviously a lie," I said. But I found myself smiling as I steadied the ladder.

201.

By noon the next day we were ready for the party to begin. But then it was five o'clock, and still, no one had shown up. The three of us had been very talkative earlier in the day, but now we were subdued, deep inside ourselves. I wondered if João and the Sociologist were thinking what I was thinking. Of how, if my aunt didn't show up, they'd have to go back to their old lives: João peddling his pornography on the streets of Stockholm; the Sociologist on the run, alone. Me back in Congress. I'd get insurance money for the house, and I supposed I'd use it to build a new house in the same spot, and restart my old life, such as it was. The thought made me tired. Not because it seemed impossible but because it seemed inevitable.

Is it any wonder we drank too much that day? Neither João nor the Sociologist had had anything alcoholic to drink since I'd met them, and neither had I. But the waiting had been too oppressive, and around five we started to drink cheap red wine. The Sociologist had bought dozens of bottles of the stuff. It was hot that day, too, and soon I became flushed with the heat and with the wine, and that caused me to drink more wine and to feel even more flushed.

Flushed and also itchy. It had now been thirteen days since I'd last shaved my head, and it itched, and so did my cheeks, and neck, which I'd also not shaved, and my beard felt gruesome and unkempt and slick with wine. Also, I was still wearing my German clothes. I'd washed them the day before in the bathroom sink, but still the shiny shirt felt reptilian against my clammy skin. I loosened a button to cool off, but I did not feel cooled off, and so I loosened another one.

202.

At eight o'clock, we were five bottles of wine in, and still no one had shown up, and the Sociologist and João began to argue about the music.

Days earlier, after João had found out the truth about his mother and father, João had seemed the ascendant one, and his father, the fallen. But their roles had reversed since: the father was once again the father; the son, the son. And the father had chosen the music. I didn't know what any of it was, but even I knew that it was painfully dated and not the kind of music you played at a party. It was the kind of music you shushed people who were talking over it so you could all admire the lyrics. Several times the Sociologist shushed João and me so we could all admire the lyrics.

"I don't hear it," João finally said during a pause in the vocals as a harmonica bleated.

"Me neither," I said.

"In order to hear," the Sociologist said, beginning to apho-
rize and also overgesticulating with his wineglass, which he then
dropped, and it shattered on the floor. I went into the kitchen
to find a broom and a dustpan. You know what it's like after a
major cleaning, when you've put away the instruments of your
cleaning so completely that it's hard to find them again. But I
finally did and was holding a broom in one hand, a dustpan
in the other, when I reentered the ballroom and saw João and
the Sociologist standing there face-to-face with Dawn. She was
wearing her black riding boots, jeans tucked into them, and
her hair was wild and springing out in all directions, and in the
moments before I remembered that she was mostly awful and
that she'd burned down my house, I was surprised at how pretty
she was and how much I wanted to say that I'd missed her.

203.

One was a fugitive from international justice and the other a
small-animal pornographer, but the Sociologist and João seemed
shy with Dawn in the room: they'd already gotten her a glass of
wine, and the Sociologist had already replaced and filled a new
one for himself, and he and his son sipped their wine and mostly
studied the contents of their glasses as though the future were
written there. Once in a while they looked up at Dawn quickly,
furtively, as though they couldn't believe she was in the same
room with them. I wondered when the last time was that either

of them had really talked with a woman. I had the distinct feeling that for them, there was no other woman in their minds and hearts than my aunt.

Dawn walked over to me. She was short, shorter than my aunt or Caroline. Her head came only up to my chest. But there was something massive about her. Her presence. Her will. Her determination. "I thought I lost you," she said, and then she produced and showed me her phone. On it was a blue dot superimposed over Lisbon. That was she. And there was a red dot over Marseille. That had been me. So that's how she'd known where I was: she was using her phone to track mine. "You left your phone in Marseilles," she said, again accusingly. As though that were my major crime. Not that I'd left her or lied to her, but by leaving my phone, I'd left her without a way of following me. She had followed me across an ocean and then through several countries. To do what? I suppose to tell me that she hated me. Or that she loved me. I suppose it was the latter. And I suppose her capacity for love was massive, too. I mean, it must have been, for her to come all that way. I should have seen that. But there was always something between the two of us: it was Dawn's capacity for producing scorn, and my capacity for absorbing it. And I thought I'd reached capacity and so was ready to say another thing I wanted to say.

"You fucking bitch, you burned down my house," I said, and I was not at all surprised to hear how much of my aunt's bright voice was in my own.

204.

Divorce, much more so than marriage, is made of the illusion that you know someone. Strangers get married all the time, but people are rarely strangers by the time they divorce. Dawn divorced me because she knew me, and I wanted her to divorce me because I knew her.

But Dawn did something surprising after I called her. Well, I'm not going to repeat it. It's enough I said it the first time. First, she looked at me, the way I must have looked at the people on this trip who spoke in Swedish, Danish, German, French, Portuguese. Then Dawn opened her mouth, started and stopped herself from saying something several times. Finally, she bit her lower lip, hard: the skin went white from the teeth. And then she began crying. Turned her head and cried, softly, into her shoulder. I'd never seen Dawn cry before. There was something demoralizing about it. Like seeing a divine being act like a mortal. Like walking into a room and catching John Calvin sniffing a dirty sock to see if he could put off doing some laundry for one more day.

"That was wrong, Calvin," the Sociologist said. This was a man who'd smuggled weapons and humans, who'd betrayed my aunt and been betrayed by her and had spent years hiding in who knows what kind of awful places, and yet from his voice I could tell he thought he'd never seen someone act so despicably. Meanwhile, João shoved me out of the way, the small-animal pornographer casting me a dirty look as he went up to Dawn, put his arm around her, and said in a gentle shushing voice, "He didn't mean it."

But I had. And Dawn knew that. And by her crying, I knew that I'd been wrong: Dawn hadn't been the one who'd burned down my house. But had I been so ridiculous in thinking so? After all, my aunt had thought the same thing. Except that I then remembered that I was the one who'd said on the drive from Paris to Geneva that Dawn had burned down my house, and my aunt had said that that made sense but not that it was true. Because that was another thing about my aunt: despite her fondness for lying, she herself rarely lied. But neither did she necessarily bother to correct you when you lied to yourself.

205.

Dawn shrugged off João's arm, walked right up to me. She pushed her wild hair out of her face, held it against her forehead with her left hand. Dawn was looking at me closely now: my half-healed head wound, my sparsely budding hair, my overgrown beard, my clothes that might have looked okay on someone else, my ridiculous shirt open ridiculously to my sternum. "You look like hell, Calvin," Dawn said.

And then she punched me, right in the mouth. I dropped my broom and pan and staggered back with my hand over my mouth, tasting blood and feeling the dislodged tooth go back into my mouth, over my tongue, and halfway down my throat before I gagged and spit it out into my hand. I looked at the tooth. Felt the space it had left with my tongue. It was my left front tooth. I did not complain or moan or anything. After all, I remembered one of my aunt's commandments: "Thou shall expect to get punched in the face for thine inappropriate acts."

Instead, I thought how funny my aunt would find it to see me with my own missing tooth. I hoped, when she showed up, that someone would take a picture of us together.

João consulted his watch and said to me, "Eight fifty-one post meridiem," which meant that at least he'd learned something from his mother when she was getting paid to slap women during their long years of exile in Ohio.

206.

Many parties end with violence, but this party began with violence, too. Immediately after Dawn hit me people started arriving. Most of them I didn't know. Among them were old friends of the Sociologist's, and I suppose my aunt's, too. Men with gray beards and bald heads, women straight from the hairdresser with hair dyed almost all the way to the roots. Criminals, I guessed. They looked at the Sociologist sideways, and he at them, but soon enough they were laughing loudly over their glasses of wine, enjoying one another's long-lost untrustworthy company. Whenever the front door opened, they, as a group, looked to it, as though expecting the police, or maybe it was just the Admiral they were expecting. I noticed the Sociologist and João closely monitoring the door, too, and of course so was I.

207.

There were almost as many pellet stove bloggers as criminals at the party. They were mostly men, mostly younger than I; they were wearing clothes like mine except that they wore them better, and many of their heads were shaved, but that seemed to speak of efficiency and self-determination and not desperation. They seemed not to be disappointed that there were no pellet stoves in the hotel; they, like the aged criminals, seemed just happy to be there and to have a chance to come in out of the shadows. They were Portuguese, and their English was good, but they mostly wanted to talk about pellet stoves, and after a while I found that I had run out of things to say about that, and to them, and so I left them to themselves.

208.

Dawn didn't seem to have much to say to her fellow industry bloggers either. She didn't to have much to say to anyone other than João. They were in the corner, leaning against the wall, deep in conversation. Dawn was holding a bottle of wine, and periodically she would refill João's glass and then refill her own. Dawn smiled, often. I stood on the far side of the room, tongued the gap where my tooth had been (the tooth itself I'd put in the pocket of my shiny shirt), and wondered what João was saying (Was it pornographic? If so, what kind? Animal or strictly human?) to make Dawn smile like that. But seeing them together didn't hurt. I wasn't jealous or sad, and I didn't have second thoughts or mourn our missed opportunities. Dawn and I had known each other for five years, had been married for two, divorced for one, and I'd thought we would never be rid of each other, and now we were rid of each other and I'd lost a tooth, but otherwise felt like I'd gotten off easy, and I was right about that.

209.

Around eleven o'clock the Reverend John Lawrence showed up. He, like me, was still wearing the same clothes as when we'd talked in Hamburg, the same clothes as when I'd unleashed my mother's fans on him in Geneva, and he, like me, seemed much the worse for wear. There were scabbed-over cuts around his eyes and on his forehead, his left suit leg was torn at the knee, he'd lost his hat, and he looked even more stooped than before. He saw me see him walk through the door, and his expression should have been triumphant, or hopeful, or angry, but he just looked diminished, like he'd lost something essential just getting there.

I grabbed a wineglass, filled it, walked it over to him. As I crossed the room, the Reverend John Lawrence's face grew angry, and he stuffed his right hand into the jacket pocket of his shabby suit as though he had a weapon in there. But then he must have seen that I was coming in peace. Because he withdrew the hand, and it was empty, not even in the form of a fist, but open, and into the hand I placed the glass of red wine. "I'm not lying to you," I said to him. "I'm not hiding anything from you. My mother really is dead."

His shoulders slumped, and I knew that he knew I was right. Maybe he'd known all along and was only now able to admit it to himself.

"I read your *blog*," he said, like he couldn't believe he'd actually uttered that made-up word.

"My ex-wife just knocked out my tooth," I said, and showed him the space. He seemed to be contemplating it, and I wondered if he was trying to think of a John Calvin quote to commemorate the event.

"I'm glad," he said instead, and he drained his glass of wine and then headed over to the table where all the bottles were.

210.

The party had evolved by this point. The pellet stove bloggers had taken over the music, had banished the Sociologist's croaky singer-songwriters, had circumvented his DVD player, his receiver, his speakers: they'd synced all their phones with one another so that from wherever they stood, all around that huge room, the same songs emanated from their pockets. I say "songs," but it might have been one song that played and looped endlessly, with a deep bass and a singer who did not croak like a human but who instead sang like a robot, an automated singer, and once again I was reminded of the Unknown Caller. I wondered if I would ever find out who he was. I wondered if my aunt would ever show up to tell me if she knew who he was.

211.

Dawn, meanwhile, had turned into the kind of person who, having run into her ex at a party, wants to time travel so as to get to the bottom of how it had all gone so wrong.

"Why did you think I burned down your house, Calvin?" she asked, her voice slurry and sweet with wine.

"Because you wanted revenge," I said, the words whistling through my missing front tooth.

"But why would I want revenge?"

"Because I'd left you and gone to Europe."

"But why did you leave me and go to Europe?"

"I went to Europe because my aunt wanted me to." Dawn frowned at that, and I knew she wasn't going to accept that answer, and so I gave her another true one. "I went to Europe because you wouldn't leave me alone even though we were divorced."

"Why did we get divorced, Calvin?"

"Because I wouldn't move to Charlotte with you."

"But why wouldn't you move to Charlotte with me?"

"Because I didn't love you enough to move to Charlotte."

"Yes, but why *didn't* you love me enough?"

"Because," and I was about to say, again, that she was a bitch except that I was acutely aware that I was already missing a tooth and I didn't want to lose another one, and so I said instead, "you didn't love me enough to stay in Congress."

"Yes, but *why* didn't I love you enough?"

"Because you thought I was a big pussy."

"Yes, but why did I think you were a big pussy?"

"Because I was afraid of my mother, who was a lot like you, who I was also afraid of."

"*That's* right," Dawn said, her eyes flickering over to João, who was standing on the stairs with a bottle of wine. Dawn waved at him, then punched me on the upper arm, but gently, as though to tell me that there was no more real violence between us, before leaving me and following João upstairs.

212.

Not long after that, Wrong Way Connie arrived.

I'd been half watching the Sociologist the entire time. He seemed happy in the company of his fellow partners in crime. I saw him hug those who were leaving, clink glasses with those who stayed. But still, there was something superior about him. Maybe it was his height, his bearing, but even when he smiled, the Sociologist seemed as though he were smiling over everyone's heads.

That changed when his sister showed up. And when I say "showed up," I don't mean that I saw her walk through the door. I mean that she appeared, in the middle of that large room, among a group of drunken dancing bloggers. I saw her whisper something to one of those bloggers, and he looked over his shoulder, and I watched her snake his cell phone out of his pocket, watched her turn off the volume, watched her return it to the man's pocket. By the time the blogger had turned back to face her, she'd moved on.

To her brother. Who'd moved on to her. When the Sociologist saw Wrong Way Connie he bounded over to her. There was nothing superior about him now. He was less like a Sociologist and more like a dog, a pooch, who, happy to see his mistress, stops bashfully a few feet away from her as though remembering he that he'd done something wrong and wasn't sure if he was yet forgiven.

Wrong Way Connie took a step forward and hugged her brother, and he hugged her back. I watched him. His eyes were closed, and remained closed until they finally stopped hugging and took a step back from each other, and I saw that the Sociologist and Wrong Way Connie had hugged so hard that they'd mangled his glasses. They hung from his neck on the string, frame bent, lenses cracked, totally useless.

I'd never wanted a sibling before. But watching those two hug, I thought it might be a good thing. I looked upstairs, where João and Dawn had gone. I assumed they were in one of those bedrooms, having sex. And Wrong Way Connie's entrance had made me so hopeful that I didn't think about João, *He's sleeping with my ex-wife*, but rather, *I'll have to go find my brother when our mother shows up*.

The Reverend John Lawrence sidled up to me. "Who's that?" he wanted to know. He was talking about the Sociologist. The Reverend had drunk only a couple of glasses of red wine, but his flat voice was already thick.

"The Sociologist," I said. I saw that the nickname didn't register for the Reverend John Lawrence, the way my mother's nickname hadn't registered for me. "The Admiral's ex-husband. She betrayed him after he'd had sex with the Conductor."

I used the nicknames intentionally. They helped me put some distance between myself and the real people and their real names. They helped me forgive, and also forget. Although it's important to recognize—and I did not recognize this—that nicknames, like alcohol, don't affect absolutely everyone in the exactly the same way.

213.

Wrong Way Connie's arrival seemed to predict other arrivals, other reunions, but then it was two in the morning, and still, Aunt Beatrice hadn't shown up. The mood of the party had changed. The young people had become aggressively drunk; the old people, wearily so. The wine had seemed infinite before, but now I could count the full bottles on two hands. The song playing on the bloggers' phones was finally over, and no one had bothered to play a new one. A few of the old people checked their watches, and indeed, it was as though the whole party had started to hear the ticking of the clock.

Dawn and João came downstairs briefly. João went over to say hello to his aunt Connie, and Dawn came over to me, hair tussled, and said (and I could tell she'd sobered up because she'd lost her slur and found her scowl), "This reminds me of one of those weekend parties." Then she looked at the Reverend John Lawrence, who was standing next to me, and said, still scowling, "Who are you supposed to be?"

I'm your ex-husband's dead mother's forsaken secret lover. That's what I wished he'd said. That would have been honest. Had he said that, he would have had nothing left to defend, nothing left to hold on to. "I'm the Reverend John Lawrence of Hebron, Iowa," he said instead. As though that still meant something. It clearly didn't mean anything to Dawn. She didn't even acknowledge that he'd spoken, just grabbed a bottle of that wine and then went upstairs, and a minute later João followed her.

I said earlier that I wasn't sad about them, but I felt sad now. Not because João and Dawn were together but because I was still alone. Caroline: she probably thought I'd stood her up in Marseille, and she'd also probably read that pornographic blog post and thought I'd written it. I knew that even if my aunt showed up, Caroline would not.

"Who *is* that guy?" the Reverend John Lawrence wanted to know. He was still talking about the Sociologist, who seemed to be arguing with his sister on the far side of the ballroom. "She's not coming," I heard Connie say, and then the Sociologist said, "Don't say that." Meanwhile, the Reverend John Lawrence still wanted to know, "Who is *that* guy?" It was clear that alcohol made the Reverend John Lawrence aggrieved, repetitive, dumb. It had been three hours since I'd first told him who the Sociologist was, and still he wanted to know.

"He had sex with my mother, who was also your lover," I told him. "All those other men who I said slept with my mother didn't. I made all that up. But the Sociologist, *Morten*, he really did it. Because she really wanted him to." We both looked at the Sociologist: even as he leaned over to argue with his sister, he seemed tall, straight backed and shouldered, detached, superior. The exact opposite, in other words, of the Reverend John Lawrence. "If he bothered to think of you," I said, "he would think he was better than you." I paused to let that sink in and then added, "But he doesn't think of you. He doesn't even know you exist."

And how did this make me feel to say this true thing meanly? Did it make me feel grown up? I don't know. I do know that it made me feel *good*. Because I'd wanted to hurt the Reverend John Lawrence again, and I'd done it again. This was another thing I'd learned from my aunt, another of her commandments: "Thou shall hurt other people because it feels good." Although of course, only for a moment, and only before those people start hurting you, and also other people.

214.

Just then, the table supporting the stereo equipment came crashing down. Everyone turned to look, and the people standing near the table began to protest their innocence. But since most of the people standing next to the table were young people, the older people seemed generationally disinclined to believe them. Recriminations began to fly, in many different languages. Only after a few minutes of this did I notice that Wrong Way Connie was no longer standing next to her brother, and right after that her brother seemed to notice the same thing. The Sociologist squinted myopically into the corners of the room and, not finding her there, ran in the direction of the kitchen. In the kitchen I knew there was a narrow set of stairs that led to the cellar, and in the cellar I knew there was another narrow set of stairs that led to a bulkhead, which led to outside.

"Calvin," Caroline's voice said from behind me. I turned, and there she was, just a foot away, looking just as lovely as she'd had on the train. And I was suddenly aware of how I looked worse—flushed, drunk, toothless, unshaven, ungroomed, unbuttoned—and how I must have looked to her when I hadn't shown up to meet her in Marseille, and how I also must have looked to her when she'd read that blog post. I suddenly wished Wrong Way Connie would come back, so she could create a distraction so that I could disappear.

"I didn't write that blog post," I told Caroline, for starters. And when she didn't respond, I elaborated: "It wasn't me."

This caused Caroline to do something odd: she put her hands on my shoulders—not as a lover might but as a parent would a child—and her eyes flickered around the room as she considered what to say next.

"Can I tell you, Calvin," Caroline said, her eyes finally looking at mine, "that not for one second did I think you were the one who wrote that blog post." She didn't say this unkindly, but still, I felt diminished, like I was all of a sudden less than a person. Because this was another thing, perhaps the main thing, that my aunt taught me: if you are not capable of surprising someone, then you are not capable of being fully human.

"I don't think you're from Sheboygan *or* that you're a seafood processor," I told Caroline, hoping to surprise her by passing off my aunt's opinion as my own. When she didn't respond I added, "I think you're Interpol."

Caroline didn't immediately respond to that either. Instead, she looked confused, and for a moment I thought she was going to confess that she didn't know what it meant to be Interpol. But instead Caroline sighed and said, "Well, shit." She removed her hands from my shoulders, then slowly lowered her arms. Caroline's eyes narrowed. She wasn't looking at me; she was looking over my shoulder at something behind me in the ballroom.

I turned to see what she was seeing. There, at the opposite end of the room, at the mouth of the kitchen, was the Sociologist. He'd returned to the ballroom and now looked blankly at the room. He rubbed his eyes, then blinked, as though he couldn't believe what he was seeing. Or maybe it was just that he couldn't see much of anything. His wrecked glasses still hung from his neck.

I say that the Sociologist looked at the room. But really he was looking at the Reverend John Lawrence, who was standing ten feet away, pointing a gun at the Sociologist. The Reverend was holding the gun in his right hand, which was shaking, and so the gun was shaking, too, and so he held it with both hands, and then it was steady.

"Who are you?" the Sociologist wanted to know. Although it didn't sound like he cared terribly much about the answer. His voice was far away, and I wondered if he was thinking about his sister and how she'd left, and my aunt, how she hadn't yet arrived. Meanwhile, Caroline had stepped to my left. She was wearing a white dress, and over that a blue linen blazer, and her right hand was in the right pocket of that blazer.

"I am the Reverend John Lawrence," the Reverend John Lawrence said, sounding very much like a drunk man trying to sound sober. Each word, each syllable, was pronounced carefully, as though being spoken for the first, or last, time.

"Never heard of you," the Sociologist said, and that was the wrong thing to say. The Reverend John Lawrence took a step closer, and I saw, out of the corners of my eyes, little movements, shufflings, as the young bloggers and old criminals tried to scurry away, like mice, along the edges of the room.

"You had sex with Nola," the Reverend John Lawrence said, and then glanced at me, because of course I was the one who'd told him so. And of course that meant I was one of the people responsible for whatever was going to happen next. I knew that then, and I know it now, too.

The Sociologist rubbed his eyes again, and while rubbing his eyes, he yelled, "Come on, man, that was forty years ago!" It was the first time I'd heard the Sociologist raise his voice. And what a thing for him to yell! What a thing for him to say, or even think! As though it mattered whether he'd slept with my mother forty years earlier or two weeks earlier. After all, John Calvin had died 452 years earlier, and right up until her death my mother still quoted him, and for that matter, so do I.

"We were supposed to go a cruise," the Reverend John Lawrence said very quietly now, and I noted the finality in his voice, and I wasn't the only one.

"No!" Caroline yelled, and she had her own gun pointed now, at the Reverend John Lawrence. But the Reverend John Lawrence didn't listen: he did the only thing that he thought was left for him to do, and then so did Caroline.

Seventeen
- - - - - - - - - - - - -

215.

At the end of my mother's famous book, my mother wrote, "We are empty shells. But even so, there is not room inside us to keep everything. If you keep nothing else from this book, keep John Calvin. Lose me. Lose my son. Lose the book. Lose yourself. Keep John Calvin, who will save you in the way I, and my son, and it, and you yourself, cannot."

It is fair to say that by this point I had lost myself. How strange, then, to turn away from screaming, the cordite (that *was* the smell I'd smelled in Paris), the bodies, the wine, and to look at the doorway and to realize that I'd been found. Because standing in the hotel doorway was the man wearing a T-shirt that read IM DIFFICULT TO KIDNAP. It took me a moment to remember where I'd seen the T-shirt before: in Paris, right after my aunt had seen the Butcher and stolen her prescription pad and procured the pills and right before she'd told me that my house had burned down. And then I saw that it wasn't only his T-shirt that was familiar. I knew the man wearing it, but his also wasn't a name that I'd thought to write on my ship cell's wall.

216.

It was Charles Otis, my old classmate and neighbor from Congress.

Charles. I had barely lived a moment, I realized, in which Charles had not been there, watching me. There he was—in preschool, elementary, middle, and high; on my father's football, basketball, and baseball teams; in the back pew in my mother's church. He'd not gone to college with me, not gone to college at all, but once I'd spotted him on my college campus's academic quad. This was during my junior year. "Charles!" I'd yelled and run over to him, more surprised than happy to see him there. The college was two hours away from Congress. Charles had looked sheepish, as though he'd been caught at something. He'd said he was there for work. "What work?" I'd asked. "Firefighting," he said, and then walked away.

Charles: he had been everywhere. And for months after that night in Lisbon, Charles stayed with me, in my dreams, and what was especially strange about those dreams is that they seemed not just to be my dreams but also João's: in those dreams, Charles was still wearing his T-shirt but was otherwise naked, and a small rodent was on top of him, moving erratically, but Charles wasn't looking at the rodent—he was looking at me.

217.

I walked toward Charles, and once I reached him we began walking down the hill, toward the river. I struggled to know what to say to him. There were too many things, and they all seemed outrageous, and so finally I decided to ask him where his father was.

"I had to leave Dad at home," Charles said.

"Why?"

"Old man stuff," Charles said, shrugging. "Bad knees. Bad back. He has these really bad headaches. He forgets things. I don't know why."

I managed to not remind him of that time he'd knocked his father unconscious with a full bottle of laundry detergent. Charles shrugged again, looking sad, trying to rally.

"No big deal. Just typical old man stuff," he said, and I could hear how badly he wanted that to be true.

I searched for something encouraging to say about his father. There wasn't much. But I did remember that news article, the one Aunt Beatrice had shown me on her phone, the one about my house being burned down. Charles wasn't in the photo. Now I knew why. His father had been in the photo, but I remembered how his back had been to the fire, not fighting it.

"Your father wasn't too old to burn down my house," I guessed, and Charles smiled. I didn't ask Charles why his father had burned down my house, because I knew that his father hadn't done it on his own behalf any more than Charles had followed me to Europe on his own behalf. I was sure now that my aunt had hired Charles's father to burn down my house, just as she'd hired Charles to watch over me in Europe, just as she'd had him and his father watch over me my entire life, keeping me safe, until she could come get me herself.

218.

One more thing about Lisbon before we left it then, and before I leave it in memory now. We walked, in silence, until we got to a plaza by the Tagus. It was only five in the morning, but even so the plaza was full of people walking in pairs. I don't mean young lovers walking together. I mean old couples. And I don't mean one old man and one old woman. I mean, two couples, together, two old men, two old women. I saw a dozen of these pairs of pairs. And always, the women were walking in front, linked arm and arm. And always, the men were behind, heads slightly down, hands clasped behind their backs, close enough to be touching but definitely not touching. This sight made me feel hopeful, and also desperate. I couldn't have told you why. Although of course I could have told you why.

"What would you do," I asked Charles, "if I looped my arm through yours right now?"

He seemed to think about it for a minute. Or maybe he'd already been thinking about it. Maybe he'd noticed the couples, too.

"I'd punch you right in your fucking head wound," Charles finally said, "and then I'd knock out your other front tooth." But it sounded like this was something he had to say, and I didn't really think he would do it. Charles's left hand was in his pants pocket, and I looped my right arm through his left and felt his skin against mine. Charles yanked his arm away, and shouted, "What the fuck!" which, in that early hour, sounded like a gunshot. But he did not punch me. He may have wanted to do. But he didn't.

219.

We'd walked down to the plaza because that was the only place to get a cab at that early hour. We got one, took it to the airport. Got on a plane. I won't tell you where the plane went. There are reasons even now why I wouldn't want you to know. But I will tell you what happened after Charles and I got off the plane, at the end of a very long wait and a very long line to get through customs.

"Look at us, Calvin," Charles said. And I thought I knew what he meant. *Look at us, two guys from Congress, here in _____, surrounded by so many people who don't know us, so many people who are so unlike us.*

But then we got to passport control. Charles was in charge. He was holding both our passports and handed them to the customs agent. The man said something rapid fire in yet another language I didn't understand, but he must have asked who was who. Because Charles pointed to himself and said, "Charles."

And then Charles pointed to me, and said, "Geeker." Which I suspect was his revenge for me looping my arm through his.

"Geeeeeeker," the customs agent said, really drawing out the middle vowels. English wasn't his first, or probably even his second, language, but it sounded like he knew exactly what the nickname meant. Although of course he couldn't have known.

220.

From the airport Charles drove for an hour, crossed a river, and a border, from one country into another, and then drove for another hour. The vegetation grew greener, the roads dustier. Suddenly, on our left the vegetation disappeared and in its place, sand, dunes, tall as foothills. On our far right, the ocean and, between the road and the ocean, shacks with corrugated tin roofs, leaning telephone poles, ancient metal signs with the names of gasoline companies that didn't exist anymore, and, underneath them, pumps that didn't have any gasoline in them. Once in a while one of these gas stations had been turned into a cafe, plastic tables scattered around the pumps. I didn't see any women. Only men, sitting at the tables, smoking, watching us as we rattled by.

Finally, we turned right off the main dirt road onto a smaller one that got narrower and narrower until it became clear that we were driving on a road that was actually a path and wasn't meant to be driven on. By the end it was too narrow to drive on at all, hemmed in by spiky, dense green shrubs on either side. We got out of the car, and the shrubs pricked me and tore through my

shiny German shirt and my already distressed jeans. In front of
us was a house. Two stories, white stucco, with a long-pitched
roof. A large window facing the path. Charles had parked the car
in front of a set of large double doors, wood, closed. It reminded
me of a church. But then, if you grow up the son of a minister
who named you after John Calvin, every building reminds you
of a church.

221.

We walked into the house. It was another first floor dominated
by one large room, although this room wasn't nearly as large as
the hotel's ballroom. And like the hotel's ballroom, there wasn't
much furniture in this room. Just a long wooden dining room
table. At the head of the table was John Calvin's chair, and on
the table was João's DVD, and the bejeweled knife my aunt had
stolen in Copenhagen, and the skull she had stolen from the
Butcher in Paris, and also several other objects that I hadn't seen
before: a hand grenade with the pin still in it; what appeared to
be our host country's national constitution, an early draft, tat-
tered, with words crossed out in faint blue ink; a capsized large
brass church bell with the clanger missing; a tennis racket signed
on the handle by I suppose the famous tennis player (I'd never
heard of him) who'd played with it; a black velvet bag overflow-
ing with ancient-looking coins; a lamp made of deer hooves; a
dozen small plastic bags full of what I guessed was marijuana.
My aunt had been busy. Although I wondered for whom all
these things were intended if they weren't for the Sociologist. I

dared, for a second, for much longer than a second, to think that maybe they were for me.

Charles yelled "Hello!" but no one responded. So we left the house and took a rutted path through more of those spiky shrubs, toward the ocean. It was high tide, and only a thin strip of beach remained. But there my aunt was, sitting on a chair, her back to us. Not a beach chair. A kitchen chair, wooden, spindle backed, with one of the spindles missing. Charles yelled "Hello!" again, and my aunt stood up—haltingly, unsteadily, I thought, and in getting up, she grabbed the back of the chair for support and the chair itself rocked back in the sand and I thought both of them were going to tip over. Neither did, and by the time we reached her, she was standing independently of the chair. I noticed that her glasses were missing, but otherwise she seemed unchanged, eternal, and all of a sudden it seemed silly that I'd ever wondered if I was going to see her again. Because of course I would.

"Welcome, Calvin," she said in her bright voice, and then smiled at me, and there, I saw another thing different about her: since last I'd seen her, Aunt Beatrice had gotten a new tooth.

"Calvin, come closer so I can see your poor face," she said. I did that, and the lines in her weathered face deepened as she squinted at me. "And now your mouth." I opened it, and she saw immediately what was missing, of course, and then she looked at Charles accusingly.

"What," he said, and I was surprised to hear how much defiance was in his voice. "You're not the boss of me." Which was an odd thing to say. Because of course she was.

222.

Charles then left us and walked back in the direction of the house. I sat down on the sand, my aunt in her chair, and we talked for hours. It took a long time for my aunt and me to go over how I'd ended up in Lisbon in the first place and then what had happened there. I expected my aunt to be saddened by news of the Sociologist's death, but no: she acted as though his violent death were preordained, and maybe she was right about that. She only had one question of her own before I started asking her mine.

"Did João see his father die?" my aunt wanted to know.

"No," I said, and my aunt nodded and said, "Good," and I was glad that I'd not told her the truth: that, after I saw Charles, I looked back at that big room and there, at the top of the stairs, was João. He'd already seen his father, lying on the floor. And now he was looking around the room with wild, desperate eyes. Finally, they came to me, settled on me, and I could tell he'd found what he was looking for: someone to blame. And I'm sure that he blamed my aunt, too, for not being there, although of course he would have also blamed her had she been there. Except that she'd never had any intention of being there.

"You never had any intention of reuniting with the Sociologist," I said to my aunt. And she agreed that, indeed, she'd never had that intention.

"You let Connie believe that you thought the Sociologist was still alive," I said. I waited for Aunt Beatrice to ask me how I knew that, and then I would tell her that I'd recorded and translated their conversation in Copenhagen. But she didn't ask, and so I added, "You let her believe you were looking for him." Still, my aunt didn't respond. "You *lied* to her."

"I let her lie to herself," Aunt Beatrice corrected. "Which is what you do, Calvin, when you don't want someone you care about to know the truth."

"What was the truth?"

"That after we'd betrayed each other, I didn't love the Sociologist enough anymore to care whether he was alive or dead." And then, before I could respond, my aunt said, "You shouldn't judge me, Calvin."

But of course I'd long ago stopped judging Aunt Beatrice. And in any case, I knew exactly what she meant: because in the end, I hadn't loved Dawn enough to care either.

223.

Aunt Beatrice closed her eyes against the rising sun, which was shining directly in our faces. There was something holy looking about her. I wanted to take her picture, but of course by this point my camera, which was also my cell phone, was long gone.

"I just have one more question," I said. "And I want you to answer it directly." Aunt Beatrice opened her eyes. As I said, she wasn't wearing her dark glasses anymore, but her milky-blue eyes served the same function: I could not see anything in them, and they would not tell me what I wanted to know.

What I wanted to know, of course, was that she was my mother. And I wanted her to tell me so herself. I did not want to have to ask her. Because I knew she would not respond directly, and then it would take several minutes, maybe hours, maybe days, for her to finally answer, and in the interim I would feel humiliated, and in the end, depending on the answer, I might feel even more humiliated. But then, life had been humiliating, right up until I'd met my aunt, whereupon she'd introduced the promise that life for me might yet be something else. And in order for it to actually be that something else, I would have do things the way Aunt Beatrice wanted them done. For as John Calvin said about his own conversion, "I judged nothing more necessary to me after having condemned with groaning and tears my past manner of life, than to give myself up and to betake myself to Thy way."

"Are you my mother?" I asked her, and then felt the humiliation, and the hope, rising in my throat.

My aunt immediately reached up to fiddle with her glasses, but of course they weren't there. She was denied that crutch, that aid. When she realized that there were no glasses to help her buy some time, she smiled, smiled so broadly that if her face were actually made of clay, it would have surely cracked. "Oh, Calvin," she said, and I said, "Mom," and then she began laughing. A ringing sort of laugh. It was the sort of sound that drew people to it. Like the bell in my old mother's church, telling her congregation that it was time to come hear her talk about John Calvin. I wished that analogy occurred to me then, at that moment, because if it had, then it would have been perfectly on cue.

224.

"What's so funny?" my mother said from behind me.

I turned around, and there she was. Very much alive. Wearing a yellow sundress, and barefoot. I'd never seen her shoeless, let alone sockless. My mother's feet were broad and block toed, like a cavewoman's. And she was tan, too: I wondered if she'd spent the entire time since she'd supposedly died on this very beach.

I should have been shocked to see her. But I wasn't. After all, I'd thought, believed, that my mother was dead. I'd *wanted* her to be dead. And it was very much like my mother to be alive just to show me that what I had thought, believed, *wanted*, was wrong. "If you desperately want something," my mother wrote in her famous book, "then that is surely proof that you don't deserve to get what you want."

Meanwhile Aunt Beatrice was trying so hard to stop laughing, making breathless *hoo*-ing sounds, like an owl. "Oh, Calvin," she said, finally getting control of herself. "I'm sorry, but no, I'm not your mother. I just wanted to spend some time with you and your mother before I died. That's all."

225.

"So you actually did it," I said to my mother, my real mother, the still-living world-famous expert on John Calvin, Nola Bledsoe. "You actually faked your death and disappeared. Why?"

"Because I was sick of John Calvin, and sick of Congress, and sick of America, and sick of my famous book, and sick of the people who read it, and sick at the thought of trying to write another one, and sick of poor John Lawrence and his talking about that cruise, and sick of myself and sick of you, too, Calvin," my mother said. And I didn't take any offense at this last part. Because I understood what she was saying: for so long, I'd been sick of me, and of her, too.

226.

My mother had been responsible for everything. She was the Unknown Caller. The Otises had always worked for her, and not my aunt; it was on my mother's behalf, and not my aunt's, that they'd watched over me. It was with the Otises' help that she'd faked her own death; she'd been communicating with them, and my aunt, regularly in _____. She'd had Leland Otis burn down our house in Congress so I wouldn't be tempted to return to it. She'd had Charles Otis follow Aunt Beatrice and me to Europe; she'd had Charles leave a copy of her famous book in my hotel room in Stockholm as a way of telling my aunt to hurry up, that my mother was waiting for us; and then, after Charles had lost me in Marseille, my mother had read the Sociologist's party invitation on my blog, and she'd sent him to Lisbon to bring me to her, to them. She'd had my aunt set up that fake real estate company website, the one that had tricked Dawn into thinking my house was under contract. She'd even had my aunt bug my phone and record my having sex with Caroline, and then my mother had written and published that pornographic post in my name.

"That *was* wrong of you, Nola," my aunt said. There was

nothing ironic in her tone, and I wondered if it was a relief for her to be able to disapprove of someone else's bad behavior.

"I never got to have any *fun*," my mother said, and I was surprised to hear how childish she sounded.

"Well, your *fun* got Calvin *fired*," my aunt said, and I was surprised to hear how adult she sounded.

"I'm glad I got fired," I said, and now it was their turn to be surprised at me. All the panic and fear I'd felt on the train to Marseille—about losing my job, about losing my blog, about losing Caroline, about losing everything—was gone, and in its place . . . well, nothing yet. Which still was better than the things I'd lost. "I would rather have had the sex than kept the job," I admitted.

"Good for you," my aunt said. She stood up on my left, and I did to her what I'd been waiting for her to do to me: I looped my arm through hers. My mother was on my right, and I did what I'd not been waiting for her to do to me: I looped my other arm through hers. And then together the three of us walked back to the house.

227.

"They were for your mother," Aunt Beatrice said. She was talking about the stolen items on the table. She and I were alone in the house. My mother had left in the car with Charles on an errand. "I knew your mother was here the entire time. But I didn't want to come without gifts."

I didn't say what I was thinking: that except for John Calvin's chair, these gifts seemed better suited for my aunt than my mother. But then I remembered all the birthday gifts my mother had given me over the years, and they'd all had something to do with John Calvin, and for that matter my father's gifts to me all had something to do with sports.

"Except for this," my aunt said, and she used both arms to gather those small plastic bags of marijuana to her. "These are mine." She produced a squat wooden pipe from her pants pocket, took some of the pot out of the bag, stuffed the pipe's bowl, lit it with a match, drew, and held a deep breath, then exhaled, smoke pouring out of her nose. "It's medicinal. Helps ease the pain," she said in that familiar pathetic voice, the one that was difficult for me to believe. I once again thought of the recording I'd made of the Butcher, the one I'd not listened to before the Sociologist's hired muscle had destroyed my phone. When I mentioned that—that I'd recorded what the Butcher had said to her but that I'd not gotten a chance to translate and listen to it before the phone was destroyed—I expected my aunt to be surprised by my sneakiness. Instead, she took her phone out of her pocket, fidgeted with it, then handed the phone to me. I knew, before I'd even put the thing to my ear, what it was: my aunt had recorded that particular moment with the Butcher also. Because not only does an old lady like being accompanied to the doctor's office, but an old lady also likes to record what the doctor says to her, so difficult is it for an old lady to pay close attention to the doctor's diagnosis at the time of its delivery, especially if the diagnosis is a bad one.

228.

"The conventional treatment is almost certainly going to fail, Admiral," the Butcher said in her clear, cold voice, translated by my aunt's phone into English. "And you will die. But I do want you to seriously consider the radical treatment. It has a smaller chance of failing, we think, we don't really know, we've done only a few, but the treatment is promising, which means that the people who've had the treatment haven't had it long enough ago to know whether the treatment will live up to its promise, but hey, you have to do everything, it's your life, let's go for this is my feeling." I was struck by how much the Butcher's voice changed over the course of her speech. If she'd begun speaking like a doctor calmly delivering bad news, she'd ended by sounding like a saleswoman at the car dealership across the street from her office, trying to talk my aunt into buying the newest model Renault. "Oh yeah," the Butcher said, in closing to my aunt, "you gotta go with the radical."

229.

"What are you dying of?" I asked my aunt. Even then, I hoped she'd say, *Nothing*, or at least not answer my question directly.

"Cancer," Aunt Beatrice said in that same sad, pathetic voice, and I realized now that that was the voice she used not when she was lying but when she was telling a particular kind of truth.

"We need to go back to Paris," I said to my aunt.

She didn't say anything to that. She packed another bowl, smoked it, exhaled into the room. And the room changed with it: before it had been filled with death, and after it was still filled with death, but it seemed further away. Or rather there was something—a curtain of smoke—between it and us. But still, I persisted.

"To the Butcher," I said.

Aunt Beatrice didn't respond to that either. She'd packed yet another bowl and handed it to me. "No," I said, but I'd already accepted the bowl. I put it to my lips. Aunt Beatrice lit the bowl, and then I inhaled. It was my first time, and I did it poorly, and my hacking broke the spell and her death drew close again. My aunt reached out, and I gave her the bowl and said through my coughing, "So you can have the radical."

Still, my aunt didn't say anything. She'd knocked the remnants of the bowl onto the table, brushed ashes to the floor, returned the bowl to the pocket of her white summer pants. Then she leaned back in her chair—it was John Calvin's chair—and stared deeply at the stucco ceiling as though it were the night's sky.

"Say something," I said.

"It's too late for the radical, and very soon I'm going to die, Calvin," my aunt said, and she said this in her normal bright voice, not her pathetic one, but that did not make what she said any less terrible to me, "but between now and when I die you and I will pretend that it is not too late and that soon I will go to Paris to get the radical and that I will not die. But I won't, and I will."

"Say something else," I said.

230.

Aunt Beatrice didn't say something else. She just sat there in John Calvin's chair, head tipped back, eyes aimed at the ceiling, as though she'd already given up, as though she was already looking toward the afterlife. I hated to see that, and so I stumbled out of the room, out of the house, back toward the beach. There were a couple of surfers out there in the waves now, teenaged boys on what looked like homemade boards with chipped noses. I sat on the sand and stared at the surfers and then, after they left, stared at the waves themselves, stared at them for a long, long time, trying to organize my thoughts, trying to think of what to do or think or say next. Nothing especially original came to mind.

"I don't want Aunt Beatrice to die," is what I finally said—to the waves, I thought.

"Me neither," a woman's voice said from behind me. I turned and there was Caroline. Her blue blazer was gone, and her freckled skin looked pale against her white dress. The dress looked freckled, too—there were red flecks near the hem that I realized were spots of blood. I scrambled to my feet. "Even though your aunt has done some very bad things," she added.

"But that doesn't make her a bad person," I said automatically.

"Of course it does, Calvin," Caroline said, and it struck me that my aunt probably would have said the same thing.

231.

I was conscious of my aunt spying on us from the house, and so Caroline and I walked away from the house, down the beach.

There was nothing in front of us that I could see, no people, no animals, just sand and water. It was the emptiest place I'd ever been, and also the hottest: I could feel my scalp prickle in the sun.

"How did you find me?" I asked her, and she put her right hand on my left shoulder, and that prickled, too. Then Caroline removed her hand and showed me a square piece of black mesh, barely visible, like a patch. It was a bug, a tracking device, I supposed, and I supposed she'd put in on my shoulder back in Lisbon. Weeks earlier I might have been surprised that such a thing existed, let alone that it had been attached to me. But now it seemed like just one of the many small wonders of the world. Caroline released the bug and it disappeared in the sand.

"Who are you really?" I asked her.

"Well, my name *is* Caroline," Caroline said. "And can I tell you something funny?"

"No," I said, but she once again ignored me.

"I *am* from Sheboygan."

"So that much was true."

"Just outside Sheboygan, actually."

"What's the name of the town?"

"You wouldn't have heard of it," she said. "It's unincorporated."

I nodded, thinking of the other lies that she might have told me.

"Were you really divorced from a man named Ron?"

"I wasn't even married to a man named Ron. Or anyone else."

"Did you have sex with me because you wanted to or because you wanted something from me?"

"Both," she said immediately, and I know now that she was telling the truth, that she was done lying to me, although at that moment I wasn't yet ready to believe her.

"I don't believe you," I said.

"Totally understandable," Caroline said. Her eyes were as usual on the move—to the sand, the ocean, the sky, my face, the sand—and I thought that whatever kind of spy you were if you were Interpol, then she was the most nervous, most guilty-seeming spy ever.

"Was that really you in the hotel lobby in Sweden?" I asked, and she said in a robotic Swedish accent, "An unfunny joke is a lie."

"But you were taller," I said.

"There are high heels, Calvin."

"Your hair was blonde." I don't know why I was so insistent on arguing against her truth. Maybe because I'd so recently learned mine. "Your face was so pale."

"There are wigs. There is makeup."

"You *lied* to me," I said.

When I said that, Caroline's eyes fixed on mine, really held them in place, the way my mother's used to when she was making what she knew was an excellent point about John Calvin. "And then your poor son died," Caroline said, and I remembered how I'd lied to her on the train about having a son and about how he'd died.

"Well," I said.

"Of kidney stones," she said.

"All right," I conceded.

"And after that," Caroline said, smiling now, but not unkindly and maybe even with a little admiration, "after that, you and Dawn were never the same."

232.

It was only after Caroline had admitted lying to me, and only after she'd made me admit that I'd lied to her, were we both fully ready to believe each other. To quote John Calvin one last time, "Not that they may believe against their wills (which would be impossible), but that they may be made willing to believe who were before unwilling to believe."

233.

It turned out Interpol had wanted to arrest both the Sociologist and my aunt and that the only reason Caroline hadn't arrested her on the train was that she'd hoped Aunt Beatrice would lead her to the Sociologist. And if she had, then Caroline had planned to arrest both of them.

"But she's an old woman," I said. "With terminal cancer."

Caroline shrugged and said, "Interpol is rules," and I said yes, I knew all about the rules.

"So you're here to arrest my aunt?" I asked, and Caroline shook her head.

"I'm done with all that," she said.

"Why?"

"Calvin, I *killed* that man," Caroline said. And I knew what she meant. After all, I had, in my way, killed the same man, and the man he'd killed, too, and I was relieved to be so far away from the place where I had done that thing to those people.

"So why are you here then?" I asked Caroline, and I felt as I had earlier, right before I'd asked Aunt Beatrice if she was my mother. It was the feeling you get when you ask a question and are afraid the answer you're going to get is not the answer you want.

"I want you to run away with me," Caroline said, then laughed at herself for saying, or wanting, something so ridiculous. "I mean it," she added, and I believed that she did.

Anyway, that was the answer I wanted! I'd finally gotten the answer I'd wanted! And it turned out, as is true of most people and of most good things, that I was not worthy of it, that I was scared of it.

"But you barely know me."

"Well, *yeah*," Caroline said in a way that suggested that her barely knowing me was my most attractive quality.

"Where would we go?" I asked, not really caring where, just trying to buy myself some time. Caroline shrugged, but I sensed that she knew where and that she wasn't going to tell me because I would find some way to object to the place even though I'd surely know not one thing about it. "To do what?" I asked, and again she just shrugged.

"I can't," I said. Caroline didn't say anything to that, didn't even bother to shrug, just fixed her eyes on me and kept them on me, just *daring* me to say something false. I realized then how she must have, in fact, been very good at her job, and that it must have cost her a great deal to give it up. But I persisted. I told her that my aunt was very sick and that I had to take care of her. And that my mother had come back into my life, that she was not dead after all, and that it would be wrong to leave her now that it turned out that she hadn't left me. I suggested that Caroline stay with us instead. That we didn't have to go anywhere. That we could make a life here in _____.

"A life here," Caroline repeated. She'd made her voice sound as Sheboygan as possible: guileless, wide open, as though she really were considering making a life in that place. "Tell me about it," she said. But she must have known I wouldn't, that I didn't need to. Because I could already see the life we'd make there. My aunt would die soon, and I would have to watch that happen, would have to bury her. And then it would be us, and my mother, in the house that resembled a church. No matter how much we'd changed, or had wanted to, we would revert to who we had always been. My mother would probably take up her John Calvin again, and I would find another obscure industry to blog for. Who knew what Caroline would do, but whatever she did, or didn't do, my mother would probably judge her for it, just as she'd judged Dawn, and they would end up hating each other, and then they would end up hating me, and me, them. It would be like we were back in Congress. It would be like we had never left or never could leave.

"Where will we go?" I asked Caroline. And this time she told me. And I was right: I knew not one thing about the place.

234.

There was still one last thing nagging at me.

"Did you really not know about my mother's book?" I asked.

"Oh, Calvin," she said, placing her right hand on my left cheek, and I closed my eyes to more deeply feel her touch. "Of course I did. Everyone knows about it. It's a very famous book."

235.

It turned out that we'd been walking toward Caroline's car the entire time, that she'd parked it down the road and walked back to the house so that no one would know she was there (it's not easy for a spy to stop acting like a spy, a thief like a thief, a minister like a minister, a blogger like a blogger). We got in the car, and she drove us back to the house. When we got there, I saw Charles's car parked out front. I assumed that my mother and Charles had returned from their errands, and I felt a strong need for closure, a need to not simply disappear, a need to say goodbye.

"You sure that's a good idea?" Caroline asked, and I knew what she was really asking was, *Are you sure you're going to be able to do that?* I didn't answer her. I just got out of the car, walked into the house. My mother was sitting at the table with my aunt, who, when she saw me, handed me her pipe and her lighter. I lit the pipe, sucked on it, inhaled, exhaled, without coughing, and then returned the pipe to my aunt. She had a bemused look on her face, and I couldn't help but wonder if she'd seen me talking to Caroline, if she knew I wanted to tell her something, and if she, like Caroline, doubted I'd be able to.

"Where's Charles?" I asked.

"Gone," my mother said. It turned out that she'd driven Charles to the airport so he could fly back to Congress to be with his father, Leland. My mother seemed melancholy; maybe she was thinking of how, for so long, the Otises had watched out for me on her behalf (my mother feared, I think, that my aunt would show up and try to corrupt me, and of course she was right to fear that) and how it marked an end of an era.

"Charles is a good man," my mother said.

The room was still thick with smoke, and my head was still thick with it, too. I've heard that smoking pot relaxes you, but that wasn't true in my case.

"Charles is an asshole," I said. And when I said that, I could feel something take root and grow within me, and I knew that I really was going to be able to say goodbye to them after I was through saying all the other things I'd always wanted to say.

"He is a good man," my mother insisted, and even though she was supposed to be a new person, I could hear the old rectitude in her voice, which made me even angrier.

"He beat his father over the head with a bottle of laundry detergent. But then, his father probably deserved it. He's an asshole, too."

"Calvin," my mother said in warning. My aunt hadn't said anything, pot smoke pouring out of her mouth the way the words were pouring out of mine.

"You were a terrible mother," I said to my mother.

"Bea," my mother said to my aunt. As though my insulting

her was Aunt Beatrice's fault. Which it might have been. But I wanted credit for it, too. My aunt may have put the words in my mouth, but I was the one who was finally saying them.

"It's true," I said to my mother. "My *father* was a better mother than you. The Sociologist would probably have been a better mother than you, too. You had sex with both of them. *And* Reverend John Lawrence. I don't know how you could have had sex with that man, if you did have sex with him, but I bet, since you did, if you did, even *he* would have been a better mother than you."

After that, there was silence. I didn't know what either of them was thinking. But I was trying to think of what terrible thing to say next. There was so many of them in me, and so many of them had been waiting to be said for so long that I didn't know which one to choose.

"Your book was boring," I finally said, taking care not to refer to it as famous. "I'm glad you didn't write another one. The first one was bad enough."

"Calvin," my aunt said, and this time it was she who seemed to be warning me about going too far.

"Oh, go ahead and die already," I said to her. My aunt didn't say anything to that, didn't seem to be affected by what I'd said at all, but my mother gasped.

"You shouldn't judge me," I said to my mother, and my aunt laughed in pleasure at hearing those words of hers come out of my mouth. Which of course was what I wanted, what I'd always wanted. *I already miss you so much*, I thought, and now, years later, I still miss her, and I've missed her for so long now that I suppose I'll never stop missing her. Meanwhile, my mother was staring at me, in horror or astonishment or admiration, I couldn't tell which.

"Who *are* you?" she wanted to know.

"Yes, Calvin," my aunt said, smiling. "Who are you?"

That was a joke. She knew who I was. Because she had helped make me. And so, in her way, had my mother. But I answered anyway.

"You know who I am," I said. "I'm Calvin Bledsoe."

Acknowledgments

This book was inspired by Graham Greene's 1969 novel *Travels with My Aunt*. Thanks to Mr. Greene, wherever he might be.

In an interview with the *Paris Review*, the fiction writer Joy Williams responded to the notion of fellow fiction writer Don DeLillo's coldness by saying, "What's wrong with that? The cold can teach us many things." That idea ended up being so important to this book that I had one of my characters repeat it. Thanks to Ms. Williams for that.

Thanks to the editors of the *Cincinnati Review* and *Great Jones Street* for publishing sections of this book.

Thanks to Jim Longenbach and Joanna Scott for their support and friendship over many many years.

Thanks to Chuck Adams and Craig Popelars at Algonquin Books, and to my agent, Elizabeth Sheinkman.

Thanks to Bowdoin College for its financial support.

Thanks to my friends and family.